THE JOSIAH EFFECT

The Power of One

D.L. Augustine

ISBN-13: 9781500552008
ISBN-10: 1500552003

I dedicate this book to you mom. I wish you could see the woman that I have grown into being. I think you would be proud of me. I love and miss you more than I can say. I understand now that you needed my love, not my anger. Please forgive me, as I have forgiven you. I'll see you on the other side.

Your loving daughter

PROLOGUE

(The Letter)

Hey God, can you hear me?

This is Josiah and I'm 10 years old. I don't know if you can help me but I figure it couldn't hurt to try. There is so much going on; I don't even know where to start. I love my mom. It's just me and her. I know she's not really happy even though she laughs a lot. I don't know how I know, but I know. She mostly laughs when her friends are over or when she's been drinking or smoking. I'm not supposed to talk about that stuff, but I figure if you're really God you probably already know. She's fun when she smokes weed. She plays with me and I don't get on her nerves. God, what are nerves? If you tell me what they are or at least where they are, I promise not to touch them anymore. I hate it when she is mad or unhappy. It's just like when you're outside playing on a sunny day and all of a sudden clouds come and it gets all dark and gloomy. That's what it feels like when she's mad at me or when she's sad. I try to make her happy but it's almost like she's gone somewhere else even though she is still here. I just love her so much. I go to school and bring my papers home so she can see all the A's and smiley faces. I give them to her hoping to bring a smile to her face but she's gone away again. She smiles, but not the real one. Doesn't she know that I know the difference? I just want her to love me like I love her, but even at ten I know I am not enough. That really hurts, too, God because she is everything to me. I don't show her my pain though because I know it will hurt her. I wonder if she knows she hurts me sometimes. I know she doesn't mean to. I think my dad hurt her. I think that is why we never see him or talk to him. Sometimes I wish he would come around or call, but I would never let her know that. I really wish he was around when I see other boys playing with their dads. It just makes me wonder why my dad hates me so much. I use to think that he probably didn't like me because I was an ugly baby and that is why he went away. I wish he would come back and see how different I look now. I don't look nothing like those ugly baby pictures. Oh well, he's probably mean anyway. My mom's last two boyfriends were mean, too. They use to hit her and make her cry. I tried to stop them but they were too big. Well at least my mom doesn't have boyfriends anymore. She just has friends. She wants me to call them auntie but I don't, except for Brenda. She was nice to me for real and not because she wanted my mom to think she liked me. My friends all tease me. They say my mom is a dyke. I don't know what it is exactly, but whatever it is, it ain't good. God, I'm not talking about my mom or nothing, but I wish she could just be a regular mom, like Keon's mom who always helps out at school and hangs out with him or like those moms on T.V. My mom is so busy. That's why she is always sending me over other people's houses. I don't know exactly what she does that makes her so busy, but she is gone a lot. She mostly tries to leave me with nice people, but when she leaves they always talk about what a bad mother she is—that's just because they don't know her. She would stay home with me more but she has to spend time with her friends. She's still young. I heard her say that once. I just wish she would spend more time with me. God, how can I get my mom to love me more? Can't she see I am all she needs? But what do I know? I am just a kid. I'm only ten years old.

CHAPTER ONE

Dr. Robin Walters could feel Josiah staring at her as she turned the pages of her calendar looking for an available appointment for the following week. He always did the same thing when their weekly sessions came to an end. She knew if she looked up he would look away embarrassed to be caught staring, so she pretended to be unaware that he watched her every move. She pretended, for his sake, that she didn't see the vulnerability that showed in his face when he thought no one was watching. She had learned through trial and error how far she could penetrate behind his nonchalant exterior. She knew if she pushed too hard it would be weeks before she would see him again, and she didn't want to jeopardize the progress that had been made in the past few months.

Slowly looking up to give him a chance to look in another direction, she smiled at him and began writing on her calendar.

"Okay Josiah, I will see you at four o'clock next Tuesday afternoon," Robin said, writing his name in her appointment calendar.

"Do you think your mom could bring you the next time?"

"No ma'am." Josiah hesitated trying to think up an excuse. "Uhhhh, she has to go somewhere." He hated lying to Dr. Walters but he knew his mom wouldn't bring him even though all she would be doing was lying on the couch watching her shows. "My teacher, Mrs. Drayton, said she doesn't mind bringing me because it's on her way home."

"Well ok," Robin absently replied, as she continued writing on her calendar. Looking up, she caught Josiah's eyes. For a moment she was able to see behind the brave façade, which was a permanent part of his protective armor. Just for a second she caught a glimpse of the 10-year-old unhappy little boy he always tried to hide, but just that quick he was gone again, replaced by the 10-year-old child with eyes that looked so weary they made her want to weep.

With a gentle look on her face she asked, "You okay?"

"Yes ma'am," he replied.

She held his gaze, but only for a moment before he looked away. Deciding to take a chance, she stood to her feet.

"I need a hug," she said. Coming from behind her desk, she walked over to him and took him by his frail shoulders and pulled him to her.

"I hope this doesn't embarrass you, but sometimes I just need a hug."

"It's okay, Dr. Walters. I always hug my mom when she's sad. She says I'm the only one who can make her smile when she's depressed," Josiah replied.

"You are such a gentleman," Robin said, giving him a caring smile.

They stood there together looking at each other. She, the world-renowned child psychiatrist, and he, the saddest 10-year-old she had ever encountered. She thought again how beautiful he was. His ash blond hair hung down almost covering eyes that reminded her of the Atlantic Ocean. They were sometimes blue, sometimes gray, going from stormy to clear, depending on his current mood. He was a child who wanted to please. A child any mother or father would or should have been proud of.

Josiah was always polite. A habit she gathered came from his Aunt Angie, who he described as his mom's best friend, casually mentioning she was black too. Robin took this to mean black like her.

"Be sure to think about what we talked about today. Promise me you won't forget Josiah," Robin stated.

"I won't," he said.

At that moment there was a soft knock on the door. Glad for the interruption, she responded.

"Come in."

The door opens and her best friend and Josiah's teacher, Tiffany Drayton, sticks her head in the door.

"Hello, anybody home?" She spied the two standing in front of the desk.

"You guys finished or did I interrupt?" Tiffany asked, stepping into the office.

Robin laughed as she returned to her desk. "Would it really have made a difference?"

Josiah greeted his fifth grade teacher as he picked up his book bag off the floor. "Hi Mrs. Drayton," Josiah said, turning his attention away from Robin.

Tousling his blond locks, she asked him, "Did you give Dr. Walters a hard time today like I told you?"

"Nah," he replied.

Suddenly looking serious, Tiffany puts her finger under Josiah's chin admonishing him.

"I'm sorry what did you say young man? I don't believe "nah" is in the dictionary, but maybe I missed it. Did you find that word in the dictionary Josiah?" Tiffany, always the teacher, was temporarily distracted by the misuse of grammar.

"Nah, I mean no ma'am," Josiah said, looking down at the ground.

"Do you want to try that again?" she asked.

"Yes ma'am," he answered.

"Okay, the question is, did you give Dr. Walter's a hard time today like I told you to?"

"No ma'am."

Trying to look serious, Tiffany responded. "Why not? Didn't I tell you she likes it when you give her a hard time?"

"Yes ma'am, but," Josiah hesitated before speaking.

"But?" said Tiffany.

"She's too nice. I didn't want her to get mad at me," he continued to say.

Suddenly, the playful moment turned serious. Robin walked over to Josiah, grabbed his hand, and spoke low so only he could hear.

"I told you, this is a safety zone—there is nothing you could ever say that would make me not like you or think that you're not the perfect gentleman. You are free to express yourself here. You don't need to worry about trying to make me like you. I already do and nothing you do will ever change that," Robin explained.

Josiah stared into her eyes willing her to confirm what she had just spoken. His eyes were so beautiful. Today they were gray and stormy. Josiah stared at her fighting back tears.

"Do you believe me?" Robin asked as she continued to hold his stare forcing him to acknowledge what she had just told him. She repeated, "Do you believe me?"

Breaking their gaze, Josiah looked down at his feet and in a voice barely above a whisper replied, "Yes ma'am."

Robin grabbed Josiah and held him close to her for a moment before reluctantly releasing him. It was if there was no one in the room but the two of them.

The silent reverie was broken by the apology of an angst-ridden Tiffany. "I'm sorry Josiah, I wasn't thinking. You know I was just teasing, right? " Tiffany spoke, looking remorseful.

"Yes ma'am," replied Josiah, with an obvious effort to pull himself together.

Tiffany and Robin briefly exchange glances as Tiffany grabs Josiah's hand making a hasty exit. Glancing back over her shoulder, she quickly waved goodbye to her friend.

"I'll see you next week Josiah," said Robin. "Don't forget to call me later Tiffany. I need to know if we are still on for the concert Saturday."

"Okay," said Tiffany, closing the door softly behind her.

Robin stared pensively at the closed door, thinking about the incident that had just occurred between her and Josiah. She realized they had crossed a line. He had made a decision to trust her. She had felt it when she held his gaze, refusing to allow him to look away. She understood for Josiah, the decision to trust instead of to retreat within himself, had been big. She knew she had to make sure she did nothing to violate the fragile offering he had sacrificed so much to make.

CHAPTER TWO

Robin finished dictating her notes from her session with Josiah and placed his file back on

the stack, piled precariously on her desk resembling the Leaning Tower of Pisa. She looked at the name typed on the folder. Thomas Josiah Martin, III. It was a big name for such a little boy.

Robin picked up his chart again and began reading some of the earlier notes.

overly protective of mother, role reversal with parent, believes he is the man and should be responsible for himself and mother, possible substance abuse problem with mother, no father involvement or male role model, possible anger issue, extremely perceptive and intelligent"

Perusing the chart, she fought hard to see beyond the black words written on white paper and tried to make sense out of the information she was reading. She tried with all her gifts to see what was not visible.

Robin Giselle Walters was 31-years-old and widely respected in her field. When her name was brought up amongst her peers, words like "gifted" and "revolutionary" were spoken in relation to her work in the field of child psychiatry. She graduated Suma Cum Laude from The Ohio State University and without so much as a summer off, she continued on to earn her master's degree, and then her doctorate in clinical psychology, all by the tender age of 24-years-old.

She was the youngest psychiatrist ever hired at the prestigious "Burke Center" in Columbus, Ohio. Their specialty was child psychology. Robin always knew she wanted to help children. Upon her completion from grad school, several Ivy League universities and numerous esteemed foundations, specializing in child psychology, had hotly pursued her, but none of them excited her like the Burke Center. The Burke Center, founded by Leonard Burke, was the only facility of its kind to specialize in treatment for all types of juvenile behavior problems. The center's philosophy was cutting edge, in that it didn't agree with the traditional therapies that kept children heavily medicated—never really getting to the root of the problem. They, instead, opted for intense individual and group therapy, along with new courses of treatment, such as Light Therapy and Interpretative Phenomenological Analysis, which is used for treatment of resistant depression and other exciting breakthrough methods for reaching scarred children.

In her seven year tenure at the Burke Center, she published two papers on alternative therapies and not once, but twice, been the recipient of the highly coveted NARSAD Award for Psychiatric research. Robin was proud of the accomplishments she had obtained, but managed to keep them in perspective.

Slowly she ran her fingers over Josiah's name thinking to herself, "how can I reach this child?" She knew she was running out of time. She knew each week she made a little progress, but Josiah still remained in crisis mode. Today had been the biggest breakthrough to date.

Turning the recorder back on, she thought of an additional observation from their earlier session. As she opened his file, she spied the letter written in Josiah's child-like scrawl. Just looking at the letter gave her goose bumps.

It was the letter that had been the impetus that brought the young charge into her life. Her friend and sorority sister, Tiffany, was Josiah's fifth grade teacher. Tiffany had discovered the letter in his book bag while assisting him in looking for his fourth" lost" homework assignment in five days. When she found the letter in his bag, her first reaction was anger. She thought that instead of doing his homework, he had been wasting his time writing love letters. She decided to teach him a lesson and started to read the letter to the class. She abruptly stopped after realizing it was not a love letter at all, but a desperate cry for help from a 10-year-old child.

After school, Tiffany had insisted on driving Josiah home so that she could speak with his mother. Robin recalled the horrific story that Tiffany told her about meeting Josiah's mother.

Tiffany sat silently across from Patricia Martin as she held Josiah's letter in her hand crying.

"I don't know what to do," Patricia whined. "He was always my little soldier man."

Wiping tears from her eyes, she picked a dirty used napkin off the equally dirty coffee table and began to blow her nose. "I thought he was happy," she sobbed. Fresh tears fell down her cheeks as she glanced at the letter again. "I don't know what to do."

She stopped for a moment and picked up a half-smoked cigarette from the overflowing ashtray. Lighting the cigarette, she inhaled deeply. Turning in Tiffany's direction, she whined, "What am I supposed to do?"

The question hung in the air like the smell of rain after a thunderstorm. Tiffany shifted on the couch, with springs barely under the surface. Squirming uncomfortably, Tiffany felt the spring snagging the silk skirt she had just purchased the weekend before from the Ralph Lauren sales rack in Nordstrom's. "Dang!" she thought to herself as she tried to twist in the opposite direction, only to be rewarded with the sound of ripping as the persistent spring continued to do its damage. Standing to her feet, she attempted to console the grieving mother.

"Can't you get him into some type of counseling?" Tiffany asked. Her eyes followed the overweight woman as she continued to pace back and forth. There was something childlike about Ms. Martin. Her hair was blonde like Josiah's but a darker shade and where Josiah's was soft and silky like a newborn's hair, Ms. Martin's was lank and greasy, and looked in need of a good wash. This only added to her general unkempt appearance.

"I can't afford nuthin' like that," she replied.

Looking around, Tiffany noticed there was no shortage of beer or cigarettes, judging by the mounds of cigarette butts and empty beer cans sitting on every open surface. Tiffany perceived in that moment that if she didn't get Josiah into counseling, he would never get an opportunity to go. After speaking with his mother, she knew if Josiah didn't get help soon he would become a statistic. She realized Ms. Martin loved Josiah and had been genuinely disturbed after she had read the letter, but her self-absorption would never allow her to probe any deeper than surface level. Tiffany knew she would ask Josiah about the letter and because he was so protective of his mother, he would tell her everything was fine and that would be the end of it, until Josiah came to a point where he couldn't take it anymore.

Josiah was not the average ordinary 10-year-old, and on some level, Ms. Martin recognized that. She also recognized that he was unusually perceptive for a 10-year-old, but what she didn't understand was the effect that it would have on his emotions. No matter how precocious he acted, Tiffany knew the thoughts and feelings he had expressed in the letter went well beyond what a 10-year-old could handle. Going out on a limb, she mentioned to Ms. Martin that she had a friend who would do the counseling pro bono. It took another ten minutes to explain that pro bono meant the services would be free. After which, Ms. Martin seemed to cheer up a little, but still seemed reluctant. Tiffany went on to explain who her friend was and her background in child psychiatry. She told her that her friend Robin G. Walters, Ph.D., was one of the top child psychiatrists in the country. None of this seemed to impress Ms. Martin until Tiffany mentioned that Robin had been a guest on Oprah, Dr. Phil, and the Montel Williams Show. She immediately became interested until she remembered she wouldn't be able to get him to counseling because she didn't have a car. Tiffany promised she would take him each week and bring him home afterward. So finally Ms. Martin consented. Tiffany felt like she had just gone fifteen rounds with the heavyweight champion of the world. Tiffany's next challenge would be to convince Robin to take Josiah on as a new patient."

In the beginning, Robin refused. "I just can't right now Tiff, my plate is full with the new wing of the center opening in less than 90 days. They have already requested that I head it up, and I have decided that I am going to accept. I just won't have the time. I can ask Rick if he can take him as a favor to me."

At that point Tiffany began pleading. "Please Robin," Tiffany begged. "It has to be you. Just read the letter then make your decision. If you read the letter and you still decide not to see him, then I won't ask anymore. Just read the letter, please."

"Okay, I will read the letter, but I can tell you right now, I don't have time to see the child."

Reading the letter had affected Robin as nothing had before. The pain she felt after she read it was visceral. Robin immediately recognized that Josiah was a child in crisis.

Now they are months into counseling and she is just beginning to win his trust. Robin knows in her heart of hearts that her desire to help children and her destiny are tied to this child. She vowed she would leave no stone unturned to help Josiah to become a healthy whole individual. Coming back to the present, she picked up the letter and began reading.

Robin slowly folded the letter as a lone silent tear rolled down her cheek. She quickly wiped it away and placed the letter back into the file. Even after all this time, the letter still affected her as when she had first read it. Robin finally finished dictating her notes from her session with Josiah, and again replaced his file back to the top of the stack. Briefly glancing at the clock, Robin is startled out of her musings as she noticed the time.

"Oh shoot!" she cried, jumping out of her seat. Taking the stack of files piled on her desk, she places them into a locked filing cabinet, frantically gathering her coat, purse and briefcase. She crashed through the glass office doors like a triathlon runner. "Hold that elevator!" she shouted as she sprinted down the hall.

CHAPTER THREE

Robin pulled her pearl white Range Rover up to the valet booth at Polaris Fashion Place mall. She grabbed her purse as the valet attendant opened the door for her.

"Hey Greg, how are you doing?"

"I'm fine, Ms. Walters."

"Ms. Walters? I told you Greg, Ms. Walters is my mother. Just Robin, okay."

"Okay, Robin," Greg said hesitantly. "Do you need a wash today?"

"No time. I just have to run into Saks real quick and pick up my dress."

"Okay, then I will just leave your car right here. Call me when you're ready to leave and I will meet you at the south exit."

"That's okay, I can walk around."

"Just call, Robin, and I will bring your car to the exit. It's not a problem."

"Alright, it shouldn't be more than half an hour."

Robin slipped Greg a $10 bill from her purse as she entered the mall and began walking toward Saks entrance.

Entering Saks, Robin smiled and nodded at a couple of salespeople she recognized. She noticed two youngish African-American females looking through the Ralph Lauren sales rack to her left. The girls caught her attention because they looked vaguely familiar. While she pondered where she might know them from, she noticed Carol, the loss prevention specialist, posing as a shopper, all the while hawking the two young women. Frowning, Robin stared at Carol who continued to dog the pair everywhere they went in the store.

The two young women were at first oblivious to Carol, but it quickly became apparent that she was following them from department to department. Robin, who had stopped at the Armani department, had a bird's-eye view of all three ladies as the pair confronted the loss prevention specialist.

The women, who before had been laughing and carefree, quickly changed to a defensive posture as Carol continued to follow them from department to department. Suddenly, the first young woman stopped, did an about face and spoke directly to Carol.

"Why are you following us?" asked the woman.

Robin could hear the entire conversation from where she stood.

"I beg your pardon?" Carol said, trying to pretend she was just an ordinary shopper and totally unaware of the two women.

"I mean you keep following us like you some kind of stalker. You're either gay, a fan, or you think because we're black, we are here to steal something."

"I have no idea what you're talking about," she replied, trying to look indignant. "I am shopping just like you. Why would you accuse me of following you? Maybe you have a guilty conscience."

Laughing out loud the other girl spoke up. As she turned to address Carol, Robin could see she was quite beautiful and appeared to be in her mid-to-late 20s, which was older than what Robin had originally thought. Long and willowy, her body was a designer's dream. Smiling at the security guard she pointed to an overweight white female about 10 yards behind the loss prevention specialist.

"Wrong perp, Sherlock! While you were dogging our every step, you missed the white lady back there in the black coat. Don't you think it's a little warm for a coat that big?"

Carol turned just in time to see the woman stick several hangers of dresses under the large black coat. Taking a walkie-talkie out of her pocket she instructed store security to block all exits and began moving toward the blonde to apprehend her. The thief, who looked like any other high-end shopper except for the ridiculous looking hot coat, nonchalantly began moving toward the exit. She quickly spotted security circling and figured out what time it was. Weighing her options, she made a fast break for the front door with security hotly in pursuit.

The two girls began laughing as they turned around and continued shopping and talking to each other. Robin decided to approach them.

"That was quite a show."

They both turn toward Robin smiling.

"Yes it was," said the taller one.

Up close, the tall one was more beautiful than Robin had first thought, with a complexion to rival Halle Berry—flawless smooth cocoa brown skin without a flaw, with cheek bones any model would have given a year's salary for. She had slanted golden brown eyes, which sparked with intelligence and fire, but also a sense of humor. Robin could see that this girl loved to laugh, but she could also tell that if you came at her wrong, she would be quick to put you in your place.

"Robin Walters," she said, extending her hand to the taller of the two girls.

"Johanna Banks, but Jo is fine, and this is my girl, Amera James."

Amera was short and curvy with a body that would stop traffic. She was what the guys called a brick house stacked on top and bottom with a tiny little waist. She possessed kind of beauty that was rare because you couldn't quite put your finger on what exactly it was that made her so appealing, but you knew she was beautiful.

"Waz up?" Amera spoke lazily, looking Robin up and down as she sized her up. She admired the $2,000 navy blue Armani business suit, complimented by a pair of matching navy and white Manolo Blahnik toe pumps Robin was wearing. Everything she wore looked quietly tasteful. The only piece of jewelry she wore, beside the diamond studs in her ears, was an understated, yet elegant Cartier watch that delicately framed her tiny wrist.

Robin looked like she belonged in this world of wealth and class. I bet they never follow her around, Amera thought, and before she could help herself, thoughts became words and she spoke out loud the words which only seconds before had been safely locked in her head.

"I bet they never follow you around." As soon as the words came out of her mouth, Amera was immediately sorry she said them. She could tell the sister was cool, but at the same time, she also looked like one of those black folk who had achieved success and escaped the ghetto, but to assuage their conscience, tried to act like they were still down.

Robin, without missing a beat, laughed out loud as she turned to Amera.

"Think again, my sister. The loss prevention specialist's name is Carol, and the reason I know that is because I had to actually report her to management for following me around. Even now, if I come in here with my jeans on like you guys, she will follow me until she gets a good look and recognizes who I am." Robin laughed softly. "That is why I stayed around to keep an eye out. I don't put anything past her, but I must say, you two had everything under control. That was classic telling her about the lady in the coat."

With a conspiratorial air they all begin laughing.

"So why do you shop here if you know this store indirectly supports racism by allowing her to continue to work here with her racist views?" Amera asked.

Without a pause, Robin answered. "Why should I be denied access to the designers that I love and service you can only get in a store like this because of the foolishness of one ignorant woman? Saks doesn't care what color I am, they just care that my money is green. I am here today to pick up a dress that I had the personal shopper select for me. If I don't have time to shop, then all I have to do is call her and let her know what the event is and when I need it. She already has all my measurements, favorite colors, and likes and dislikes. She emails me pictures of some dresses and by the time I get off from work, we have it narrowed down to two or three dresses, and because she is so good at what she does, at least one of them will be perfect if not all of them."

"Wow that's hot!" said Amera. "You must be balling to be able to do that."

Robin looked at Amera's Chanel purse, which she knew was not a knockoff, and the $200 Seven brand jeans Amera was wearing and smiled.

"Girl, you may have fooled Carol with those jeans on, but that bag that you have thrown so casually over your shoulder is a genuine Chanel Limited Edition hobo sack, which by the way, retails at $3200. And you got to be connected because they don't hit the stores until Friday." Amera and Jo burst out laughing, again, and it was in that instant that true friendship began.

"Girl, that's way too much information," said Jo.

The girls begin talking together like old friends and chatted for several minutes before Robin remembered she still had to pick up her dress and get her hair done.

"I would love to hang out with you guys a little longer but I have this charity event I have to attend this evening."

"Sounds stuffy," said Jo.

"You have no idea," replied Robin. "And I still have to pick up my dress and get my hair done."

"So where in this town can a sista get her hair done? Amera asked. We both have natural hair and have a problem finding qualified people to do our hair when we are on the road."

"What do you guys do for a living?" asked Robin.

"We are in the entertainment industry," Jo replied.

Robin, who was distracted trying to figure out how she was going to recoup the time she had lost, absentmindedly replied. "What type of entertainment?"

There was silence as the two girls looked at each other, speaking without words as they debated whether or not to divulge their identities.

"You really don't know who we are," stated Amera.

"You guys did look familiar when I first saw you, but I wasn't sure how I knew you." Suddenly, a thought occurred to her. "Hold up—you guys aren't strippers are you? I mean if you are, that's okay. I didn't mean to say it like that."

Robin began stammering as she tried to apologize for any unintended slight. Amera and Jo began laughing until they both were bent over with tears coming from their eyes. They laughed so hard it was a couple of minutes before either could speak. "Strippers, oh my God, that is hysterical!" Jo said, as they both continued to laugh holding their stomachs. "No girl, we're not strippers," Jo continued, "We are singers." They both continued to laugh wildly, which made Robin laugh simply because the two were so out of control.

"Singers? Do you guys have anything out that I might recognize?" Robin asked.

Amera, answered, wiping tears from her eyes. "Have you ever heard of "I Do," "In the Morning," "Say Goodnight or Say Goodbye?"

Robin was stunned. For a moment she couldn't even speak. Each song Amera mentioned, Robin not only was familiar with, but she knew every word to every one of them. She had been playing that same CD for quite a while. The two girls together formed a group known to just about everyone in the modern world as Truth. Their CD was number one on both the Pop and R&B charts, which was almost unheard of. There have only been a few artists who had multiple number one singles off the same CD. The fifth number one single off the CD was released over a month ago and it was like its predecessors—triple platinum. Standing before her was her favorite group on the planet and she didn't even recognize them. Robin was suddenly star struck.

"Oh my gosh! Oh my gosh! No way, you are not Truth! I thought you guys looked familiar, but I would have never imagined that I would be standing in Saks, in Columbus, Ohio, kicking it with my favorite group! I can't believe I didn't recognize you! What are you guys doing here? I know you have a show tomorrow night in Cincinnati because I have tickets, but there is no show in Columbus." Robin noticed she was babbling. "Sorry, I know I'm babbling, but I just can't believe I am actually meeting you guys in the flesh. Wow! Wait until I tell my friend Tiffany. She loves you guys, too."

Amera and Jo, who now had finally stopped laughing about the stripper remark, looked at Robin smiling. "It's cool," said Jo. "We get that a lot. We still flip out over celebrities that we meet as well."

"Yea," said Amera. "We met Denzel Washington last January at the Dove Awards and girl, he thought I had a speech impediment."

"Oh yea," said Jo laughing. "You should have seen her. Every time he would ask her a question she would answer, but she would leave words out of her sentences," she said jokingly. "Then she would just stare at him all starry-eyed. I had to go grab her and explain to Denzel that when we were nine, Amera had always said she was going to marry him. He was so cool! He spoke with us in length about our new CD and said his wife, Paulette, loved our music. You won' believe what he did.

By now Robin's eyes were as big as saucers as she listened to the two young women describe a personal encounter with someone whom she had only seen on the movie screen. Jo asked her to guess what Denzel had done.

"I have no idea," Robin said, in a celebrity-induced daze.

"Girl, he asked us for an autograph! Can you believe that Denzel Washington asked us for our autograph?"

"What did you do?" asked Robin.

"Girl please, we signed his program!" said Jo, with a sassy expression. All the girls began laughing at that point.

"I could talk to you guys all night. I hate to leave but I am already super late for my hair appointment and my stylist doesn't play favorites or overbook, so I might be twisting up my own hair tonight," said Robin.

"Is your event black-tie?" asked Amera?

"Actually white-tie and very conservative."

"Well you may be in luck," said Amera chuckling softly. "Before Jo became the infamous JoJo with the group called Truth, she was the stylist extraordinaire Lady J."

Robin looked at Jo and then back at Amera, with questioning eyes. "So what are you saying? Are you telling me that you will do my hair?"

"If you don't mind, I don't mind," replied Jo. "Besides, it will give us a chance to hang out longer."

"I would love that!" said Robin.

They all realized in that moment that something special was being born. What they didn't know was that the friendship which had started so casually, would bind the girls together for a lifetime. Like a three-fold cord which is not easily broken, the strength of their friendship would sustain and keep each girl through their own personal storms of life.

"So how do we do this?" asked Robin. "I still have to get my dress and then you guys can come back with me to my house."

"Today is a free day for us, so your place is fine. We can have our driver follow you," said Amera.

"If you guys don't mind, we can all ride together in my car and you can just give your driver my address. That way we can talk and get to know each other better," Robin suggested.

"Normally we don't go anywhere without Cliff. He is our bodyguard but I am comfortable letting him go back to the hotel if you are Amera," said Jo.

"I am okay with that," replied Amera.

At that point, both girls began looking at something behind Robin. Turning around, Robin saw what she had missed before—one of the biggest men she had ever seen in her life. He looked like a professional wrestler. As the girls caught his eye he began to move in their direction. Walking up to the threesome, he spoke directly to Amera and Jo.

"Are you ladies ready?"

Cliff stood in front of the three ladies with his six feet six inch, 250 pound muscular frame. His hands were demurely folded in front of his stomach which had not an ounce of fat anywhere. He looked to be in his forties, but very well preserved and quite handsome in an older dignified way.

"Cliff, we have made a new friend and we are going to her house to play beauty shop," Amera said laughing.

"I'll get the car," he said, turning to exit the store.

"Not necessary," said Amera. "We are going to ride with Robin and we will call you when we are finished to be picked up."

"That's fine. I will follow and just wait in the vehicle until you are finished."

"No Cliff, we can't let you do that. Do what we're doing. Take a free day to do anything you want to do. We will be fine," said Amera. "I don't think Robin is a mass murderer."

"By the way Robin, we told you what our occupations are, so what do you do for a living?" asked Jo. "Oh yea Cliff, remind me to tell you later what Robin thought we did for a living," chuckled Amera."

All three girls begin laughing hysterically as Cliff looked at them quizzically.

"May I ask if you ladies were acquainted prior to today?" Cliff asked.

The girls still amused all answer at the same time. "No!"

Cliff gave Robin the once over before responding. "Then I will have to insist upon accompanying you. I will just follow and wait in the car."

"We will be fine, dad," said Jo, as she pretended to punch Cliff in the arm.

"I'm sorry, ladies, but I cannot let you leave all alone with someone you just met today. Even if it is a woman, I just can't do it," Cliff insisted.

CHAPTER FOUR

Robin, Amera, and Jo all laughed and talked like old friends as they left out through the south exit, with Cliff quietly bringing up the rear. Greg, the valet was waiting outside the door, standing by Robin's car. He quickly moved to take the packages from Robin and her friends as they came outside, placing their packages in the trunk of Robin's SUV.

Just as he closed the trunk, a black Hummer with chrome rims and all the trimmings pulled up behind Robin's car. The attendant got out and went around to the passenger side of the Hummer to open the door.

"That's okay, we will be riding with Ms. Walters," said Amera, as she placed a bill in the attendant's hand.

Cliff climbed into the Hummer as the ladies all piled into Robin's vehicle laughing like schoolgirls. Robin opened the window and yelled back to Cliff.

"I'm going to text you my home address to put into the GPS, in case we get separated on the way to my house."

"I already have it," replied Cliff.

"What!" said Robin, with a bewildered look on her face.

"Don't worry," said Amera, "That's just Cliff doing his thing. He used to be with the FBI, CIA, or one of those I-Spy organizations. He has all kinds of connections, including the Bureau of Motor Vehicles."

"Oh," said Robin hesitantly. "Wow, that's a bit scary, but I must say, he does know his stuff."

The girls talked the entire way to Robin's house. Turning into a hidden entrance off the main road, they drove down a long driveway avoiding a turnoff, which would have taken them to Robin's four-car garage. They, instead, followed the road that ended in a circular driveway in front of the home's main entrance. They piled out of the car chattering like magpies. They looked around at Robin's estate and their faces had a look of amazement. To call it a house wouldn't have done it justice. Amera and Jo were blown away by the beauty of Robin's home.

"Wow, your house is absolutely beautiful!" said Jo, as she looked around at the lush landscaping and the beautiful glass mosaic doublewide entry door.

"Girl, we know movie stars who don't have a house this nice; you must make a great living," said Amera. "By the way, you never did say what you do for a living?

"You're not a drug dealer are you?" said Jo.

Robin stopped in her tracks. "What!" she looked at both girls with an incredulous look on her face. They burst out laughing. Robin relaxed and laughed as well. "You guys had me going for a minute," she said opening the door.

As beautiful as the house was on the outside it couldn't compare to the beauty of the interior. From the entry way to the right was a beautifully decorated formal dining room done in an Asian theme. Japanese prints graced the walls while authentic 18th century Japanese art pieces sat on beautiful teakwood tables and sideboards. The table was set with exquisite delicate pieces of hand-painted china. To the left was a formal sitting room and no expense had been spared in decorating. It was obvious that every piece had been personally hand selected for that room only.

Both rooms were beautiful, but neither could compare with the actual foyer which was huge with a soaring high ceiling. The most amazing thing about the open space was that the entire foyer was painted to look like the picture "The Last Supper" by Michelangelo—everywhere you looked was a feast for the eyes. Amera and Jo were speechless. Cliff walked up the steps and came inside the house. You could tell that even he was momentarily blown away.

"This is incredible! This is absolutely incredible," Amera said repeatedly.

They all stood in the foyer entranced by the painting that covered every wall.

"It's a little overwhelming at first," said Robin. "You either love it or hate it, but there is no in between. The Last Supper is my favorite painting. Whenever I get stressed I come out here and I sit right there on that settee and I just soak it all in. For me, it has such a calming effect. Come on let me show you the rest of the house."

All the girls go up the spiral stairway with Cliff following closely behind. Robin showed the girls and Cliff to their own beautifully-decorated guest suite. Everyone agreed to meet downstairs after Amera and Jo changed into the sweats and tee shirts they had purchased in Saks. The Jack and Jill bedrooms Amera and Jo were in allowed them to go back and forth between each other's room through the shared restroom. Robin had offered them each an individual guest suite with their own lavatory but they had refused saying they loved the easy access to each other's room.

Both bedrooms were exotically beautiful with each sporting queen size beds and fireplaces. The rooms were decorated in jewel-tone colors, creating an oasis of beauty, which beckoned to the occupant to curl up in front of the fireplace with a cup of hot chocolate and a good book.

"Very nice," said Amera.

"Thanks," said Robin.

"Who is your decorator?" asked Jo.

"Yours truly," replied Robin, blushing slightly.

"Wow!" Jo proclaimed. "I can't believe you did this on your own. It looks like these rooms were done by a professional decorator."

"Decorating is my second love. I wouldn't mind doing it for a living if I wasn't already working in the field which is my first love."

"Which is," replied Amera. "We never did find out what you do for a living—that is, once we determined you're not a drug dealer." All the girls started laughing again.

"My first love is children," said Robin.

"I would never have guessed you had children," said Amera. "This house looks like a child-free zone, with all the expensive art pieces everywhere," she continued.

"Oh I don't have any children."

Both girls look at Robin curiously.

Cliff spoke up at that moment. "Ms. Robin Giselle Walters or should I say Dr. Robin Giselle Walters is a very well-known child psychiatrist."

All the ladies were stunned into silence for a moment, but all for different reasons.

"A child psychiatrist. Wow!" said Amera.

Stammering, Robin asked, "howwww did you know that, Cliff? I never told you what I did." She looked at Cliff with a little fear in her eyes and Cliff quickly assured her that all was well.

"I meant no disrespect, Dr. Walters, but my job is ensuring the safety of Miss Amera and Miss Jo, and I take my job very seriously. Although you guys are all going on your gut instinct regarding each other, I would have been remiss in my duties if I had done the same. I will say, my gut was also telling me you were okay, but I still have to do my job and make sure that they are always in a safe environment. Before I became a personal bodyguard, I worked for the FBI and some other government agencies which, due to national security, shall remain nameless. Needless to say, I have many contacts and resources for accessing databases which detail individual backgrounds. Again, I meant no disrespect."

The room was silent for a moment as the ladies processed the information.

Amera broke the silence. "Girl, don't be offended, I told you that was just Cliff doing his thing."

There was a tense awkward silence as Robin stared intently at Cliff. She finally broke eye contact with him and smiled. "Cliff, you are one scary individual. I wouldn't want to get on your bad side," she said.

With that, the awkward silence was broken, and the girls went back to discussing the pros and cons of doing Robin's hair, in a classic chignon or a sexy upsweep. They all moved toward the kitchen where Robin poured everyone a glass of wine, except for Cliff who was still on the clock.

CHAPTER FIVE

Three hours later, Robin was dressed to impress with her hair done up in a classic chignon. Her $3000 classic black Vera Wang cocktail dress, with its simple design, came to life on her slim frame only to be complimented by square cut emerald earrings and a matching necklace.

The girls and Cliff had agreed to watch movies and veg out until she returned and then they were going to play scrabble. Cliff's eyes had even brightened upon discovering he was not the only avid scrabble fan. Robin promised she would make her exit from the stuffy event at the first available opportunity.

As Robin made her way to the front door, her cell phone began ringing. She took it out of her purse to put on silent but noticed the number calling was from Children's Hospital. Curious to know who was calling, she answered.

"Hello."

"Robin, is that you?" said a feminine yet familiar voice on the other line.

"Yes, it's me," said Robin.

"Thank God I found you! This April from the hospital and I thought you would want to know that Josiah has been admitted to the psych ward. He tried to kill himself earlier tonight."

There was momentary silence on the line as Robin processed the news she just received.

"He took a bottle of Excedrin," April said. "His mother told the paramedics it was a new bottle with only a couple missing, so he had to have taken close to 100 pills," April continued. "They've pumped his stomach and did a charcoal treatment on him, and it looks like physically he is going to be okay, but he's going to need some help. I knew he was your patient from the clinic and that you would want to know."

"Thank you so much for calling to let me know April. You wouldn't happen to know whose patient he is at Children's would you."

"Yes," replied April. "I figured you would want to know that as well. They have him listed as Dr. Kirker's patient. I went ahead and got his number for you."

"Thanks April! You are a godsend," Robin replied, as she wrote down the number.

Amera, Jo, and Cliff all stared at Robin as she ended the call. It was obvious that the call had disturbed her. Robin looked at them all and saw genuine concern in all of their eyes and a question. "What can we do to help?"

Though the words were never spoken out loud, Robin knew, without it being said, that she only had to ask and they would do whatever they could to assist. Silently, she thanked God for sending her these two extraordinary young women, and also for Cliff, whom she knew would also do whatever he could to help her, based on her relationship with his two charges. They all stared at her expectantly. She thought to herself how much she could share without violating doctor-patient confidentiality.

"It's about one of my patients. He is in crisis and needs my help. I don't like to drive when I am upset and I was wondering, Cliff, if you would be willing to drive me to Children's Hospital?"

"Of course," he responded without hesitation.

"It looks like all your hard work is going to be for nothing, Jo," Robin continued. "It doesn't look like I will be going anywhere tonight," she said, as she walked back up the stairs she had just come down. "Give me five minutes to change my clothes, Cliff, and I will be ready. I'm not sure how long I will be gone, but I will be back as soon as I can."

Amera looked intently as Robin spoke. "If you don't mind, sis, we would like to ride with you. We understand we'll need to fall back at some point, but let us ride with you and support you for as long as we can."

Jo seconded Amera's suggestion. "Yea Robin, let us at least ride with you. You can let us know when to step off."

Robin closed her eyes and when she opened them they were moist with unshed tears. "I don't know why God hooked us up today. He must have known I was going to need a friend." A lone tear slid down her cheek.

Both Amera and Jo quickly scurried up the stairs and sandwiched Robin with hugs.

"Go change your clothes while Cliff brings the car around," said Amera.

"Okay, I will be right back," Robin replied.

Robin left to go change, while Amera and Jo joined hands in prayer.

"Father God, we ask you to give us the spirit of discernment and we pray for your guidance, Lord, this we ask in Jesus name, Amen."

Moments after they finished praying, Robin returned, now dressed in jeans and a small black leather jacket. The Hummer was awaiting their arrival, with Cliff already behind the wheel looking large and in charge. The ladies all climbed into the vehicle and Robin told Cliff where to take her.

"I need to go to Children's Hospital in downtown Columbus."

"Don't worry, the navigation system will get us there," Cliff replied.

They take off and the girls began talking. Robin told them as much as she legally could about her young patient's current situation.

"I appreciate you all coming with me. One of my patients has been admitted to the hospital." I am not usually this emotional about my patients, but for some reason this little boy has gotten pass all my professional barriers. There is something in him that calls to me. It is like there is a pain in him that only he and I can feel, and I know this may sound crazy and I don't even know why I feel this, but it's like I know that his well-being is tied to my well-being. I believe that God sent him to me. He is my greatest joy and my greatest pain. My greatest joy came when he opened up to me for just a crack and allowed me to see his pain. I knew it was there but I knew he needed to trust me first. He was so use to hiding his pain. For months during our weekly sessions we both pretended that it wasn't there—ignoring the elephant in the room. Again, I knew until he trusted me enough to show me his pain we could not move forward. Today, he finally let down his barrier for just a moment. It was almost like for a moment he ran out of strength and just couldn't hold his shield up any longer. My greatest pain is to now know just how much pain that child is in. It broke my heart. He is such a great kid! I won't rest until he is a free and a healthy10-year old." Tears slid down her cheeks as she spoke about Josiah.

Jo, who was in the back seat with Robin, put her arm around her comfortingly. "Let's all pray together," she said.

Quietly the three women held hands and began to pray. They prayed until they felt the vehicle come to a slow stop. Looking up, Robin saw they were at the emergency entrance of the hospital. Robin got out and was quickly followed by Amera and Jo.

"You guys don't have to go in with me; you've done enough already," stated Robin.

"If you don't mind," said Amera. We would like to go with you as far as we can."

"Okay," Robin replied. "Let's go."

They all walked in through the emergency room, stopping at the desk where they were directed to the elevator and told that the psych ward was on the third floor. Upon arriving on the floor, Robin left Amera and Jo in the waiting area while she went back to Josiah's room.

Quietly she entered Josiah's room, careful not to make any noise that would startle him. Josiah laid in the hospital bed still and silent. She only knew he was alive by the beeping of the monitors. His breathing was so shallow his chest barely rose. He looked so small lying in the hospital bed. His hands were in restraints. Robin moved closer to the bed and glanced down at his face. Only half of his face could be seen because he lay at a right angle with his face turned toward the wall. His beautiful ash blond hair covered his one exposed eye. He looked so fragile. Not wanting to wake him, she stepped back and took a seat in the chair next to the bed.

CHAPTER SIX

Robin cracked one eye open, quickly closing it because of the sunlight streaming through the window facing her chair. Her body was stiff and protesting as she moved around trying to find a comfortable spot. After several seconds of seeking that which could not be found, Robin finally gave up trying to go back to sleep and began to take in the reality she found herself dealing with. She was both cold and sore. She opened her eyes to try and find out why she was so uncomfortable and that was when she realized she was not in the comfort of her own luxurious king size bed, but somewhere foreign, somewhere unknown and suddenly it all came back to her.

"Josiah!" Jumping up she looked toward the bed and her eyes locked with his. He had been watching her for over an hour. For a moment they just stared at each other.

"Hey," said Robin.

Josiah was silent, but he didn't break eye contact.

"I know you're probably scared and wondering where you are, but don't worry, you're going to be okay," said Robin.

Josiah remained silent, but he never took his eyes off Robin.

"How are you feeling? Can you at least tell me that? Are you in any kind of pain?"

Josiah held her stare for a few seconds more before blinking and looking toward his restrained wrist.

"Don't worry about those, I will have them removed. We just need to make sure that you will not try to hurt yourself if we remove them. Will you promise me that if we take them off, you will not try and hurt yourself?"

Josiah looked away. Robin put her hand under his chin and turned his face back toward hers, forcing him to again look into her eyes. Locking eyes with her, he spoke for the first time. His voice was raspy and barely above a whisper.

"I promise," he said quickly looking away.

"Okay then, let me get the doctor," Robin said, as she moved toward the door. "I'll be right back. Are you hungry?"

Josiah shook his head no in response.

Robin left the room and that was when she remembered that she had left Amera and Jo in the waiting room all night. "Darn," she thought to herself. "I know they're probably gone, but I really wanted to thank them." She knew their concert was that evening, so she understood if they needed to leave. She entered the waiting room and to her surprise she spied Cliff, Amera, and Jo all asleep, leaning on each other like each one was the other's body pillow. As she approached the threesome, Cliff's eyes opened as if he hadn't been sleeping at all and locked eyes with her. Even though Cliff never moved, the change in his energy woke Amera, which in turn, awakened Jo. The girls quickly leapt to their feet group hugging Robin all the while asking her a thousand questions. Cliff quickly took control of the situation, settling everyone down.

"Okay ladies, give Robin a chance to answer the first question before you ask her another," Cliff said.

"So how is he?" said Jo.

"First I would like to say I'm sorry. I didn't mean to fall asleep in his room," Robin said apologetically.

"We don't care about that," said Amera. "Just tell us how he is doing."

"Physically, he will be fine but this was a definite setback to the work we have been doing. The child in that room is even more fragile than when I first met him. It's like all the progress we made has been undone. Something set him off. I need to find out what."

"Did his parents tell you what happened? Why he did what he did?" asked Amera.

"I haven't seen his mother since I have been here," replied Robin.

There was silence for a moment as everyone processed this piece of information.

"I am so sorry about how our evening turned out. I know you all have that concert in Cincinnati tonight and need to leave. I'm not even sure if I am going to be able to make it with these latest developments," Robin stated disappointedly.

"Don't worry about any of that. Cincinnati is less than a two hour drive, which means Cliff can get us there with the lights and siren in less than that, so we are okay" said Jo with a smile.

"We just need to know what we can do to help?" she said.

"You all are unbelievable," said Robin. "Let me get my patient straightened out and then I will ride back to the house with you so that you can get your stuff and I can get my car."

Cliff left to get everyone coffee from the hospital cafeteria. After about 20 minutes, Robin rejoined her new friends and they headed back to her house.

After arriving at her home, the girls gathered their belongings while Robin made phone calls. When the time came to say goodbye, an awkward silence fell over them. The girls could see Robin was a thousand miles away. As they got her attention, she snapped back to the present and realized she was actually going to miss them. She observed that somehow, she felt stronger when they were all in it together and now that they were about to leave, she was experiencing a sense of loss. She thought to herself how crazy that was, because she had just met them the day before, but they had all fit together like missing pieces to a puzzle.

They hugged longingly at the door's threshold, not wanting to let go. Amera was the first to break from the pact.

"I can't believe how I feel. It feels like I am abandoning you," said Amera.

"I'm glad you said it because I was just tripping about how much I hate to leave. You need us. I can feel it," said Jo.

All three girls had tears in their eyes. Robin wiped the tears from her eyes before speaking. "I know I'll be okay, but I feel like part of my strength is leaving and for the life of me, I can't explain it. It's like you guys are my long lost family and we have this really deep spiritual connection."

"I feel that, too," said Amera.

"Me, too," said Jo.

Cliff looked on in amazement as he witnessed the intimate moment between the ladies. Cliff had done everything from undercover work, to presidential detail, but had never witnessed anything quite like this. He knew what the girls were saying was unexplainable, but he also knew exactly what they were talking about because he could feel it, too. He knew that these three ladies paths were destined to cross again. The only thing that remained to be determined was the purpose of this connection. Shaking his head in amazement, he interrupted the emotional moment the girls were sharing.

"Remember ladies, you are only a plane, a car ride, or a phone call away from one another," Cliff stated.

"Actually, we are closer than that, because we are just a prayer away," Amera responded. All three girls continued to hold hands and, in that moment, the three musketeers were born. All for one and one for all! Hugging each other one last time, the girls and Cliff left, and Robin jumped into her car and headed back to the hospital.

CHAPTER SEVEN

Robin arrived back at the hospital and rushed to Josiah's room. She entered the room to find the resident physician notating Josiah's chart. She began to pepper him with questions, which at first didn't seem to bother him, but after answering several questions, it became apparent she was starting to irritate him.

In a nasty, condescending tone, the resident ceased documenting on the chart, and turned to address Robin directly.

"Ms. Martin, the chart indicates that your son is currently under the care of a mental health provider. I would suggest you follow up with them for the rest of your questions."

"My name is not Ms. Martin, my name is..." he interrupted her before she could finish.

"Oh, I'm sorry, Ms. Martin I..." Robin returned the favor.

"You what?" Robin asked. You don't listen? I told you last night I was Dr. Walters, and I am, as you put it, his mental health provider." Robin gestured doing air quotation marks with her fingers.

The young doctor begins stuttering. "I am sorry Dr. Walters, I meant no disrespect. I just pulled a double shift so I am just a little tired.

"I understand double shifts are a part of your residency but forgetting can cost you a life."

"Yes, you're right of course, but I just thought, since you spent the night at his bedside, that you were the mom."

"Are you saying you haven't seen his mom since he was admitted?" she asked.

"The only person I have seen with this patient besides hospital staff is you. That is why I assumed you were his mother. I am sorry I forgot about meeting you last night but I was all over the place, even though that is no excuse," the young doctor explained.

Robin, feeling somewhat mollified, turned from the doctor and looked closely at Josiah to make sure he was still sleeping soundly. His breathing was deep and even.

"May I see his chart please?" she asked.

The young doctor quickly handed her the chart, which she perused and handed it back to him.

"I see a child services representative is scheduled to see him later today," she said, moving around the bed checking Josiah's urine output and legs for swelling. "Would you happen to know what time that is scheduled to take place?"

"No I don't, but the nurse on duty would be able to tell you that. I will tell her to step in and talk to you."

"Thanks, but that won't be necessary. I can go out to the nurse's station myself." Robin left Josiah's room and headed for the nurses' station. After providing her hospital credentials, Robin got the information she needed and quickly headed back to Josiah's room where she found him awake.

"Hey you!" she said. "Are you feeling better after your nap?"

Josiah just stared at her and she noticed how tired he looked. There were black circles under his eyes and he was as pale as a ghost.

"Would you like something to drink? It said in your chart you are allowed to have clear liquids. Would you like some water?"

Josiah nodded his head affirmative.

"I'll be right back," Robin stood to leave but a look of stark terror crossed Josiah's face. Opening his mouth to speak, his words came out in a hoarse croak.

"Don't go, please."

"I wasn't leaving. I was just going to get you a drink."

His eyes filled with tears as he repeated, "Please don't leave me, Dr. Walters. I promise I'll be good."

Robin felt like someone had kicked her in the stomach and she had no air to breathe.

"Josiah, I won't leave you. Don't you ever worry about that."

Sitting back down, Robin pushed the call button for the nurse's aide, but she never took her eyes off Josiah's face. Tears continued to roll down his cheeks. It was as if a dam burst. Robin took tissues out of the box and began dabbing his tears.

In all the months he had been in therapy, she had never seen him cry, and it was devastating. He cried like his tears had no off switch. They had been there all along, but Josiah had refused to let them out, always thinking he had to be strong. Always putting his mother's needs before his own, he knew she couldn't handle his tears so he learned to lock them away deep inside, and to smile because she loved his smile. She had told him that once, so even when he wanted to cry, he smiled because that was what she wanted. He just loved her so much. He always tried to make her happy no matter what, but today, for some reason, he couldn't keep them in.

The more he tried to stop them, the harder he cried. He wanted to stop, he really did because he had come to love Dr. Walters too, and wanted her to like him—no, he needed her to like him. He didn't know what he would do without her. She was the only person in his life that he felt really and truly cared about him. He understood his mother. He knew she loved him on some level, but he also knew she was unable to give him the unconditional love his young soul needed in order to be free, to be himself without fear of rejection. At 10 years old, he knew his mother's love was inadequate, but it was better than his father's love which was nonexistent, so he tried to make sure that he did everything in his power to keep her love around. Sometimes it just got to be too much and that was why he couldn't stop crying.

He felt overwhelmed and afraid. He hadn't seen his mother since they loaded him in the ambulance to bring him to the hospital. They had done all kinds of scary things to him in the emergency room. He kept telling them he wanted to wait until his mother got there but she never came so they stuck him with needles, put a tube down his throat, which made him feel like he was going to die because he couldn't breathe. They had given him something to drink which was so nasty it made him throw up until he felt like he was throwing up the inside of his stomach. Still she never came.

He knew he had run her off with his weakness. She didn't like sadness. She said she had enough of her own and couldn't bear it if he was sad. He was sorry he took the pills, but he just felt like it would be better for everyone if he were gone, especially for her. He knew he was a burden to her even though she never said so, but she often mentioned how she wished she had waited to have kids. Josiah cried and Robin cried with him.

Josiah noticed Robin was crying and he immediately tried to go into protection mode and began apologizing. "I'm sorry, Dr. Walters, I didn't mean to make you cry. I don't know why I'm acting like a stupid baby," Josiah remarked.

"Is that what you think Josiah? You think if you cry, that you are acting like a baby?"

"Yes ma'am."

Robin crawled into the bed with Josiah, put her arm around him, and hugged him close. "Then let's be babies today."

Josiah laid his head on her shoulder and cried like a baby.

He cried for all the times he needed his mom and she wasn't there.

He cried for all the times she was there but he was invisible to her.

He cried for the father who had rejected him for reasons he could not fathom.

He cried for the woman who was his doctor who he wished was his mother.

Josiah cried for all that was unfair in his 10-year-old world. He cried until no tears remained and promptly fell asleep.

CHAPTER EIGHT

A couple of weeks later, Robin kept her standing appointment at Lifetime Fitness with her best friend, Tiffany. This routine started years ago with the understanding that only a nuclear holocaust would be an acceptable reason for missing their weekly carved-in-stone appointment.

"I can't believe you spent the night with my favorite group in the world and you are just now telling me," said Tiffany. She adjusted the incline on her treadmill, while walking at a moderate pace.

Robin, who was on the treadmill next to Tiffany's, continued to jog, picking up speed while Tiffany decreased hers.

"Girl, you are going to have a heart attack if you don't slow down. Do you realize you have been running for over an hour? There are only two things that make you try to kill yourself on the treadmill, your mother or Josiah. Which is it today? I'm guessing Josiah," Tiffany rambled on. "I called his mom to find out how he was doing and she told me he is still in the hospital but he's being released tomorrow. She also said he wouldn't be coming back to school, but would be going into foster care. Can you tell me what happened without violating patient confidentiality?"

"Unfortunately, I can't, but I can tell you to please keep him lifted up in prayer," said Robin.

"You know I will," said Tiffany, wiping the sweat off her forehead as her machine went into the cool down interval.

"PLEASE STOP RUNNING!" she spoke loudly to Robin who had put her ear buds back in her ears and increased the speed on her machine, as if she was intent on completing a marathon run on the overworked treadmill.

Robin, glancing over at Tiffany, smiled as she lowered the speed on her machine, silently acquiescing to Tiffany's demand.

After the obligatory five minute cool down and another five minutes of stretching they headed toward the locker room, both tired and sweaty.

"So do you think Amera and Jo will ever call you again?" asked Tiffany.

"They have called every night since they left just to check in and see how I'm doing. I'm telling you, Tiff, it was as if we had known each other all our lives."

"I think I might be a little jealous. After all, I was your best friend first," Tiffany spoke cautiously, making it sound as if she were joking, but Robin could hear the ring of truth in her words.

"Girl, we have been best friends since freshmen year in high school. We have shared everything from breakups to failed quizzes," Robin said.

"Robin, you have never failed a quiz in your life," said Tiffany.

Robin quickly responded. "Yea but I was there for all of yours." Both girls laugh hysterically.

"What I am trying to say is that you will always be my best friend, Tiff. Nothing will ever change that," said Robin trying to catch her breath.

"I'm just saying, if Oprah decides one day she wants me to be the new Gayle, I might have to kick you to the curb," said Tiffany smugly.

"Funny!" said Robin.

"I'm serious, if you call me and all of a sudden I don't have time to work out with you anymore, then just know, Oprah's in town," said Tiffany, pretending to be serious.

"Oh you are so dead." Robin took the towel from around her neck and began winding it up to pop Tiffany who took off running towards the locker room with Robin in hot pursuit. Their loud laughter followed them down the hallway.

Robin and Tiffany slowly walked back to their cars, each relaxed and happy after a thorough workout followed by a long, deep tissue massage. Robin's cell phone rang. She looked at the caller name on the screen and her face grimaced.

"Well I guess I know who that is," said Tiffany. "Tell mommie dearest I said hello."

Robin quickly opened her car door and started her engine while she took her mother's phone call.

"Hello, Carmen." Her mother's birth name was Dorothy but as long as Robin could remember, her mother answered only to the name of Carmen. She insisted that not only should her friends all refer to her by her alias, but her only daughter should as well. She was NEVER allowed to refer to her mother as mom, mommie, mother, etc. Carmen advised Robin that she was much too young looking to be labeled as anyone's mother. Carmen was indeed a beautiful woman, even now at close to 50. Her entire life had been about preserving, maintaining, and parlaying her one asset, or rather her two assets, which were her face and body. Carmen was on her sixth marriage, each one to wealthy men who quickly fell out of lust when they saw behind the shallow vain facade which was Carmen Walters.

"Hello darling," Carmen begin. "I saw you on CNN last week. You were looking a little peaked. I see you haven't been using that under eye concealer I suggested."

Robin made no reply to the caustic comments her mother continued to spit as she had become quite accustomed to her never ending criticisms.

"You really need to drop about 10 pounds if you are going to go on television dear. You were looking absolutely pudgy on the one segment. I see someone's been skipping the gym," Carmen continued, with a fake little titter. "Darling, all I'm trying to say is that it is great that you got an education, but a man doesn't want a diploma in his bed at night. He wants a beautiful, sexy, vivacious woman which you certainly could be if you would just put forth a little effort. Why don't you come out to California so I can introduce you to a few of Robert's friends? They're all multimillionaires, and too old to be much of a nuisance, if you know what I mean," she tittered again. "Darling, you could have a ring on your finger within a few months if you follow my instructions."

Carmen didn't even notice that she had been talking for a full ten minutes, and with the exception of her answering the phone, Robin hadn't spoken one word.

"Things are growing a little weary here. Robert is hardly ever home and when he is, he barely even speaks to me. I am bored out of my mind. So needless to say, I've been getting in a lot of retail therapy and spa treatments." Carmen took a quick breath before continuing.

"Maybe we could meet at this lovely quaint little spa in Arizona. You certainly look like you could use a vacation. How about we make it my treat? I know you working women have to budget your pennies."

Carmen had no idea that her daughter was wealthy in her own right due to her books, speaking engagements, and the generous salary she makes at the Burke Center. Not to mention a very savvy investment in Google stock. Robin didn't have to worry about "pinching pennies" or trying to marry a wealthy benefactor.

Carmen believed the only way a woman got wealthy was she was either born into money, or she married into it. Since the first didn't apply, Carmen had put all her eggs in one basket. She believed her face and body would always be enough to get her through, but Father Time waited for no one and the day was coming when the surgeries would no longer stave off Father Time and the men would look for younger trophy wives. Carmen's day of reckoning was right around the corner, but she refused to see the handwriting on the wall.

"Sorry, Carmen, I would love to but I have to work," Robin said, as the white lie slipped out before she could stop it.

"But I didn't even give you a date yet," Carmen said, sounding surprised.

"I don't have any more vacation time left for this year," said Robin.

"See that is why you should be independent like me and have your own money."

Robin had to bite her tongue to keep from reminding her that she didn't really have her own money. Each marriage came with a prenup. This meant as long as Carmen remained married, she lived a lavish lifestyle but the minute she divorced, she was returned to her former state with only a meager allowance. This caveat forced Carmen to constantly be on the prowl. She had to continue to find fresh bait to put her back into the lifestyle she craved.

"Well, I guess we can't all be as lucky as you, Carmen," said Robin. Robin shook her head because she knew this comment would just go over her mother's head. She wouldn't hear the sarcasm hidden behind the words. "Some of us have to work for a living. I hate to cut you off, but I have another call coming in. Take care of yourself," Robin said, as she ended the call.

With that, Robin hung up the phone, sadly shaking her head as she pulled out of the gym's parking lot. Her mother was clueless. Robin tried to push down the anger she felt whenever she spoke with her. Robin didn't hate her mother, but the history they shared kept Robin tied to the past. Her grandmother had always taught Robin to respect Carmen because she was her mother; to try to see the real Carmen behind the glitz and glamour.

Robin didn't understand how she could just ignore their history and pretend like she had been a real mother to her. She prayed for God to help her come to a place of forgiveness because she realized now she had moved on with her life, but she had never really forgiven her mother.

CHAPTER NINE

The staccato tap of high heels made rhythmic sounds on the hardwood as Robin and her assistant briskly made their way down the hallway. Simone, who was Robin's assistant, juggled her tablet in one hand and her cell in another, easily keeping pace with Robin after years of practice. Each of the ladies multi-tasked as they moved toward the door marked "Conference Room A" at the end of the hallway. Robin was the first to break the silence.

"This is our third meeting today and it is not even noon yet. I am exhausted. "

"Tell me about it," replied Simone.

Simone was old enough to be Robin's mother even though you couldn't tell that by looking at her. She, like Robin, was dressed conservatively in a dark business suit but where Robin finished hers with a pair of sexy black Stuart Weitzman stilettos, Simone had chosen a black pair of understated yet sexy Anne Klein sling backs. Her natural hair was thick and beautifully coiffed with a touch of gray around her hairline. When the two of them were in meetings, it was often hard to tell who the assistant was and who was in charge. There was a shared intimacy that seemed to go beyond the traditional business relationship. Oftentimes, Simone was the one who seemed to wield the power but that was just because Robin absolutely trusted her and left many details in her hands to handle. Over time, Simone had come to be something of a surrogate mother, confidant, and a very close personal friend to Robin.

"Simone, I am going to need you to stay and run the power point presentation since I will be using props for this one."

"Yes, I've already figured that out. I've got everything set for your 3 p.m. staff meeting, but your 4 o'clock meeting with the board still remains a mystery. Nobody, and I mean nobody, has a clue about who or why they have called this meeting. You know there is nothing that goes on in this building that I can't find out but I have exhausted all my resources, and either no one knows anything or everyone is afraid to talk, which is a first."

"I know, it's got me a little paranoid," Robin warily replied.

"Why? Have you done something questionable?" Simone curiously asked.

Laughing Robin replied, "Do I ever do anything questionable?"

"That's a discussion for another day," said Simone dryly.

Both ladies laughed as they entered the conference room.

It was five minutes before 4 o'clock when Robin arrived at the main conference room where only the board met. She still had no clue what the meeting was about. As soon as she entered the space, her guard immediately went up. The room's décor was meant to intimidate. The room was definitely masculine with leather chairs, cherry wood paneling and a wall of bookshelves which went from floor to ceiling. It was a beautiful room but did not inspire warmth. Looking around the room, she noticed the entire board was present and accounted for, except for its chairman and founder Leonard Burke. Robin found it strange that she was the only staff in attendance.

"Hmmm," she thought to herself. "I wonder why I am the only staff member in attendance." Robin's stomach growled reminding her that she had missed lunch with all the meetings earlier. Grabbing a cookie and a bottle of water, she took a seat next to the one board member that she was the most comfortable with.

"Hey Mitch, how are you? I haven't seen you since the golf outing last month. How are Sara and the children doing?"

Mitch smiled with his lips but the smile never reached his eyes. "Sara and the children are fine. Thanks for asking." Mitch replied, but turned his head away from Robin instead of engaging in their normal friendly banter.

Robin looked at Mitch curiously. Thanks for asking? She immediately thought to herself, what is really going on? It was in that instant, that Robin knew something was rotten in Denmark. At the moment of that revelation, Leonard Burke walked in the door and the meeting was officially called to order.

After the minutes were read, Leonard Burke was the first to speak.

"Robin it has come to our attention that you have a pro bono case that you are working which did not come through our normal channels, and by that I mean there was no referral from the agencies that we traditionally work with for our pro bono cases," he said. "Are you familiar with what I am referring to?" Dr. Burke paused looking at Robin for a response.

"Yes, I am familiar with the particular patient you are speaking about, but if you will look at the notes in his chart you will find that he fits the criteria perfectly for the program he is in, and I can assure you that he qualifies financially as well."

"Yes, well that may be but the fact remains, this patient came to us without our normal vetting process being applied and now it seems we have somewhat of a situation."

"A situation?" asked Robin. What do you mean we have a situation?"

Then entire board was silent as they all looked accusingly at Robin. Robin glanced around the table at each of the faces and noticed not one of them would look her in the eye. These were the same men who sat with her in this boardroom and begged her to accept the position at Burke, explaining why working with them would be so much more beneficial than working for the other six companies who already had offers on the table. Two of the offers they couldn't compete with financially so they had sold her on the cutting edge work they were doing in her field. Robin had loved the work the Burke Center was doing and Dr. Burke had appeared not to care about protocol, but seemed to genuinely want to help children. That is what swayed her in the end. Fast forward seven years and here she was in this same room for a very different reason. Now her champions were her accusers and she still had no idea of what she was being accused of.

"Somebody better tell me something quick," Robin said, looking directly at Leonard Burke.

"Two days ago, the mother of your pro bono patient filed a lawsuit against the center."

Robin felt like she had been kicked in the stomach. Her eyes looked around the room at each of the men willing them to tell her that this was a joke, a prank, yea that was it, she was being punked. Where was Ashton? This couldn't be real, but as she looked around the room at the unsmiling faces of her judges she knew that this was too real.

"What? What do you mean a lawsuit? For what? What reason could she possibly have for filing a lawsuit?

"She is stating in her suit that she gave you a healthy, happy 10-year-old and after working with you, her son became depressed and tried to commit suicide. She went on to say that she never wanted to put her son in counseling but she felt pressured by you after you interviewed her and her son. She also stated you told her that she and her son would be on the Dr. Phil Show. I think they just threw that one in as an afterthought."

Robin was speechless. Josiah's mother hadn't said much of anything the entire time he had been in counseling. She continually missed the appointments Robin made for her to come in so they could lay out a strategy for home to help Josiah manage the deep emotions he dealt with on a daily basis. It was as if she couldn't handle knowing that Josiah was fragile. Whenever Robin tried to talk to her about it, she would act like Robin hadn't said a word, and change the subject.

Robin arranged for one of her colleagues to agree to do counseling with Ms. Martin on a pro bono basis, but she never kept one of her appointments. After she broke three appointments, Robin sent her colleague a check to pay for the three broken sessions and tried to figure out a new strategy to reach Josiah's mom. When she didn't show up at the hospital after Josiah's suicide attempt, Robin's frustration with Ms. Martin grew to a whole new level.

Robin wasn't surprised when Josiah hadn't been allowed to go home after his release from the hospital. She knew Child Protective Services always opened a case when a child tried to commit suicide. During Josiah's seven-day hospital stay, Ms. Martin had only visited once. Robin tried to warn Josiah's mother that if she didn't visit Josiah, the hospital staff would document that, and Josiah might not be allowed to come home with her. Ms. Martin totally misunderstood the nature of Robin's call and became defensive and very angry. That was the last time Robin had spoke with her. No doubt she found an ambulance chasing attorney, and now here they were.

Robin was silent as her mind ran back over all that had happened since Josiah's suicide attempt. Even after he had been placed in foster care, she was able to see him daily. What happened to Josiah at the hospital had been a breakthrough.

When Josiah broke down and freely cried with her, it had been like a catharsis for him. It was almost like a funeral where he buried the idea of the mother he wanted, and accepted the mother he had. This was remarkable for a 10-year-old. Josiah had not been the same since she had held him in his bed and they had cried together—he was stronger. Yes, he was still Josiah, showing a strong face to the world and Robin knew he wasn't as strong as he pretended, but he had turned a corner.

Robin watched as his world was turned upside down and inside out but Josiah had fought for life, in spite of everything. She noticed openness in Josiah that had not been there before. Josiah's spirit was as wobbly as a newborn colt but it was up, standing on its own. Robin was determined to do whatever it took to help Josiah become whole and complete. They had forged a new level of trust through the fire of his trauma and Robin was ecstatic that they had turned a corner in his treatment.

Bringing her mind back to the present, Robin processed the new information she had just received.

"This is a mistake," she said. "I will speak with Ms. Martin to get this cleared up."

"You absolutely will not speak with Ms. Martin under any circumstances," Dr. Burke said expressively. "Our attorneys have advised us to speak with no one. They want to keep a lid on this so the press doesn't find out. Thank God she didn't hire a more high profile attorney because we would certainly have been a sound bite on the evening news. So far so good as far as press coverage goes, but you will need to cease and desist from treating Josiah immediately and no further contact is to be made with this child until the attorneys clear it."

Robin looked in horror at Leonard Burke. "I can't do that, Dr. Burke. We are in a crucial part of his therapy. If I walk away from this child it will cause irreparable harm."

"I'm sorry, Robin, I understand, but our hands are tied. There is no way the Burke Center can continue to treat Josiah with an impending lawsuit. You know how I feel about children, but we would just be setting ourselves up for more litigation if we allow you to continue to treat him. Additionally, you would have to get the court's permission to continue to treat him and they are already recommending his care be transitioned to another therapist."

Robin chose her words carefully. "You don't understand! This is a child who has just returned from the brink of death. He is in the midst of grieving the loss of his mother who was his only caregiver.

I don't mean a literal loss because she isn't dead, but the dream he has held onto for all these years—the fantasy mom—is who he just buried." Robin continued. "Dr. Burke, he trusts me. If I just suddenly stop showing up, it will undo all the progress we have made, and it may push him back to thoughts or attempts of suicide. I can't live with that on my conscious. I, at least, have to see him to explain what is going on and why all of a sudden I won't be around."

Dr. Burke stared intently at Robin and she right back at him. Neither broke the gaze for several seconds. Dr. Burke was the first to look away.

"I'm sorry Robin, but for now you cannot see Josiah. I will speak with the attorneys to see if you can have an exit visit to transition his care to another doctor, but don't count on it Dr. Walters." He called her by her title, something he had never done before.

Robin closed her eyes in pain before replying. "Please do whatever you can, Dr. Burke. My next appointment with him is tomorrow and I would like to be able to keep it. I don't want to push but I really think if I could be allowed to speak with Ms. Martin I may be able to head this thing off at the pass. Will you at least pitch that to the attorneys as well?"

"Don't press your luck, Robin. You are treading on very thin ice right now and if I were you, I would be grateful that you still have a position here instead of pushing."

"You are right, Dr. Burke, but you knew when you hired me that the children come first. Respectfully, there is no way that I will ever harm a child in exchange for the safety of my job or even my life. They will always come first."

Dr. Burke softened, "I know that Robin, that is what makes you so good at what you do. I am just asking you to tread softly until we can figure this out."

"I can do that," replied Robin.

"Then I guess we have an understanding."

"Yes, we do," Robin replied, as she stood up and exited the room.

CHAPTER TEN

Robin's mind was going a thousand miles a minute as she moved down the deserted hallway toward her office. It was going on 6 p.m. The office was officially closed and the place looked like a ghost town.

As Robin opened the door to her office, she spied Simone at her desk working on the computer. Simone, never taking her eyes off the screen, spoke out to Robin as she entered the office.

"That bad huh?"

"How can you tell?" Robin sighed wearily.

"Your energy speaks volumes."

"Simone, you are not going to believe what happened." She quickly caught Simone up on what had transpired in the boardroom over the last two hours.

"Wow, that's bad. Poor Josiah can't catch a break, and just when he is beginning to accept his lot in life, he gets another blow. It is so unfair."

"I know," said Robin. "I don't even know how to tell him this latest bit of news. He is just starting to really open up to me for the first time. How do I tell him that now I, too, will be abandoning him?" Robin sat down behind her desk massaging her temples.

Everyone he has ever loved has hurt him. First his father, then his mother, and now me," Robin said sounding like she was going to cry.

"This is not your fault Robin," said Simone, bringing her a box of tissues.

Robin dabbed at her eyes as she sprawled in her oversized chair. trying to think of a solution to this complicated issue.

"He's not going to understand. Who will tell him why I've stopped coming to see him?"

"It really doesn't matter who tells him, he won't understand. He will only know that another adult has lied to him again and let him down," said Simone.

"I can't do this to him. We have to think of a solution."

Simone, looking thoughtful, sighed wearily. "Well it looks like it's going to be a long night. I'll make the coffee while you get the take out menus."

For a moment, both women are temporarily distracted from the burdensome task which was before them. The mundane chores of ordering takeout and making coffee provided a momentary stay of execution for the onerous task they were each reluctant to face.

An hour and a half later, they were no closer to a solution, even though they had drunk two pots of coffee and demolished a table full of Chinese takeout.

"Robin, I don't know about this. If you try contacting Josiah's mother while we're in the midst of litigation, you could lose your job."

"At this point I don't care about my job. I care about Josiah and what is best for him. His mother is not acting in his best interest right now, but I don't think she knows that. If I could just talk to her one-on-one without her attorney being there to whisper in her ear, I really think I might be able to get through to her."

"What if you can't? What if she tells her attorney you were trying to pressure her to change her mind? You would practically be making their case for them."

Robin pondered her words silently while chewing on her pencil as she tried to think things through.

"I have to call the girls," she said out loud, to no one in particular, but realizing they would be a great sounding board at a time like this. After offering their opinion, they would do as they always did at the end of each of their conversations, they would end with prayer and ask God for guidance.

"What did you say?" asked Simone.

"I need to call the girls. I always get clarity after speaking with them. Right now I feel like my head is stuck in a bowl of pea soup. Everything is thick and cloudy and I can't see what is in front of me so I don't know which way to go."

Taking out her cell phone, she tapped in the speed dial number for her two new friends—no, they were more than that. They were her sisters. She put the phone on speaker. It rang, sounding hollow in the quiet office space. Jo answered just as Robin was about to hang up.

"Hello? Hello? Robin, are you there?"

"Yes, I'm here. Can you hear me?"

"Yes, I can hear you just fine. Hold on let me get Amera and Cliff."

There was silence on the phone but not for long. Suddenly, Robin heard Amera's voice in the background, along with Cliff and Jo's, all saying hello.

"What's wrong, Robin? It's one a.m. here. Are you okay?" asked Amera.

"I'm sorry, I will call you tomorrow," Robin said sounding sheepish preparing to hang up.

"That's okay, we are still up, just getting in from a late rehearsal. Why are you still up?

"Believe it or not guys, I am still at the office;" Robin replied.

"No way," shouts Jo in the background, "Why are you still there? Is it your one patient?" Although the girls knew general details about Robin's connection to Josiah, they didn't know personal information such as his name, age, or his illness due to doctor-patient confidentiality.

"He's okay for now but unless I come up with a solution, he won't be for long."

"What do you mean?" said Amera.

Robin quickly brought them up to speed about what was going on, careful not to share any personal information that would reveal Josiah's identity. Pausing for a breath she listened to the silence on the other end of the phone.

"Are you still there?" said Robin.

"Yes, we are all still here. We're just trying to absorb the shock of these latest developments," replied Jo.

"How are you holding up?" asked Cliff. "I know how much you care about this patient."

Cliff's voice, which was normally businesslike and authoritative, was so gentle that for a moment, Robin almost didn't recognize it.

"Cliff, I would like to say that I am just fine but I'm not. I know we are supposed to stay detached from our patients, but Cliff, the thought of him being faced with another disappointment is breaking my heart. He tries so hard to be brave, but he's only 10-years- old. Every adult in his world has let him down and now I am about to do the same. He trusts me. I cannot just stop seeing him." She could hear the girls talking in the background.

"Cheer up, sis. Are you forgetting who has the last say in everything? It's not those doctors or those lawyers, but your Heavenly Father."

Robin couldn't tell if those words came from Jo or Amera, but she felt the power of them uplifting her.

"I know you're right, I just needed to be reminded."

"Are we ready?" said Jo. "Cliff, will you lead us in prayer tonight."

"It would be an honor," replied Cliff.

Robin and Simone joined hands and each of the women closed their eyes as Cliff began praying.

"Father God, we come before you knowing you are the only one who can give us direction on how to proceed in this situation. We all have opinions and ideas of what should be done and how this situation should be handled, but God you are the only one who truly knows what comes next so God we are asking you to show us what to do. Show Robin how to proceed, to protect her patient and show us Father, what to do to support Robin. God, we believe with all our hearts, minds, souls, and bodies that you brought us together for your purpose, so we ask you God to order our steps in your word. In Jesus name we pray, Amen."

After the prayer there was silence on both ends of the line for a moment.

"Thank you for that prayer Cliff," said Simone. I don't know how the rest of you feel, but deep on the inside, I feel like everything is going to be alright. I don't know how, when, where, or why, but it's going to be okay," Simone spoke, sounding emotional.

"Me too," said Robin.

"Girl, we have to go to bed before we're late for sound check in the morning, we have a concert tonight," said Amera.

"I am so sorry, where are you guys?" asked Robin.

"We are in London, England" said Jo.

"WOW!" Robin said. "Sorry for calling, I had no idea."

"Don't you ever say you are sorry for calling. We told you that we are here for you and even if we cannot physically be there, we are always just a phone call or a prayer away and don't you ever forget that."

"I know," said Robin. "Thanks for being there for me. I really needed you guys tonight."

"Call anytime, day or night, and make sure you keep us in the loop," said Amera.

"Okay, girl, we have to go. We will call you tomorrow," Jo added.

The call disconnected, leaving Robin and Simone in a room full of silence, looking at one another.

"I don't know about you," said Robin, "but I feel better. I feel calmer, more at peace. It doesn't feel as overwhelming as it did before we prayed."

"I feel the same—that was a powerful prayer," replied Simone.

"For now, let's just wait and see what tomorrow brings," said Robin, rising to her feet.

Both Robin and Simone were deep in thought as they cleaned up the office in preparation for the following day, still feeling the power of the prayer they had all just prayed. Simone recited James 5:16 in her head:

"The effectual fervent prayer of a righteous man availeth much."

CHAPTER ELEVEN

The sunlight shining through the window in Robin's bedroom refused to be ignored. Robin slowly opened her eyes acknowledging its presence, as she slowly shook off the last remaining vestiges of sleep. Robin noted that she felt rested, which was surprising considering the emotional rollercoaster she had been on after finding out about the lawsuit.

She had gotten in late last night, tired to the bone but so wired she couldn't fall asleep. She remembered thinking as she finally began to drift off, that she just knew she would sleep poorly and wake up exhausted, but to her surprise she awoke feeling refreshed. She remembered feeling the sensation of being wrapped in a cocoon as she slept soundly and peacefully.

"Hmmmm," she said aloud remembering the sensation of someone holding her as she slept and soothing her troubled mind every time worry threatened to bring her conscious back to the surface.

"I feel great!" Robin said as she sat upright in the bed, marveling at the clarity of mind and rejuvenated physicality she was experiencing.

Swinging her legs over the side of the bed, she made her way to the restroom. She looked around at the beauty of her bedroom. It was almost as if she had never seen it before. She noted the soft blues and browns along with the lush green of the live plants which were all strategically placed to give her room the feeling of an outdoor space. Robin knew her home was beautiful and she was proud of all the work she had done to make it so, but what she was most proud of was that she had bought it herself, with money she had earned. She had not used her beauty or body to achieve her goals, but instead, used her mind and hard work. Robin knew if Carmen had been able to have her way, she would have been a chip off the old block, but Robin had refused, being horrified by the lengths that Carmen would go to just to maintain a certain lifestyle.

After losing her father when she was five years old, Robin had been sent packing to live with her paternal grandmother whom she came to love deeply. She had been the only parent Robin had ever really known besides her father.

Memories of the time when she and her father, Delano, had lived with Carmen came unbidden to her mind. She recalled how as a child, she pitied her father because he absolutely loved Carmen, while Carmen, with equal fervor and passion, had despised him.

Her father had played the acoustic guitar and had a beautiful singing voice. It was that which had drawn the beautiful Carmen to him when they were both in high school. All the girls had wanted Delano Walters, but he only had eyes for the beautiful Carmen, so they had married young.

It wasn't long before Carmen came to hate the blue collar life her husband, Delano the romantic, could only provide. She thought often of all the men with money she could have chosen who could have showered her with all the things she desired. Delano was hard working and faithful to a fault, but had only his heart and devotion to give. Unfortunately for him, it would never be enough for a woman like Carmen.

When Carmen had become pregnant, she vowed Delano would never touch her again. After the baby was born, Delano waited and waited for Carmen's heart to return to him, for her to love him again, but he waited in vain. Although they lived together, Carmen lived a totally separate life. She barely acknowledged her young daughter and totally ignored her husband except for when she needed cash. After several years of this lifestyle her father began drinking, but even at his worst, he loved his young daughter. All the love he wanted to give Carmen was lavished on his young daughter, so father and daughter grew close until life and tragedy came to take it away.

Robin remembered coming home from school one day, and as she entered her front yard, she could hear her mother yelling and her father crying and begging Carmen not to leave. Robin turned and noticed a shiny red Cadillac parked in front of her house with a man in the driver seat who looked like a movie star. Although she was curious about him, she turned back toward her house to hear why her parents were arguing.

"Dorothy, please don't leave," she could hear her father pleading.

"I told you, don't ever call me by that name. My name is Carmen."

"You know I love you and your daughter loves you, too. We've been waiting for you to come back to us. I have let you do whatever you wanted all this time because I thought it was something you needed to get out of your system, but Dorothy, we are your family."

"Stop calling me by that name!" Robin heard her mother screaming.

"You can't just walk out on us," Delano pleaded.

"Oh no? Watch me."

Carmen snatched up her suitcase and moved toward the front door. Robin watched them through the screen door in horror as her mother moved to open the door. She understood then why the shiny red Cadillac waited outside with the handsome man who looked like a movie star. Robin ran to her mother just as she stepped onto the porch and grabbed her around her legs begging her to stay.

"Momma, please don't leave us. We'll be good, please, momma." Robin cried like she had never cried before. She had always thought that sooner or later she would do something that her mother would like, or find interesting, and maybe then she would pay attention to her. She had often heard Carmen tell her father that kids just weren't her thing. She thought she had time, but now her mother was leaving and even though she had ignored her and barely spoken ten words to her, Robin realized she wanted her to stay. She realized she loved her mother, even if her mother didn't love her, and if she left she would never have a chance to get her mother to notice her.

"Please, momma." Burying her face in her mother's dress, she cried and held on for dear life.

Carmen began disengaging the tiny fingers from her dress with a disgusted look on her face. The neighbors on each side of their house came out on their porch, watching the drama unfold.

"Robin, I told you to never call me momma. Call me Carmen."

With a look of disgust, she pried Robin's young fingers from her dress. Robin dropped to the ground grabbing Carmen around her ankles, continuing to beg.

Looking down at her dress she noticed that Robin had left a trail of snot and tears on her beautiful dress.

"Look what you did!" she shouted. You've got my dress all nasty."

"Carmen I'm sorry. I won't do it again. Just don't leave, please."

Tears streamed down her young face as she begged and begged her mother to stay. She felt hands lifting her up as they removed her hands from around her mother's ankles. She began to fight.

"Let me go," she cried. "She's going to get away." Robin fought frantically, trying to escape the arms that held her. Who was this trying to help her mother get away? She looked through her tears and saw it was her father who was holding her and he was crying as much as she was, all the while trying to comfort her.

"It's okay Robin bird, she will be back. It's okay," her father whispered in her ear.

He called her by the pet name he had called her for as long as she could remember. Robin fought until her young five-year-old body had no more energy. She collapsed into her father's arms totally spent, quietly sobbing until there were no more tears.

Time passed and finally the neighbors came over and helped them into the house. Her father looked shell-shocked. Miss Anna from next door fixed Robin a plate and tried to take her from her father to feed her, but she refused to get down from her father's arms and she also refused to speak.

Weeks later, Robin still hadn't spoken a word since the day her mother had left. Her father stayed up all night drinking and playing his guitar and singing the love songs he had written for his love, until he passed out. An atmosphere of heaviness and gloom hung over the house. The neighbors continued to bring food over. Every day was like someone had died and they were having the wake. Delano refused to eat but insisted Robin try to eat, but they were both too deep in their own darkness to comprehend the need.

Robin's mind is unlocked and she is flooded with suppressed memories from the past. Suddenly she is able to remember the day her father left like it was yesterday.

It had been on a Friday and she should have been at school but since her mother had left, she refused to go. She had known her father didn't have the strength to fight her. She was in her bedroom lying on the bed staring at the ceiling when her father had come into her room. He stood in the doorway for several moments just staring at his beautiful little Robin bird. She looked so much like her mother. Delano walked over to the bed and scooped her up in his arms. He just sat on the bed holding his daughter, remembering better times.

"Listen, Robin bird, I have to tell you something and it's important. I know you can hear me even if you don't answer back so just listen and do what I tell you. First, I want you to know that you are the light of my life and I love you so much. I don't ever want you to forget that."

Robin remembered feeling uneasy after he said that. She remembered thinking to herself why would he tell me not to forget that I love him like he is going away. She remembered the fear coming back and she began trembling. Her father continued.

"I know you miss your mother as much as I do, and I know I told you she was coming back," his voice broke and Robin could hear the tears he was trying to hold back. "Robin bird, I hate to say it, but I don't think she is coming back." At that point he really began to cry. Deep wracking sobs coming from deep in his soul. Robin wanted to comfort him and tell him everything was going to be okay, but she had lost the words. It had been over a month since Carmen had left and there had been only darkness for both she and her father.

Robin could not speak so she sat in her daddy's arms as he confessed to her that he was unable to go on without his love, Carmen. He told her that he had called his mother and she was catching the greyhound bus and would be there by 4 p.m. that day.

"Mama will know what to do when she gets here. Just stay in your room until she comes to get you."

With that her father kissed her on the head and put her back on her bed and left the room. She wanted to call out after him because she could hear the ring of goodbye in his words, but she was unable to speak so she lay there with tears rolling down her cheeks and did exactly what her daddy told her to do. She waited.

Many hours later she heard her father stumbling around and then she heard a loud crash. The sound frightened her but the silence which followed frightened her more. She wanted to call out to her father because she was afraid, but she had no words, so she cried instead because that was something she had gotten good at.

The shadows in her room lengthen until finally her room grows dark. The darkness outside tells Robin something is wrong. Her father hadn't come to her door to try and make her eat. She knew he should have at least stuck his head in the door to check on her by now. She got off the bed and opened her bedroom door. The entire house was dark and there were no sounds at all. No television, no guitar playing, nothing. Even the sounds of snoring which her father frequently made after passing out, could not be heard.

Sticking her head out the door she peered into the darkness of the long hallway and hesitated. She wanted her daddy to come and get her, but couldn't call his name. It was as if her mouth had been glued shut. Bolstering up her courage, she began to move down the darkened hallway. She remembered thinking to herself if she could get to the living room she could at least turn the light on. Navigating the long hallway she turned the corner and entered the darkened living room moving toward the end table where she knew the lamp sat. As her hand felt the end of the sofa, she reached for the end table stepping in that direction, only to trip over something on the floor. She fell and hit her head on the coffee table. She began to cry because it really hurt. Standing up, she slowly felt her way along the sofa again locating the lamp on the table. As she clicked the switch, the room was instantly illuminated. Once her eyes adjusted to the light she began scanning the room to determine what she tripped over. She saw her father's body lying on the floor, which in itself, was not so unusual since many times before she had found him passed out drunk on the floor, but something was a little odd. He lay on the floor in a liquid pool of red and even though his eyes were wide open, he did not move. She knew the red was blood and Robin remembered the feeling of terror that overtook her. Robin spoke for the first time in over a month crying out.

"Daddy!"

Running to her father's side, she sat on the floor next to him and tried to cradle his head in her arms, but his cold and lifeless body refused to bend. His wide open eyes stared at her but they were lifeless. Robin understood on a visceral level that her father was dead, but being only five years old, her mind refused to accept what her mind could not handle. She cried his name over and over again until she became hoarse—until she finally accepted he was not coming back, just like Carmen wasn't coming back. She laid down beside him with her head on his chest. That was how her grandmother found her only son and her only grandchild. Him dead, and her alive, barely.

Robin snapped back to the present, shaking her head as the floodgate of memories unleashed. She had forgotten that day. Until this moment, she had completely blanked it out of her mind. When her grandmother had questioned her about that day, all she could say was "I don't remember." Why now, after all this time, would these particular painful memories surface. Robin remembered something else she had forgotten. Her father committed suicide. She remembered people whispering about it. They said he overdosed. Everyone was angry at her mother. They all said Carmen was the blame, but she still had wanted Carmen to come back. She didn't care what they thought.

She remembered the day of her father's funeral. She had prayed to God, begging Him to send Carmen back to her. She remembered promising God she would do anything He asked if He would just make Carmen walk through the doors of the funeral home where her father's service was being held. She knew they were all whispering about Carmen and blaming her for her father's death, but Robin told God she could forgive her mother if He would just send her back home.

The service ended and Carmen never came. Her grandmother had been so patient thinking Robin hadn't wanted to leave her father, but Robin had been waiting for Carmen. They stayed until the undertaker at the funeral home informed them they had to get ready for another service and politely asked them to leave. Her grandmother grabbed her and hugged her as she whispered in her ear, "don't worry baby, grandma is here, and I promise you, I won't leave you until God say so and by then you will be ready, she said in her deep southern drawl.

Robin remembered her grandmother's words like it was yesterday. They resonated through her mind as she took the trip down memory lane. She went to live with her grandmother when she was five and had been devastated at 29 when her grandmother finally went home to be with the Lord. Her grandmother had been her rock, teaching her right from wrong and always giving her the unadulterated truth.

She recalled being a teenager and romanticizing the relationship between her mother and her father. Her grandmother had nipped that in the bud, immediately telling her that both her mother and her father had been selfish. Her dad because he had refused to fight knowing he had a daughter to raise and Carmen because she only did what pleased her, never considering if or how her actions affected others.

Her grandmother raised her to put other people's needs before her own and to trust God no matter what. Robin grew up to be a remarkable young woman because of her. She was smart, beautiful, and kind. Robin's grandmother had been a deeply spiritual woman and one who truly understood the Savior she loved and served.

She knew her granddaughter was angry with God, believing that He took both of her parents, but she also knew Robin was totally unaware of this fact, so she said nothing putting it into God's hands to reveal it to her at the appropriate time.

Robin thought about the time Carmen had come back several years after the death of her father. She had been an impressionable 11-year-old and Carmen had been beautiful and glamorous like the women on television. She had wanted Robin to come live with her. She had pumped Robin's head full of fairy tales about the big house she lived in that looked like a castle and all the magical places they would travel to, once Robin came to live with her. Robin was so excited but her grandmother instinctively knew Carmen was up to no good, and immediately got an attorney and filed for full custody.

The lawyer's private investigators discovered the reason Carmen was so desperate for Robin to come to live with her, was because her new husband had agreed to adopt Robin which meant he would have been financially responsible for Robin, even if he divorced Carmen.

For Carmen, it was always about the money. Robin never saw Carmen after that until she was an adult and was of some renown. It wasn't until then that Carmen decided she would claim her only child.

Robin, coming back to the present slowly tries to gather her wits, but she felt shaken to her core. Why had the ordeal with Josiah shaken loose painful memories that her subconscious had managed to keep buried for years? As a psychiatrist, Robin knew there was a connection between the two events, but for the present, that connection eluded her.

"Why now God?" Robin thought to herself. She recalled the connection she had felt to Josiah at their first meeting. Early on, she had known intuitively that her relationship with Josiah was going to be out of the ordinary, and she had welcomed the challenge. She now realized, that she hadn't fully understood the nature of the 'out of the ordinary.'

Something was going on. She wasn't sure what exactly, but could feel it. Even her new friendship with Jo, Amera and Cliff seemed to have come just at the right time. She found herself leaning on them and drawing strength from their resources. She noticed since meeting them, she talked to God a lot more.

Their faith in God had amazed her in the beginning. Robin believed in God and went to church faithfully, but she knew immediately that there was a vast difference between her relationship with God and Amera's, Jo's and Cliff's. At first, she had tried telling herself that there wasn't a difference but the more they talked and got to know each other, she had to admit, there was a familiarity that they all shared with God the Father that she just didn't have. It had been the same with her grandmother and Simone, but she hadn't quite been able to put her finger on it. Her relationship with God seemed a little more formal, more reserved. Robin thought that was because she respected who God was, but they all seemed to have God on speed dial. That was probably why she called them for prayer all the time.

She wasn't sure why, or what it meant, but Robin got the feeling that there were forces in play that she was unable to comprehend, but she knew God was with her. She could feel Him. She knew then it had been Him that had comforted her during the night and woke her up refreshed. Robin was blown away by this comprehension and for the first time in her adult life, God felt real.

Robin began moving toward the kitchen to start her day but her mind was busy, filled with both past and current events. She began making coffee and looking in her refrigerator for some morning sustenance. Suddenly her phone rings. Robin picked it up on the third ring.

"Hello."

"Good morning, Sunshine" Simone replied cheerily.

"Hey Simone, why are you so chipper this early in the morning with all the foolishness we have to deal with today."

"I told you last night, I just feel like somehow, this is all going to work out. Where is your faith, Robin?"

"I know, I know, it's just that sometimes God doesn't work things out like we think He should work them out. I guess I'm just hoping this isn't one of those times." Robin felt shame flood her being. She had just had an intimate encounter with the Father for the first time, and here not five minutes later, she was sounding like...Simone interrupts her silent reverie.

"Robin, you can trust and believe that however God decides to work it out, it will be the right decision for everyone involved. That means Josiah, you, and Josiah's mom. You have to believe that."

Robin hesitated before responding. "I know," she paused. "I do believe that for the most part, but God can be a little tricky sometimes."

"Girl are you crazy?" Simone became indignant. "What do you mean God is tricky? God doesn't play tricks on people and He doesn't lie. Where is all this coming from Robin? Correct me if I'm wrong, but aren't you a Christian?"

"Of course I am. I didn't mean it to sound like that. I know God doesn't play tricks on people or anything like that. What I meant was somctimes it is hard to figure out what God is doing. That is all I meant."

"Well girl say what you mean and mean what you say," said Simone sounding relieved. It sounds to me like you got some unresolved issues you need to be discussing with your Father and don't forget, I am here for you as well if there is something you need to get off your chest."

Robin replayed the conversation she just had with Simone and was surprised by her own words. Simone was right. It did sound like she had some unresolved issues. She wondered if it had something to do with the unlocked memories she had experienced this morning. She was thoughtful as she replied to Simone.

"Thanks for having my back, Simone. I really appreciate that. You know you are like a mother to me. You have loved me unconditionally since the beginning and I am grateful to have you in my life, but I think you are right about me having some unresolved issues. I am going to have to look into that. Thanks though for loving me enough to bring that to my attention. I'll let you know what I find out. I'll see you in about an hour."

CHAPTER TWELVE

Josiah stood silently surrounded by a circle of eight boys. Although they were on the playground at school, the group of boys had isolated Josiah and wrangled him to the far end of the open play area. Josiah could hear the voices of the other children playing only yards away from him, but he had never felt more alone.

He had been transferred from foster care to a group home which the social workers had explained was more suitable for long-term care. He wondered what that meant. He had no idea where his mother was or when she would visit him again. He had only seen her once since he had been transferred here. He hated to admit it, but he was afraid here. The boys were either mean or indifferent. Every day was like walking through a mine field with random attacks coming from different groups of boys. He never bothered anyone, but they still wouldn't leave him alone. He was so tired of the bullies and their demands. He wished for the hundredth time his mother would come and get him, but he knew he wished in vain.

He warily looked around at his tormentors, because that is exactly what they were, and as always with bullies there stood the ringleader.

Keshawn was the biggest boy in the group home with mean eyes and a temper to match. He continued to push Josiah and to taunt him as the crowd of boys continued to push him back into the center of the circle. Josiah knew the fist would be next and didn't really understand why Keshawn hadn't hit him yet.

All the boys at the school knew that Josiah had tried to kill himself. It was that fact which had made him the latest target of the bullies. They thought he was weak. He was unable to return home to his mother after his suicide attempt. The doctors were concerned that his mother had not bothered to visit him while he was recovering in the hospital. Because he was a minor who had tried to commit suicide, Children Services was brought in from the beginning. They demanded he not be released to his mother, but instead to foster care with intense therapy sessions required for both mother and son; however, but his mother had continued to be a no show. They decided it would be awhile before Josiah would go home and now he found himself in another fight of his life.

"Hit him! Hit him!" The boys all taunted as they pushed Josiah toward Keshawn; Keshawn continued to push Josiah, but would not hit him. Out of the blue, Keshawn turns, and begins walking away from the circle of boys.

"Come on guys, let's go. I want to play football," Keshawn said.

All the boys were momentarily stunned as they watched their leader turn and begin to walk away from what they all hoped would be a really good beat down.

Josiah was one of only a handful of Caucasian children in this particular group home and for that alone, he caught flack, but once they found out he tried to commit suicide they really began tormenting him. Ultimately, this got the attention of the undeclared group home leader Keshawn.

But things hadn't turned out quite like they thought. Instead of Keshawn beating the slop out of the new kid, he was giving him a pass and the rest of the bullies didn't understand. One of the bullies named Quentin decided he wasn't satisfied with the pass Keshawn was giving the new guy and decided he would take the pound of flesh he felt was due. He walked up to Josiah and pushed him in his chest. For a moment Josiah had thought that God was actually answering his prayer, but now, here he was looking into the eyes of his new tormentor. Suddenly, Josiah felt weary. All he wanted was to be left alone. He hadn't bothered anyone, but still they attacked him. "Why?" thought Josiah. "Why do they keep bothering me?" All the pent up emotions Josiah felt came to the surface as he faced Quentin returning his icy stare.

Quentin sense of bravado began to waiver as Josiah returned his stare. The look in the new kid's eyes was a little intimidating. It was as if another kid had taken his place; only this one wasn't afraid of him. As a matter of fact, this Josiah now looked as if he wanted to fight—no correction, as if he was itching for a fight. Quentin tried to figure out a way he could back down without his boys knowing he had a change of heart. But the new Josiah at that point, got in his face and pushed him in his chest. The tables were now turned.

"Ooooooooohh!" The crowd yelled excitedly, getting pumped on the action that was soon to jump off. This was going to be better than they thought. The new kid was going to fight back, instead of just curling in a ball as they all kicked and beat him. Quentin stumbled back, tripping and falling from the impact of the push. Quickly he jumped up and charged directly at Josiah.

Bammm! Quentin felt like he'd ran into a brick wall. In a daze, Quentin tried to figure out what just happened. He shook his head, trying to clear the red haze. He stood up to see the brick wall he must have run into, and saw that the brick wall in question was Keshawn's very solid 220 pound frame.

"Leave him alone man." Keshawn spoke as he pushed Quentin back.

"Uh uh, man—I'm gonna beat that white boy down.

The crowd, loving the elevated drama, began egging Quentin on.

"Beat his ass man!" yelled one of the young boys in the crowd.

"Don't let him disrespect you like that!" yelled another.

Josiah stood still as he held his ground, face red, nostrils flaring, shivering slightly; whether from fear or cold was unknown, but the look in his eyes told them all he would not be bullied today.

Keshawn, standing as a barrier between Quentin and Josiah, turns his head toward Josiah.

"You okay man?"

Josiah didn't speak, but instead nodded his head in the affirmative.

The dynamics in the crowd begin to shift. Upon understanding that Keshawn had publically made an alliance with the new kid, the desire to egg Quentin on began to wane.

"Come on Q, just forget about it man," a boy named Drake said.

"Yea man, let's go play football," another said.

At that moment, another voice cut through the crowd.

"You need to kick his white butt!" a fat boy with a pimply face named Michael yelled moving to the front of the crowd. Michael was a bully and not well liked by any of the other boys.

"You gonna let him push you like that?" he said getting in Quentin's face. "How you gonna let a little skinny white kid disrespect you on your own home turf? If you don't kick his butt, I'm gonna kick yours," he said poking Quentin in the chest then standing nose to nose with him.

Keshawn, who remained quiet up to that point finally spoke.

"Man, you sure you wanna do this?" he asked quietly, while slowly walking toward Michael.

Michael, turning in Keshawn's direction, momentarily allows Quentin to catch a reprieve.

"Mind your business Keshawn! Ain't nobody scared of you. You might have all these little punks around here in your hip pocket but you don't..."

Before he could finish, there was a loud crack, and before anyone could even figure out what the sound was, they looked and Michael was on the ground out cold.

"Anybody else got something to say?" Keshawn looked around the now silent crowd and no one spoke a word.

The crowd began to disperse into groups of two's and three's. Before they all could leave, Mrs. Dixon came running toward the crowd of boys sensing trouble. As she got closer, the boys seeing her, began to run. Noting the faces of the boys who were running away, she moved to the general area they had just abandoned. The only boys who remained were Josiah, Keshawn and Michael, who lay on the ground not moving. Mrs. Dixon quickly took out her cell phone calling 911.

Michael was taken to the hospital with a mild concussion, but was otherwise okay. It was obvious that he had been struck by one of the other boys but they were all questioned and no one had seen anything including Josiah and Keshawn.

Michael said his memory was impaired due to the concussion and had no recollection of what had transpired, so the situation remained unresolved by the group home but things began to change after that.

The first noticeable change was for the first time in the four years Keshawn had lived at the group home, he had a friend. An unlikely sort, and it was spoken about during staff meetings, and in the kitchen, and administrative offices. The two made an odd pair but were inseparable. The rest of the boys had fallen in line when they saw how far Keshawn would go to defend Josiah. They didn't understand why Keshawn had become Josiah's protector, but they all knew and accepted that Josiah was untouchable. To harass or victimize him was the same as challenging Keshawn and no one wanted to do that.

A new peace arose for the first time in the group home. Everyone just kind of got along, and those who couldn't, just stayed apart. The staff walked on eggshells in the wake of this new peace not understanding the source, but not missing that the timing aligned with the new friendship between Keshawn and Josiah.

Mrs. Dixon looked out of her classroom window observing Keshawn and Josiah walking by. Keshawn was not the same sullen boy she had struggled to work with over the last four years. As the boys walked past her window, she noticed their book bags hanging lazily off their shoulders as they seemed to be in deep conversation. She had never seen Keshawn voluntarily engage in a conversation with anyone, much less laugh or smile, but he was doing all three and she marveled at the change that had come over him. She was not sure of why these two had connected, but she could see the positive outcome of the connection on both of the young boys.

Keshawn was only 12 but he was already six foot three inches tall, easily weighing over two hundred pounds. Keshawn was as dark as Josiah was light. Josiah looked liked a bean pole while Keshawn looked like a mini Hercules. As different as these two boys were, they had found each other and where one was weak the other was strong and vice versa.

Josiah bloomed under the friendship, gaining not only confidence in himself, but in others as well. Trust had come to Josiah first by Dr. Walters and now Keshawn. He wasn't sure why Keshawn decided to be his friend, but he was grateful. Josiah was thankful to have someone in his life that seemed to understand his pain.

All his life, Josiah had been a loner. It had always been just he and his mother and he feeling like he always needed to defend her to others. He knew they didn't get her, and that he understood, because they didn't get him. Dr. Walters was the first person in his young life he felt could actually see him—Josiah. Not the Josiah he showed the world, but his true self. He had learned that he didn't have to pretend with her. She had seen him at his worse, but she had stayed. The same could not be said about his mother and this time he hadn't made excuses for her. He loved his mother to the core of his being, but he had finally accepted the truth about her. Josiah realized at that moment that something in him had changed.

Although he still loved her as much as he ever had, his expectation of his mother was not the same. This change had allowed him to look at her almost clinically. Not in a cold way, but in a realistic one. Instead of devastating him, he had allowed it to make him stronger. Yes, he still wished his mother was different, but he realized she was who she was and he had to face the reality that she may never change.

As he walked along with his friend, laughing and talking, he was momentarily puzzled. He didn't understand why, but for the first time in his young life he felt hopeful. He hadn't seen Dr. Walters for over two months and he missed her desperately. He didn't know what had happened or why she had stopped coming to see him, but he believed, without a shadow of a doubt, that he would see her again. He knew that she loved him. Dr. Walters loved him the way he wished his mother would, but that was a story for another day. Without being told, Josiah knew that someone or something was blocking her from seeing him, but he knew she would figure it out and he would see her again because at ten, Josiah had come to know and understand one of the great truths in life. True love always found a way. No matter what, it just did. So he waited.

CHAPTER THIRTEEN

Robin, Amera, Jo, Simone and Cliff were all seated in Robin's Florida room sipping tea and making plans. It had been more than two months since Robin had last seen Josiah and it had really been a test of Robin's faith in God to believe that she would ever see him again. She sat quietly in her seat, looking around at everyone in the room thinking to herself as they talked among themselves.

Looking at Cliff and Simone, she cocked her head curiously as she watched them in conversation. There was nothing unusual going on. They weren't whispering or acting overly familiar with each other, but she sensed something there. Observing them, she discerned that both of them were totally oblivious to whatever was going on between them.

She looked at Simone, and realized she had become the mother she had always longed for. Simone possessed every quality she had ever desired in a mother. There was a quiet strength in her that without even realizing it, Robin leaned on in times of crisis.

She had been with Robin every day since the court had ruled in Josiah's mother's favor and she had been denied any further visitation to see Josiah, not even to say goodbye. She had been a mess. Simone hadn't asked, but had just stepped in and took over. Cooking and cleaning, suggesting that Robin take some time off to clear her head and regroup. Robin acquiesced to her suggestion without protest.

Simone became a temporary conduit between the girls and Robin, until Robin was strong enough to shake off the grief which prevailed since her abrupt disconnection from Josiah. She grieved like a parent who had lost a child and with each day that passed, she realized she had.

Robin loved Josiah. Their relationship had gone far beyond that of the typical patient and doctor. She knew what her colleagues would say. They would tell her to back off so that she could gain some perspective, but all she could think about was him somewhere thinking she had abandoned him like his mother.

The lawsuit had yet to be settled and she was forbidden to contact Josiah's mother while the case was still pending. She stepped down from her job as director of the new wing at the Burke Center, but continued to work with the clients she maintained. She refused, for the time, to take on any new patients, both by choice and by silent agreement from the board of directors. They were in a temporary holding pattern concerning her career at the Burke Center, awaiting resolution of the lawsuit. To put it simply, her life was a mess.

"A penny for your thoughts," said Jo, as she glanced at Robin and saw her staring into space.

"You wouldn't want to pay for what I am thinking," replied Robin, as she forced a smile.

"Come on sis," said Amera.

Robin smiled, but it never reached her eyes.

"Cheer up, we got some ideas we want to run by you," said Amera excitedly. "We think we know a way that we can either get a message to Josiah or maybe get you and him together, even if only for a short while."

For the first time in two months life flashed in Robin's eyes as hope blossomed in her heart.

"What? Are you serious? How? I mean how, how could you?" Robin stammered.

"I am going to let Jo do the honors since she came up with the plan along with a little help from Cliff," said Amera.

"Please tell me your plan," said Robin sitting up eagerly in her chair.

"Okay, now keep in mind this is just a plan," said Jo. "We don't know if any of this will work but we've got to do something," she continued. "What we have in mind is either a benefit concert or we adopt the group home."

Robin's eyes widened in surprise. "How quickly can something like that be put together?" she asked.

"That's a good question. Honestly, I am not sure," said Jo. "Cliff may be able to streamline a lot of the red tape."

"You know what would work better?" said Cliff excitedly.

All eyes turned in Cliff's direction waiting for him to continue.

"The girls know NBA players and so do I. We can get some of them to invite the boys from the house to a game, to meet some of the players, etc. Robin, there's no law that says that you couldn't just happen to be at that same game. Jo and Amera, you guys will partner with the players on this outreach project which will allow you to sit and interact with the boys. Robin could just be your invited guest. If for some reason they don't allow Robin in the reserved section then at least you two would be able to get a message to him from Robin, just to let him know that she is still out here fighting to see him."

Everyone began to get excited as the plan continued to evolve. Simone looking at Robin noticed for the first time since Josiah had been gone that Robin was showing some enthusiasm.

"I think that is a great idea," said Simone.

"Me too," said Amera.

"Me three," said Jo.

Everyone looked at Robin waiting for her to respond. "I think it is a FANTASTIC idea!" Robin said with much excitement.

She stood to her feet moving to the center of the group as they began to perfect their plan.

Three weeks later, it was a gloomy, rainy Thursday evening and Robin and Simone were on their way to see the New York Knicks and Cleveland Cavaliers game in Cleveland, Ohio. Both Robin and Simone prayed silently as they entered the arena to locate the preferred seating which was in the same area the boys would be in. Robin thanked God for the speed in which the plan had come together, and silently thanked Cliff as well since his connections had come through in a big way. Her seat would be next to Josiah's and Simone would be next to her. Jo and Amera would perform during half-time and would then join them for the remainder of the game. Robin had prayed more in the three-week span it took to get all the details ironed out than she ever had in her life, except for when she asked God to send Carmen back at her dad's funeral. She had hoped she would get a different result.

The boys arrived early and watched the teams do warm ups. Robin and Simone arrived to find Josiah already in his seat. Robin's heart leaped as she looked down and saw Josiah animatedly talking with a boy much larger than himself. It was apparent that he and the boy were friends because they laughed a lot and talked back and forth. Robin felt relief wash over her. Josiah was not a ghost of himself as she had imagined, but instead he actually seemed to be happy, and to her amazement, he no longer seemed introverted. He not only spoke with the boy sitting right next to him, but she observed him leaning forward and speaking with several of the boys further down the row. They all seemed to be excited and happy as clams.

Simone watched as Robin observed the child she had come to love. She saw many emotions in Robin's face but the strongest of them was joy. She continued to stare at Josiah as he interacted with the other boys, with a look of wonder on her face. Simone shook her out of her reverie. "Are you ready?" she asked Robin.

"Yes," said Robin, gathering herself as they began to descend the stairs to the row where the boys were sitting.

They entered the row and began to move toward the seat next to Josiah. As they got closer, Josiah who had been engaged in conversation with his friend, turned briefly to acknowledge their presence. Raising his eyes to meet hers he was momentarily stunned.

"Dr. Walters!" he exclaimed, jumping to his feet as he rushed to her side and hugged her for dear life. He held her until she began to feel slightly uncomfortable. Not because she didn't relish the hug, but because she knew the chaperones would become curious and start asking questions and she wanted to be able to stay for the entire game.

Gently pushing him back she looked down at his face and noticed the emotions in his eyes. They were clear today. They were as clear as she had ever seen them. She smiled down at him.

"Hi Josiah."

"Hi Dr. Walters," he replied. "I knew you would find me, I knew you would." His smile was so big, it looked like his whole face would explode. "I want you to meet my friend Keshawn. I talk about you all the time to him." Josiah turned around and Keshawn is all eyes. "This is her Keshawn. This is Dr. Walters."

Keshawn looked from her to him with a goofy smile on his face. "You didn't tell me she was black." They all broke out laughing at that. Simone, Robin, Josiah and Keshawn all took their seats and Josiah's smile never left his face.

Amera and Jo came over and introduced themselves to all the boys who were excited to meet them. Josiah couldn't believe that they were friends with his Dr. Walters. They had a good 30 minutes to talk before the game.

Although it was noisy, Robin was able to find out about Josiah's stay at the home and his friendship with not only Keshawn but a few of the other boys as well. It was obvious to her that Keshawn and Josiah had formed a bond that was very much like brothers. He had brought out qualities in Josiah that Robin had only guessed were there. The Josiah who sat beside her now was not the same one who had tried to commit suicide a few months ago. There was a strength that ran through him that wasn't there before. After she explained to him about why she wasn't able to see him, as much as she could without violating any laws, he surprised her again by telling her not to worry.

"I knew that you would find a way to see me. That's what I told my friend, Keshawn. I said to him that I wasn't sure why you hadn't been to see me, but there must have been a good reason because there was no way you would just stop seeing me and not tell me goodbye. I knew you would never do that and just knowing that made me feel better."

"Josiah, I am glad that you knew that because all this time I have been going crazy worrying that you thought I abandoned you. I wasn't allowed to see you one last time to explain why I couldn't see you anymore. I was so concerned for you. Have you seen your mother?"

"Not since the first week that I got to the home. They told me she called a couple of times, but it's okay," Josiah replied.

"Josiah, I just want you to know that some way, somehow, I will find a way to come and see you. No matter how long it takes, just know I have not forgotten about you and I am working on getting us back together."

"I know and God said everything was going to be okay. He even told my friend Keshawn that."

"He told me the same thing. Let's enjoy the game" said Robin.

So they did and they all had a blast and all the kids loved Dr. Walters and Ms. Simone and were sad to see them leave.

The following day, as Keshawn and Josiah walked to school, they were particularly excited. They talked about the game, Dr. Walters, and their NBA email pen pals. The boy's relationship had been forged by sharing each other's deepest darkest secrets. Keshawn knew that Josiah secretly wished that Dr. Walters was his mother. The boys never lied to each other so they felt totally comfortable exposing their vulnerabilities. Keshawn knew that Josiah actually believed that one day Dr. Walters would be the mother he had always longed for and he prayed it was so.

After meeting her, Keshawn understood why Josiah was so attached to her. It was apparent even to him that her feelings for Josiah went far beyond that of doctor and patient, and they were genuine. He was surprised by this discovery thinking that Josiah was believing what he needed to believe to help him deal with his current situation, but it appeared his faith in the doctor was grounded in reality which made Keshawn breathe a sigh of relief. He only wanted the best for Josiah. "He deserves a break," he thought to himself. Heck! They both did.

His story was similar, but different than Josiah's. His mother was a diagnosed schizophrenic, father unknown. From the time he was five years old his mother had left him alone for days and weeks at a time in abandoned buildings overrun with rats and roaches, or condemned houses full of crack heads. In one of her more lucid moments, his mother had left him at the home of his maternal grandmother. For a brief period, he had experienced normalcy. He went to school every day and came home to regular meals, until one day he came home to find his grandmother passed out on the kitchen floor and the pot of beans she was cooking on the stove for his supper burning. He tried unsuccessfully to wake her. Not knowing what to do, he ran next door and told the neighbor who had called an ambulance.

His grandmother was diabetic and her blood sugar had dropped very low, causing her to go into a diabetic coma. She also had a sore on her foot which hadn't healed and was full of infection. She was taken into surgery immediately, but it was too late and the doctors had to amputate her right leg to just below the knee. Everything just went downhill from there. The neighbor, at first, was kind enough to allow him to stay at her house thinking his grandmother would be home in a few days; but after learning that her prognosis was not good, and that no one really knew when she would be home, she decided she could no longer keep him. She sent him back to his grandmother's house, but agreed not to call children's services. She told him that she would "keep an eye on him."

Keshawn again found himself at eight years old living alone. The neighbor somehow managed to finagle his grandmother's food stamp card and brought him food he could microwave or cook on top of the stove. He mostly ate chips and junk. He got up each morning and washed his face and went to school and returned each day. He wanted to see his grandmother, but didn't know how to get to the hospital.

The neighbor never checked on him other than to give him the few dollars of groceries she bought for him with his grandmother's purloined food stamps.

He was alone again, until one day he came home from school and there was a man sitting at his grandmother's kitchen table. The man had a can of beer and a bottle of liquor in front of him.

"Who the heck are you?" he said drunkenly.

"My name is Keshawn."

"What are you doing here and where is my mother?" the man asked.

"I don't know who your mother is, but this is my grandma's house."

"Your grandma?" he replied confusedly.

"Yes sir," said Keshawn.

"Who is your mother?" the man asked.

"Lynette."

"So you Lynette's boy—huh," he snorted and took another swallow of gin from his bottle. "So where is Lynette?

"She gone," Keshawn replied.

"What do you mean gone? Gone to the store? Gone to work? What do you mean?"

"She just gone."

He looked blearily at the kid, frustration evident on his face. "So where is Sadie?"

"You mean Grandma Sadie?" Keshawn asked.

"Who else would I be talking about? Where is your grandmother, my mother?"

"She's in the hospital."

"What?" Fear was evident in his voice.

"She is at OSU Medical Center. They say she won't wake up."

The man looked stunned. "How long has she been in the hospital? What's wrong with her?"

"I don't know," Keshawn answered.

"What do you mean you don't know? Haven't you been to see her? If she is in the hospital and Lynette is gone, who's staying here with you?"

"Nobody."

"What do you mean nobody" How old are you? You can't possibly be staying here by yourself. By the way, I am your Uncle Ralph."

With those words a new era was ushered in. Keshawn referred to it as the Uncle Ralph Era. Uncle Ralph was well intentioned, but was a hard core alcoholic and was either drunk or going through withdrawal or in layman's terms, DT's. Grandma Sadie never came home again. Keshawn was devastated but there was no one to tell—No one who cared. She had given him the only normalcy he had ever known. He was sorry to see it come to an end.

Uncle Ralph tried, but he was in worse shape than him so Keshawn continued on as if nothing had changed. The social security check which came in the mail was cashed each month by Uncle Ralph. The neighbor's generosity with his grandmother's stolen food stamps had ceased once they learned his uncle had moved in so he had to rely on his uncle to buy food for the house. Unfortunately, food was not a priority for Uncle Ralph. He did buy a few groceries, but most of the money was spent on liquor. Keshawn didn't mind.

He was just glad to have someone else in the house besides himself. He helped Uncle Ralph as much as he could by fixing coffee for him and sandwiches, or bringing him aspirin and cold wash rags when he was hung over. He came to love his Uncle Ralph after a fashion because at least he was there. The Uncle Ralph Era lasted about six months, until one night he fell asleep with a lit cigarette. The house caught on fire and Uncle Ralph later died from smoke inhalation. Once again, Keshawn was alone, but this time the authorities were aware and it was from that point he wound up in the group home. It was suppose to be temporary until they located a relative, but they were unable to find his mother and his father was a question mark in everyone's mind but his mother's, and maybe even hers' as well. Four years later, he was still at the home with very little chance of leaving before he turned 18.

He hoped that Josiah might have a chance. The thought that he might didn't make him jealous in the least because he had come to love Josiah like a brother. Keshawn did something he hadn't done in a very long time and that was to pray. He prayed that Josiah's Dr. Walters would be everything Josiah thought she was. Keshawn prayed that God would give Josiah the life they both prayed for but he no longer believed was possible for him.

"God, please help Josiah get out of here. God, he didn't ask for none of this. You know I don't ask you for nothing no more, but God, he is not as strong as me. He's a good kid. Please help him."

Keshawn prayed silently in his mind as he walked along with his only friend and suddenly he felt very hopeful.

CHAPTER FOURTEEN

Carla Dixon, the school guidance counselor sat in her office organizing her desk. It was perfectly straight and not in need of organization, but rearranging things is what she did when she was confronted with situations which had no good answer.

She was one of the school chaperones for the trip to the Cleveland Cavaliers basketball game two weeks earlier. What a blessing she had thought when the school had been contacted by the agent of one of the players. He had stated that his client and a few of the other NBA players wanted to help needy kids. The players donated $25,000 to the school and proposed an athlete adoption program where the participating players would each have a pen pal to email, and the kids were invited to home games three times per year.

Everything was going great at the game! Everyone was having a great time. During the game, she had seen Josiah talking animatedly to a woman he seemed to know. Carla continued to watch them and noticed that not only did some of the players come into the seats and speak with the woman, but the half-time entertainers had as well and she knew they were two of the hottest artist performing anywhere. That told her the woman was someone of significance, but who? Carla decided since she was a chaperone it was her duty to find out who the woman was so she introduced herself. It was that step that was now causing all the consternation.

The woman had turned out to be Dr. Robin Walters. Although the Burke Center had succeeded so far in keeping the lawsuit out of the local news, when Josiah arrived at the group home, all the background information, including the lawsuit, had been provided to the school. She knew who Dr. Walters was and all the details of the lawsuit.

Carla thought again to herself, "This should be easy. There was no ambiguity here." The right thing to do was to report the incident to school administrators and let them do whatever they felt was right, but for the life of her she couldn't make herself do it.

Carla thought again of the look on Josiah's face and not just on his face but Dr. Walters' as well. She had never ever seen Josiah look like he had that night. There had been such a look of joy on his face and a peace in his eyes that only came from a feeling of security deep within. Dr. Walters had done more for Josiah in one night than his mother had in 10 years. Carla saw something else as well. Dr. Walters was a well-known professional but that was not who she was that evening. She saw a mother reuniting with a long lost child.

Carla met Josiah's mother Ms. Martin when Josiah first came to the group home. She had known instantly why Josiah was in the state he was in. Her heart had gone out to the young boy. Josiah had been with them for several months and Ms. Martin had only come to visit him once. She decided at that moment to take a little extra interest in him. Josiah was just a shadow of the boy he was today, but from the beginning, she sensed something of the fighter in him.

His friendship with Keshawn had brought Josiah out of his shell and had the added bonus of bringing Keshawn out of his. Both Josiah and Keshawn were on the road to recovery but what she saw between Josiah and Dr. Walters had shaken her. As a professional she knew instantly that Josiah needed Dr. Walters and Dr. Walters needed Josiah. With this piece of knowledge in store, she tried to reconcile it with what she knew was right morally and what was right legally.

She knew the right thing to do was to report the interaction between the two at the game. She also knew that if she did that then steps would be taken to ensure no further contact would be made between the two. Josiah wouldn't be able to see Dr. Walters anymore. She knew in her heart that was not the right answer. They needed each other like they needed oxygen to breath. She saw it instantly. She wondered if Dr. Walters had finagled that whole NBA adoption program just to be able to see Josiah. She pondered a moment and thought to herself, "I wouldn't be surprised."

Knock! Knock! Her office door opened and she saw the smiling face of Maria Rodriguez, the school principal.

"Hola."

"Hola, Maria," responded Carla.

Maria Rodriguez was short and round with curly unmanageable hair that was as red as her face, which kept a perpetual smile. She was as Irish as they came but was married to a Hispanic man, hence the last name Rodriguez. She had been principal for over 20 years at the school and had seen many come and go. Very few people knew that she earned her degrees from the prestigious Princeton University and that she double majored in Education and Psychology. Princeton University was the first university to offer a "no loan" policy to financially needy students, giving grants instead of loans to accepted students who needed help paying tuition. She had been one of those students. Upon achieving her degree, she had wanted to give back. Grateful for the opportunity she had been given, she decided that she would impart all that she had learned to any hungry, young mind who was willing. It had been her choice to come to the group home and it was by choice she stayed. She loved helping children. As principal, her capacity to help children was increased even though she no longer taught. She now had the power to oversee and to weed out teachers who had no true compassion for children.

"Maria, what is wrong with you?" said Carla. "Why is your face so red?" She stared at Maria moving in her direction.

"Karen and Shantrell were just in the hall about to fight over that new boy Dante. The girls are getting harder to get under control than the boys," Maria said, laughing out loud.

"That is so true," Carla absently responded, continuing to rearrange the items on her desk.

"You know we haven't had a real incident with the boys since Keshawn and Josiah became friends," Maria said, as she combed her fingers through her hair trying unsuccessfully to restore some order to it.

"Yea I know," said Carla. "That in itself is amazing."

"Well if you think that's amazing you won't believe what just happened. I was just on my way to tell you about it when I ran into the girls in the hallway about to come to blows."

"Oh yea? What happened? Was it good or bad?" Carla asked.

"It was better than good," said Maria.

"Spill it, Maria! You got me busting at the seams now."

"Guess who came to see me?"

"Maria, I don't feel like guessing. Just tell me."

"Oh alright! You are such a party pooper. Well, anyway I just got a visit from Keshawn and Josiah."

Suddenly, Maria had Carla's full attention. "You mean they came to see you?"

"Yes they did."

"Why?" asked Carla.

"You're not going to believe this, but they want to start a mentoring program for the younger boys."

"What!"

"Yea that's what I thought at first," Maria said.

"What made them come up with this idea? Did they say?"

"If I hadn't been in that office with them I wouldn't have believed it. It was Keshawn's idea. He said he thought it would help with the bullying and with integrating the new kids. I could see he had given it a lot of thought. He didn't actually say integrating, I am paraphrasing there, but that's what he meant."

"I kind of figured that but what is amazing is that this is the same kid that we were thinking of sending to juvie this time last year," said Carla.

"It's the Josiah Effect," Maria said laughing. "Ever since he arrived here, things have been changing and for the better," she said. "What is it with that kid? There's just something about him."

Carla laughed out loud. "It's so funny you should say that because I was just thinking about Josiah when you walked in. Let me ask you a question Maria," Carla leaned forward. "What do you think about Josiah's mother?"

"I think the worst thing that could happen is for him to go back under her custody." Without a pause Maria continued, "Why do you ask?"

"He has made a lot of progress here which, in itself, is incredible. Usually when kids come here they deteriorate, but Josiah seems to have thrived and his success is spreading to some of the other boys and not just Keshawn. Everybody is calling it the Josiah Effect."

Both the ladies laugh softly for a moment as they thought about all the changes which had occurred since Josiah arrived.

"He does seem to bring out the best in people, doesn't he?" Carla stated.

"Yea, in everyone except his mother, and that's a shame because he really is a great kid," responded Maria.

"Maria, Josiah hasn't been a kid for a long time or haven't you noticed."

"Yea I've noticed. I just wish there was something I could do about it."

Carla thought about everything for a moment. She considered the pros and cons of telling her friend, who was also the overseer of the school, what she knew about Josiah and Dr. Walters, and how that knowledge had placed her in a dilemma. Making a decision, she decided to confide in her friend.

"Sit down Maria; I've got something to tell you."

An hour later, Carla and Maria sat in her office quietly contemplating what had been shared. Each woman was lost in her own thoughts. Carla felt the relief as only someone can who is not use to keeping secrets and is finally allowed to reveal it without penalty.

"I kind of wish you hadn't told me this, Carla," said a very subdued Maria. "It really puts me in a difficult position."

"How do you think I feel?" replied Carla. "I know what I am supposed to do, but it feels wrong. Maria, if you had seen them together then you would know what I mean. The dynamics between them are not doctor-patient, but I swear to you, it is mother and child, and not in an unhealthy way. We both have degrees in Psychology and you already know who Dr. Walters is by reputation alone. I get that she has stepped way over the boundaries of a healthy doctor-patient relationship but Maria, as sure as I am sitting here, I know in my heart that her and Josiah are supposed to be together—rules be damned."

"That is easy for you to say, Carla, you're not the principal. Your job is not—"

Carla interrupts, "What Maria? What? My job is not on the line? The hell it isn't. By me withholding this info for two weeks, I am already in trouble but I love these kids and I know you do too, and no matter what, I will always put what is best for them before job security and anything else."

"Are you saying that I don't, Carla?" Maria sounded hurt. "You know that isn't true. I've been offered positions at some of the best public and private schools in the country. I stay here because I love the children."

"You don't have to prove that to me, Maria. I know that already, but this situation may force you to prove it to yourself. Pray about it, Maria. That's what I have been doing and whatever you decide to do, I know it will be the right thing. I am so confused at this point, I just don't know what to do."

The ladies sat silently in Carla's office afterwards, pondering the predicament which lay before them. Each of the women knowing, for this dilemma, every answer was wrong and every answer was right.

CHAPTER FIFTEEN

Josiah's mother, Patricia Martin, looked at her face in the mirror trying to see if the dermabrasion treatments she had gotten really made her look younger. She felt like she was looking better than she had in years. Her attorney's office had been advancing her cash in anticipation of the settlement for her lawsuit against the center.

Her lawyer had assured her that the settlement would definitely be upward of $100,000, and for Patricia, that was more money than she had ever seen in her lifetime.

Of course, that was before the lawyer's share and expenses were taken out but she would still be left with a tidy sum. For a moment she thought about Josiah and what the lawsuit meant to him. Because of it, he could no longer see Dr. Walters. Patricia felt bad about that because she knew her son loved Dr. Walters. She also knew Dr. Walters loved her son and that he was more to her than just another patient. It had been that which had made her file the lawsuit in the beginning.

When Josiah tried to kill himself it shocked her tremendously. She was left speechless and immobilized. After they had taken him by squad, she had been unable to go to the hospital to check on him because she felt so guilty. She knew it was her fault that Josiah tried to kill himself. She knew it was her own inadequacies which made Josiah so unhappy so she just stayed away. It was that day that she knew in order for Josiah to live, the best thing for him was to get away from her. It never occurred to her to change her life so that Josiah could thrive. As always her motivations were permeated with self-absorption.

"I should never have had a kid," she thought to herself, as she put on her bright pink lipstick. "I was never the motherly type."

Patricia had a new boyfriend, Ace. He was young and wild just like she liked them. He stood just above six feet, with a lean almost skeletal frame. His sharply chiseled features and pale white skin were a striking contrast to his long black hair which resembled a raven's wing.

Since she had started getting the monetary advances from her attorney's office, it seemed like she had no shortage of friends or admirers. As she finished dressing she wondered how Josiah was doing. She hadn't seen him for over five months. She stopped taking the calls from Children Services when they would try to arrange visits with Josiah. She also refused to open any written correspondence from them. Ignorantly she thought if she didn't talk to them or open their letters she could always say she didn't know what they wanted if they asked. She missed Josiah at first, but each day that went by, it became easier and easier to pretend he didn't exist. That he never existed. She pretended that she was a single woman without a child. She liked being free and not having to worry about getting home so she could get Josiah up for school in the mornings or cooking dinner for him even if it was only microwaving something which is all she ever did.

She liked her new life and wasn't sure she wanted to go back to the old one.

Vrrrmmmmmmmmmm Vrrrmmmmmmmmmm, she heard Ace's motorcycle outside just as she finished dressing. She began to hurry because he had a temper and got angry if she made him wait. She knew he was already going to be angry because she only had $20 in her purse. She hoped he wouldn't hit her. She thought to herself how lucky she was to even be with him. He was young and good looking and could get any girl he wanted but had chosen her. Her friend, Angie, had stopped speaking to her months ago when she found out she had not been going to see Josiah. She had also told her the only reason Ace was with her was because she was running around flashing money everywhere like a fool. The day she met Ace, she had gotten a $5,000 advance from her attorney; and yea she had been setting up the bar, and flashing money everywhere, it felt so good when everyone looked at her like she was someone important. Ace came up to her and asked her to buy him a drink and they were pretty much together from that night on, but strictly on Ace's terms of course. She didn't care though, she was just glad to be with him on any terms.

Patricia remembered that first night when they had been talking and he had asked her if she had any crumb snatchers—she understood that to be his phrase for kids. He said he didn't do crumb snatchers. She lied and said no, thinking when the time was right, she would tell him about Josiah. But every day that went by, Josiah seemed to be a part of another life and one she wasn't sure she wanted to go back to, so she just kept pretending.

Grabbing her leather jacket off the floor she quickly ran out the front door just as Ace was about to open it.

"Hey baby, I'm ready" she said nervously surveying his face to see how angry he was.

"You know I don't like to wait, what the heck took you so long?"

"I was trying to get beautiful for you," she said, smiling at him trying to coax him out of his mood.

"Well you should try harder the next time because you look like slop warmed over," he said looking her up and down and shaking his head like she was a lost cause.

With just that one comment, he had wiped out all her confidence. She thought the new lipstick brightened up her face and the new highlights in her hair made her look hip and modern, but it seemed they were having a difference of opinion.

"Don't you like my new lipstick," she asked with doubt exuding from every pore.

"You can put lipstick on a pig, Patricia, but it's still a pig."

Patricia was crushed by his words. Hot tears came to her eyes.

"Are you crying?" He spoke, with contempt in his voice.

She knew he hated it when she cried so she quickly tried to call the tears back.

"Of course not silly, you know I have allergies. Where are we going? Can we stop and get something to eat? I am starving.

"That depends on you. How much money do you have? I wanted to go to Wild Pony and look at some new tires for my bike. Let's do that first."

"I only have twenty dollars," she said.

"We can stop by the bank," he replied.

"There is no money in the bank. I only have $20 left."

"What do you mean there's no money in the bank? Do you need to call your lawyer to get some more money?"

"No, he won't advance me anymore until my case is settled. I was hoping you would help me until my lawsuit pays out."

"Are you crazy? What do I look like helping you?"

"Ace that's not fair, when I had money you know I shared without question. I have more money coming but I have to wait for my case to settle. Why can't you help me until then? You are my man, who else am I supposed to call on?"

"Since when did I become your man? Have you looked in the mirror?" He grabbed her by the face and dragged her over to the mirror. "Look at you and look at me. Do I look like I should be giving you money or does it look like you should be giving me money?" He forces her to stare at their reflections to see what she had all along refused to acknowledge. He was a 27 year-old, beautiful male specimen but 100 percent jerk. She was an overweight, 32 year-old, unemployed, uneducated woman who really had nothing to offer anyone. Looking in the mirror she saw not only her flaws but his as well. She realized that Ace had nothing to offer anyone either.

"Call me when you get your settlement," Ace flung back over his shoulder as he walked out the door.

Patricia stood in front of the mirror long after Ace had left. The mirror told her things she didn't want to see—Things she wanted to deny but couldn't. She realized she had made many mistakes which would have been okay if she had only learned from them but she hadn't. She could see clearly now in the mirror the course her life had taken and it wasn't pretty. She saw how all her life she had been full of self-pity and selfish to the core. The mirror showed her the type of mother she had been to Josiah. When she was young, she said when she had children she would never be like her mother. How had she missed it? She had turned out to be just like her mother. Her mind brought back to her remembrance something one of those TV preachers said one time. He said that the very definition of insanity was doing the same thing over and over again hoping for a different result.

Patricia did not like the person who looked back at her from the mirror. She looked around her apartment. There were beer cans and overflowing ashtrays everywhere. Plates of half-eaten food sat on the table as if someone was coming back to finish them but they were full of mold. She looked around and realized for the first time that she lived in filth and disorder. The room was a reflection of her state of mind, pure chaos.

Taking the back of her hand she wiped the pink lipstick from her mouth. She took off her jacket, moved to the kitchen and grabbed cleaning solutions from under the sink. Fixing a bucket of hot, soapy water she went into her living room and began to pick up the trash from all the surfaces and to put things in order. She began to hum a song to herself as she cleaned and realized it was a song she had learned while attending a little storefront church when she was a child.

"Jesus loves me, yes I know, for the bible tells me so. Little ones to him belong. They are weak but he is strong. Yes, Jesus loves me, Yes Jesus loves me."

Patricia cleaned and sang. She could feel years of depression lifting from her as if someone had removed a heavy weight. She sang it louder.

"YES JESUS LOVES ME BECAUSE THE BIBLE TELLS ME SO."

She began to cry with abandon, but the tears she was shedding were tears of release.

YES JESUS LOVES ME, YES JESUS LOVES ME.

The more she sang the words, the more she felt the truth in them. She sang the song until she knew it was more than a song she had learned as a child. It was a personal message to her in her time of crisis and God wanted her to know that He loved her. No matter what! He actually loved her—the totally messed-up, screwed-up-in-the-head her. The one who made all the mistakes, the one who totally ignored God was the one whom God loved.

This realization was mind blowing! God loved her! He knew everything she had done yet He still loved her and was still offering her a way out. Patricia fell to her knees at that moment in total submission to the will of God. On her knees, she fought for her life as she prayed and cried, wrestling with the many demons from her past. Many hours later, the woman that got up was no longer the same woman who had gone down.

CHAPTER SIXTEEN

Patricia looked around her small apartment with new eyes. Every surface had been cleaned, dusted, and polished. Every dish had been washed and put away. She had gone to the store with her last twenty and bought a few groceries, and for the first time, she felt like she had a home.

Patricia slept for only an hour last night but felt amazingly energized. When she had gotten off her knees the evening before, she knew she was a changed woman. She never had much use for religion in her life, choosing instead, to believe that she was the master of her own fate whether it was good or bad. She had grown weary with life and her constant poor choices. For the first time ever, she considered what her choices had done to Josiah and hadn't liked what she had seen.

Her son tried to commit suicide and it was her fault. That was a reality that she had to accept. He was desperately reaching out to her, but she was too absorbed in her own problems to pay attention to her son. She had taken a long look back and saw all the boyfriends and the girlfriends and the total lack of attention that she paid him because she was too busy with her current lovers. She shuddered as she remembered that and much more. Shaking her head she tried to dislodge the images that were tormenting her mind, but then she heard a voice within her speaking.

"There is therefore now no condemnation to them which are in Christ Jesus, who walk not after the flesh, but after the Spirit."

She knew that in order for her to become whole she would need to face the past and then let it go. If she didn't, it would torment her continually. She allowed her mind to run through all the memories, good and bad, since she became a parent. She knew she had not done right by Josiah, but what to do going forward eluded her. Definitely an apology was in order, but she owed him so much more.

She decided to put that subject on the back burner for now and picked up the bible on the table which before had been littered with beer cans and overflowing ashtrays. Opening her bible, she began to read as she prayed and asked God for clarity. While she was reading, her doorbell rang. Putting the bible, down she got up to answer the door.

"Hey girl, missed you at the club last night."

One of her "Johnny-come-lately" friends, Allison, entered her apartment and stopped with a gasp.

"OMG! Did you get new furniture?"

"No, I didn't get any new furniture," Patricia quickly replied.

"Then what in the heck happened in here?" Allison asked. "It looks like a totally different place."

"I just decided to clean up a little bit."

"Well, girl you should clean more often—I can't believe your place looks this nice."

"Thanks, I think."

Allison laughed, "I didn't mean anything by that. I am amazed at the difference. It doesn't even look like the same place." Allison spoke as she looked around the room marveling at the change. She noticed the picture on the wall of a young boy with blond hair and the most beautiful gray blue eyes she had ever seen.

"Who is that in the picture? Is he your nephew? He looks like you."

Patricia stared at the picture before commenting. "Yea, he's my nephew," she said, remembering none of her new friends knew she had a son. They knew Patricia, the party animal, who brought the drinks and partied hard and who had no children. The fantasy her, but the fantasy was quickly turning into a nightmare and she was tired of it.

"Actually, he is not my nephew, he's my son." Patricia admitted. "and I haven't seen him in over five months—I miss him."

"So your mom got your kid, too?" Allison responded casually, as if Patricia was talking about the weather. "My mom has had my three kids for over two years now. Soon as I get myself together I am going to get them back."

She said this as she put a blunt to her lips, and pulled out a lighter from her purse. Inhaling deeply she choked slightly but it quickly turned into a coughing fit. She attempted to hand the blunt off to Patricia who just stared at it. Allison stopped coughing long enough to notice Patricia was not taking the blunt from her outstretched hand.

"Here girl" she gestured again for Patricia to take the blunt, but she continued to stare vacantly at her outstretched hand. Finally coming out of her musings, she asked Allison a question.

"Do you ever miss your children, Allison?"

"What? Why are we talking about my children? Girl you blowing my high." She put the blunt back to her lips, taking another pull on it. "Girl you gonna hit this or what?"

"Or what," said Patricia

"What did you say?"

"Or what," I said, "or what," Patricia repeated. "You asked me if I was going to hit the blunt or what. I am saying or what. I won't be hitting that blunt, drinking, or anything else that will keep me from getting my son back. Or what, Or what." She repeated the phrase like a mantra.

Allison looked at Patricia like she was crazy. She had never really liked Patricia, but she was so disliked by the crowd in the little dive bar where they hung, that Patricia had been the only one more eager than her to have a friend, so she took what she could get. But this Patricia was not the same one she had known. First clue was her apartment. In the entire time she had known her, it had never been clean. What had happened all of a sudden to make her just wake up and start cleaning? "What was her deal tonight anyway," Allison thought to herself. Ever since she had been here, Patricia had seemed as if she was in a daze. This was definitely not the same Patricia she had known and dealt with.

"Don't you miss your children?" Patricia repeated the question mechanically.

"What is wrong with you today? Why do you keep asking me about my children?"

Allison's voice was becoming slightly shrill under the pressure of Patricia's penetrating question. Her question began to get under her skin, making her feel uncomfortable. Allison began to feel almost hostile. She thought to herself, "Why does this stupid chick keep asking me about my kids? It's none of her business if I miss my kids. It's a stupid question anyway." Of course she missed her kids. She hadn't seen them for over two years. She had lost them when she and her husband started smoking crack.

She couldn't believe how quickly that drug had changed her life. Allison and her husband, Hank, had both been supervisors at the General Motors automobile plant, each making good money and living the American dream. Unfortunately, they had both like to party after hours. A friend turned her husband onto crack and he had fallen instantly in love with the drug, like so many others. When his behavior became somewhat erratic, she started questioning him about the changes in his demeanor and physical appearance. In the beginning, he had denied anything was going on until one night she walked into the bathroom and found him hitting the pipe.

He confessed everything but he had also fixed her up a hit, and she too fell in love. She remembered when they first began getting high together, it seemed to bring them closer, but soon they began missing work after staying up all night smoking. They both ended up losing their jobs and the $300,000 home they worked so hard to purchase.

Before too long, they were at each other's throats and stealing from one another. Their children walked around shell-shocked, not understanding what had happened to their happy suburban lives with their PTA mom and dad.

In the midst of all the chaos, she ended up pregnant again. Allison continued to smoke all day, every day, so her baby was born crack addicted. She and the baby both tested positive for crack cocaine, so her children, including the baby, were taken out of her custody. Her husband Hank was long gone by that point and no one knew where.

Allison's mother agreed to take custody of her two children. The baby was going through withdrawal and too sick to leave the hospital. Eventually, all three of her children would go to live with her mother, who was elderly with health issues. She remembered even through all of that, the only thing she thought about was getting high. She had known her kids would be safe with her mom, but she also knew her mom was in no shape to take the three young children which were being thrust upon her, but the drug had controlled her then and she hadn't cared.

Over a year later, she had finally gotten clean, the word clean being relative. After being arrested for shoplifting, she was given the choice of jail or rehab, and chose the latter. She had finally stopped smoking crack, but had turned to alcohol instead and there was never an attempt to stop smoking weed.

She meant to get her children back after she stopped smoking crack, but she knew she wasn't ready. Was she better than before? Yes, she was but she knew in order for her kids to come home, there were things that needed to happen which she hadn't done.

She had no place for her children to come to. She stayed in a rat trap with two guys as roommates sleeping on the couch. She still hadn't found a job, but she knew she hadn't really tried. Why hadn't she gotten her children? She made excuses and denied the truth but it looked like today was going to be her day of reckoning. Bringing her mind back to the present she looked at Patricia.

Allison stared at Patricia as if it were the first time she had ever seen her, and in many ways, it was.

Patricia held her gaze. There was an openness and vulnerability that neither of the ladies was use to seeing in the crowd they ran with. They held each other's gaze—their emotions naked before the other. Patricia close to tears, walked over to Allison and grabbed her hand. She looked deep into her eyes. "I miss my son so much it hurts. I pretended he didn't exist and tried to erase his presence from my life and now that I have, I am afraid I won't be able to get him back," Patricia stated sorrowfully.

Tears rolled down her face. There was so much pain in her voice that it affected Allison as nothing had since the day she lost her own children.

Patricia's confession not only pulled the scab off of her own wound, but it pulled the scab off of Allison's as well. They both were left with a shared pain so deep that it forced them to console one another.

The two women clung to each other, as they cried uncontrollably. Allison shared her story of how she lost her children and Patricia shared hers. Emotions spent, Patricia made a pot of coffee for them both. As they pulled themselves together and sipped on their coffee, they looked at each other and spoke simultaneously.

"What are we going to do?" They smiled looking at each other.

"I think we should pray," said Patricia.

"I don't even know how," replied Allison. "I am willing from this moment on to try anything."

"It was prayer that made me take a really good look at myself. I am going to be honest, Allison, I didn't like what I saw, but it forced me to take off my mask. I have to tell you, the world without my mask is a scary place, but for the first time maybe in my life, I feel like I am on the right path."

"I can see the change in you. I want what you have," Allison spoke quietly, looking toward heaven. "God, if you are real I want to know you. I need your help and not just for my kids, but for me, God. I need your help for me. Please show me what to do."

Both ladies kneeled down and continued to pray, not even noticing the room getting brighter and brighter, but each of them noticed their burdens getting lighter and lighter.

CHAPTER SEVENTEEN

Robin had been back to work full-time for a little over two weeks. After seeing Josiah at the basketball game in good spirits and mentally stable, she was able to return to a semi-state of normalcy within her own life.

The center tried to block her return, but she pushed back knowing that even with the lawsuit, they had no real basis for letting her go. She negotiated a great exit package in the event she was released from employment for any reason other than malfeasance. She knew her tenure at the Burke Center was now date stamped but she was okay with that. Lately, she was thinking more and more about opening her own practice. She discussed it with Simone who had agreed that it was time, and had told Robin that she had 100 percent confidence in her ability to make it a success.

Jo and Amera had agreed with Simone that maybe it was time for Robin to go out on her own, and offered to invest in her practice by providing a low-interest loan if she needed it, but Robin had assured them that "if" she decided to go that way she was more than able to start the practice on her own.

No one, not even Simone, knew that when Robin's grandmother died, she left Robin a $1 million insurance policy. The only time the money had been touched was when it was placed in a hedge fund account where it performed quite well. Robin's other investment accounts had also done well, so Robin knew that when and if she decided to go out on her own, she would be okay.

They had all agreed to pray about it and wait for God's leading. Robin thought to herself how much she had changed since meeting the girls. She prayed more, and relied on the council of others more than she ever had in her life. The difference was, the council she received from her new family, was always the same, and that was to seek God for answers before doing anything.

She had been a Christian all her life but she realized now she had never been close to God like Cliff, Amera, Jo, and Simone. She began to wonder why. She considered her friend, Tiffany, who was also a Christian. Tiffany's walk with God was similar to her own, in that it seemed more casual in nature. She knew Tiffany believed in God and went to church just about every Sunday. Morally, Tiffany was a good person. She didn't drink, gossip, lie, steal or do any of the things that most Christians use as a measuring stick to indicate holiness. Robin considered the contrasts between her old friend and her new ones. In all the years she and Tiffany had been friends, on the rare occasion she had sought Tiffany for advice, she never advised Robin to pray or read her Bible for guidance. She knew that this didn't make Tiffany any less than her new friends, but the contrast was startling in that she could see herself in Tiffany which was causing her to become an object of self-examination.

Why did it matter? What difference did it make? Her best friend had been there for her when she had first lost Josiah. She had come after work and brought food trying to coax her out of her sadness; but it had been Simone with her tough love, tempered by scripture and prayers, Cliff and the girls praying without ceasing, which had given her the strength and the strategy she needed to get through one of the worse times of her life. Robin had literally stopped fighting, choosing instead to allow depression to take hold. She, the big hot shot psychiatrist, was fully aware of what she needed to do to stave off depression, but she was powerless to call upon her education or any of the tricks of the trade that she knew and had taught others. When Simone saw her refusal to fight, she had called Cliff and the girls who had come straightaway. They were concerned about the state they found her in and immediately went to work.

The four of them surrounded her with prayer day and night. Each of them taking shifts and reading the bible to her and for two days she never said a word.

It was like the time when she was a child and Carmen had left. It had just been too much and she had shut down, but fortunately, this time she was surrounded by warriors of God's word who knew what to do, and they refused to allow her to sink deeper into her depressed state.

After two days of Robin being in what closely resembled a catatonic state, Simone, Amera, and Jo decided enough was enough. They undressed Robin and put her in a lukewarm shower. Robin remembered the coolness of the water shocking her and bringing her back into the present as she loudly protested, but they paid her no mind as they cleaned her body and washed her hair and then wrapped her in big fluffy towels.

Simone combed her hair like she was a child while the girls had oiled her skin and dressed her. Robin cried the entire time they were working on her. She remembered them singing and humming hymns and praising God as they took care of her. At first she cried for the loss of Josiah which she understood, but there came a point when she began crying for herself as a child. She cried for the day when her mother left with the man in the shiny red car and she cried for the day she found her father dead. They both left her. She had always known Carmen was never really a mother to her but her father always said he loved her. Then why did he leave? She realized in that moment, that question had niggled at the back of her mind for many years. If he had really loved her, then why hadn't he stayed with her?

She remembered then something her grandmother told her many years before. She said that both her father and mother were selfish. Her mother because she only did what pleased her and her father because he had given up, even though he knew he had a daughter to raise.

"Why did you leave me daddy?" Robin sobbed through the tears. "You were all I had after Carmen left, daddy. Why did you leave me? I thought it was because of me. I blamed myself. All these years I thought that if I had been able to speak I could have helped you and maybe you wouldn't have killed yourself. Maybe you would have stayed for me," Robin broke free from the others. "I realize now your suicide had nothing to do with me. I was just a child. Grandma was right."

Both of her parents had been selfish and she had suffered because of it. She had not been responsible for her father's suicide. As she accepted the truth of this revelation she felt release wash over her and her tears changed to tears of cleansing.

Simone and the girls immediately sensed the shift and all of them gathered her in a group hug and rocked and prayed over her until her sobs quieted down and she collapsed in total exhaustion. When she awoke, she was on the road to recovery. Robin knew that she would never be the same after that day. Something in her had been broken, and something else was released. She felt restored.

Robin thought about the journey she had been on ever since Josiah tried to commit suicide and she realized that her journey started long before all of this. When she read Josiah's letter, she knew instantly that her destiny and his were tied together. She wasn't even sure of what that meant, but they shared a spiritual connection. Josiah was a kid much like she had been at his age; he was old before his time due to circumstances and the hand he had been dealt, and like her, he showed a good face on the outside but inwardly he suffered damage.

She had determined in her heart that she would do her best to make sure the rest of his childhood would be better than what he had experienced to date.

The basketball game had been a life saver. She was grateful to find him well, but shocked to see the level of faith he had in her ability to find him and to set things straight. When she was abruptly cut off from all communication with him, she thought it would cause him a setback, but Josiah surprised her by seeming to thrive in a hostile environment. She gave Keshawn a lot of credit for Josiah's turnaround and she promised herself to look into his case when she was finished with their current situation, but for now, her focus was on Josiah.

She was mildly concerned about the chaperones from the group home who had attended the game. She remembered one in particular—a Mrs. Dixon. When Josiah introduced the two ladies, Mrs. Dixon's eyes widened slightly. She didn't say anything or act in any way to indicate that she knew the history between Josiah and her, but Robin knew she had felt something when they met. She hadn't heard anything and the game was more than three weeks ago. Mrs. Dixon seemed nice and Robin could tell she genuinely loved the kids.

There was another game scheduled for the following month and Robin couldn't wait to see Josiah again. Cliff, Amera, and Jo were going to be there as well, but would just be fans and not performing. Amera and Jo got permission to take all the boys to an indoor waterpark after the game, so Robin was very excited. She decided to call the girls to see how they were doing.

"Hello," Jo answered the phone in her normal cheery tone.

"Hey big sis," replied an equally cheery Robin.

Since that day Simone and her spiritual sisters snatched her out of the devil's grip, she had taken to calling Jo 'big sis' and Amera 'little sis.' They each were a year apart from the other with Robin being in the middle.

"Hey girl, what are you doing? You sound happy," said Jo.

"You know I am, I can't wait until the next game."

"Me neither. Hold on girl, bugaboo wants to holler."

A second later Amera's voice could be heard getting in on the conversation.

"Are you excited about the game next month?" Amera asked.

"You know I am," Robin replied.

"We are going to fly in early Wednesday evening before the game so we can have some 'us' time."

Jo spoke up in the background, "Pajama Party!" They all giggled like school girls.

"Why don't you invite Tiffany? We still haven't met her yet," said Jo.

"That's a great idea," said Robin. "I will call her when we get off the phone," she continued. "Where is Cliff? I don't hear his lovely baritone harping in," Robin said laughing.

"Believe it or not, he said he was going to see a movie and we are not to go anywhere until he gets back."

They all burst out laughing at this comment.

"I'm trying to picture Cliff sitting in the movies all by himself," said Amera. A roar of laughter erupts from all three girls.

"Who said he was alone?" said Jo mysteriously. There was stunned silence on the line lasting for some seconds.

"Talk about things that make you go hmmmmmmm," said Robin "I'm going to leave that one alone."

"I think that would be wise," said Amera.

The girls talked about nonessential things for several more minutes before hanging up. As soon as Robin hung up with the girls, she called Tiffany to invite her to the pajama party. Tiffany was subdued when she answered the phone.

"Hey girl what's wrong with you?" said Robin. "Why do you sound like you lost your best friend and I am right here," she said this hoping to elicit a laugh from her normally perky friend, but no such luck. "What is wrong with you, Tiff?"

With that Tiffany released the floodgates and allowed her tears to flow. She was so upset she was unable to speak. Robin told her she was on the way and hung up the phone. Taking a moment, she dialed Amera and Jo back explaining what had just happened and asked them to pray before quickly leaving the house.

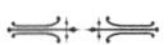

Robin pulled into Tiffany's driveway noting her car was haphazardly parked with the driver's side door sitting open making a loud dinging sound indicating she left her keys in the ignition. Robin took a moment to move Tiffany's car into the garage, closing her door and removing her key. Moving through the garage door she entered Tiffany's kitchen. She had always loved her kitchen. It was normally bright and homey feeling with beautiful hardwood floors and brick backsplash, but today she could see shadows of darkness lurking in every corner. She began to pray silently to herself.

Moving through Tiffany's home, she called out her name. Tiffany's husband, Walter, didn't appear to be home because his car wasn't in the garage. It was dusk and the house was growing dark. Robin turned on lights as she moved through her best friend's home, knowing the layout as well as she knew her own. Robin reached the winding staircase and began to ascend, all the while calling Tiffany's name. The closer she got to the top, the more apprehensive she became. This was more than a simple fight between husband and wife, more than a problem at work, she could feel it. Moving quickly now, Robin headed toward the master bedroom. The double doors were closed and locked.

"Tiffany, are you in there? Open the door!" yelled Robin. Shaking the door knob she began to beat on the door. "I know you're in there, Tiff. Open this door!"

Robin felt terror coursing through her body like a fever. Just when she was on the verge of panic something told her to call the girls. She took out her cell and dialed Amera and Jo's number. Jo picked up on the first ring.

"Are you okay? What's going on? The spirit just told me to pray and not to stop. Robin, are you okay?"

"Yes, I am fine but something is wrong with Tiffany. She is locked in her bedroom and won't answer me." Robin sounded like she was about to cry. "Something is wrong, I can feel it."

Jo could hear the apprehension in Robin's voice. "Knock on the door and tell her you're going to call 911," said Jo.

"What good is that going to do if she won't open the door? I am going to try and kick the door in," Robin replied.

Jo very calmly repeated, "Knock on the door and tell her you're going to call 911. Robin, do you trust me?"

"You know I do," said Robin, her voice heavy with unshed tears. She didn't know why, but knew she needed to listen to Jo. Walking up to Tiffany's door, she knocked loudly. "Tiffany, if you don't open this door in five seconds I am going to dial 911," she began counting. "One, two, three—"

She heard the door handle turning and the door cracked slightly open. The room was pitch black and even knowing the layout of the room, Robin couldn't make out anything as she entered the dark room. Moving toward the wall she ran her hand up and down the wall feeling for the wall switch. Finding it, she flipped on the light and made her way toward the bed where Tiffany lay looking like a broken ragdoll.

She tried to roll Tiffany over so that she could see her face. She had long suspected that Walter may have been hitting Tiffany but had no evidence to support that theory. Tiffany refused to cooperate and rolled away from Robin's hand.

"Please go, Robin," said Tiffany. "I'm okay. I will call you tomorrow." Tiffany's voice sounded hollow and broken, which only made Robin more determined to see her friend's face.

"I'm not going anywhere, now turn over and let me see your face."

"Just leave, Robin! I don't need you. I don't need anyone. I just want to be alone," protested Tiffany.

"Well, too bad because I am not going anywhere," said Robin.

"Oh so you have time for me today. Where are your famous friends? What's the matter? They don't have time for you today?"

"What? Why would you say that, Tiffany? You know you are my best friend. Why would you even question that?"

"Just get out Robin. I don't want you here and I don't need you."

"Tiff, whatever I have done to make you upset with me, I apologize. We can talk about it later, but right now I need to make sure you are okay. Let me see your face."

"Oh alright!" Tiffany quickly turned over and sat up in the bed and looked Robin in the face. Robin was stunned when she looked into Tiffany's face. There were no bruises or black eyes or blood of any kind, but the look in Tiffany's eyes was frightening to behold. Tiffany's eyes were as bleak as a winter's day—cold and void of life. Robin gasped as she looked into them. "Tiffany, what happened? Who hurt you?"

Robin had never seen this Tiffany and they were friends since high school. They had been through many ups and downs but Robin had never seen this hollowed-out version of Tiffany. She was honestly afraid for her friend.

She grabbed Tiffany and hugged her and told her everything would be okay. Tiffany, at first was stiff and unyielding in Robin's embrace, but after several minutes, she began to cry and cling to Robin.

"Robin, I can't make it through this. This is more than I can bear." Her sobs turned to mournful wails as she clung to Robin as if her life depended on it.

"Make it through what? Tiffany, please tell me what happened," begged Robin.

Tiffany continued to cry, unable to speak. Robin just held her like Simone, Amera, and Jo held her during her moment of crisis. When Tiffany began to calm down, Robin got a wet rag and wiped Tiffany's tear-stained face.

"I am going downstairs to make us some tea. While I am downstairs, I want you to jump in the shower and put on something comfy and I will be back up so we can talk."

She helped Tiffany to the shower turning on the water and adjusting the temperature. As she helped her into the shower, Tiffany continued to cry silently. Robin wanted to cry at seeing her friend's devastation. She knew that whatever was happening had wounded Tiffany deeply. She silently prayed, asking God for direction.

Robin returned with the tea. She looked into Tiffany's face and although it was clean, her eyes still had no life in them. She fixed tea for Tiffany and for herself, and they took their time allowing the tea to work its magic. Finally, Tiffany was ready to speak.

"You already know that Walter and I have been having some problems but you don't know how bad things have gotten. The Walter that I am living with now is a complete stranger to me. He treats me like he hates my guts. We haven't made love in over a year and believe me I pulled out every trick in the book to pique his interest but he has no desire for me whatsoever," Tiffany explained. "I was at my wit's end. Around this same time, my co-worker, Sheila, was going through a divorce. She started talking about how her husband had totally started ignoring her and treating her coldly and she didn't know why. It sounded familiar since I was going through the exact same thing with Walter so I continued to listen."

Robin listened intently and allowed Tiffany to tell her story.

"So I shared a little with Sheila about what I was going through with Walter. Immediately, Sheila said that Walter was having an affair. She shared more details about her marriage—private phone calls and sudden trips to the store that took hours. These were the exact same things I was experiencing with Walter, and suddenly it all made sense. I'm not stupid, Robin; it crossed my mind when he stopped making love to me, but I've never seen Walter so much as look at another woman our entire seven years of marriage. He has always had a low sex drive so I dismissed that theory, but now the truth was staring me in the face. Sheila said that she later found out that her husband had been sneaking around with one of the single mothers in the neighborhood. It got me so worked up, I couldn't even work anymore. I was furious! All this time I am thinking I was doing something wrong. but to find out he was having an affair," Tiffany said, becoming angrier by the minute.

"Correct me if I am wrong, but at this point, you didn't know he was having an affair, right?" Robin asked.

"True, but she had me so gassed up in my mind that it had already become a reality. I could see him making love to this other woman and now I am obsessed with trying to figure out who it is. Is it someone I know? Was she prettier than me?" Tiffany asked herself. She placed her cup of tea on the night stand.

"I was a mess. Sheila told me I needed to go home and confront him immediately but I didn't need any prompting. I left work early and went home to finally get the truth out of him. His car was in the garage so I figured he was home. His friend Russell's car was in the driveway so I knew right away they would be in the game room playing that stupid Wii, so I went in the game room but they weren't there. I looked in his home office and they weren't there so I figured that they both must have gone out with their other friend, Mitchell, and took his car."

Tiffany took a deep breath. "I decided to go upstairs and take a shower and get ready for the confrontation when he came home later. I headed down the hallway toward my bedroom but as I got closer, I heard noises that sounded like someone making love. I think to myself, no this fool did not bring this tramp into my house and screwing her in my bed. Girl, I go storming through the door like commando ready to kick some tail." Tiffany pauses as the tears return and she tries to regain her strength. All I can tell you is that I wish with everything in me that I had stayed at work," Tiffany shuddered.

"Who was it? Was it someone you knew?" asked Robin.

"Yep, unfortunately it was," replied Tiffany.

"Do you want to say who? If you don't, I understand," said Robin gently.

"You've got to hear the whole story to understand. So your question is, was it someone I knew? The answer to that is yes it was," Tiffany lowered her head into her hands. "I walked in on my husband and Russell making love like a man and woman."

"Oh my God!" Robin gasped. She sat back and covered her mouth with her hands.

"Yes my thoughts exactly. I can't even wrap my mind around it. My marriage has been a lie this entire time." Tiffany leaped off the bed and began to pace the floor. "There was one good thing that came out of it."

"What was that?" said Robin, perplexed that Tiffany could find any good in the situation.

"At least I know it wasn't me. I always knew something was off in the bedroom department, but I thought Walter was a man who was focused on business and that he loved me for me and not because of my looks or my bedroom game. Boy was I ever naïve."

"How can you even say that?" said Robin. "There is no way you could have known that. Shoot, I am a trained professional and I didn't pick up any clues, at least not about that. I did sense something about him was off, but I thought you were covering up that he was hitting you."

"What! You should have known better than that."

"The truth is bad enough. You know what you're going to have to do right?"

"Yea, I know," said Tiffany. "I will call my doctor tomorrow and trust and believe I am going to be tested for everything!"

"I can go with you if you want."

"Nah, this is one walk of shame I need to do alone."

"Tiff, would you mind if we prayed together? When I went through my crisis, prayer was the only thing that pulled me back from the edge. I know you will be okay, but God is able to comfort you in the midst of your storm."

"Yes, I'd like that," Tiffany agreed.

Robin and Tiffany joined hands and bowed their heads. Robin not knowing where the words came from began to pray like she never had before. As she prayed, Tiffany began to cry as she joined in the prayer, calling on God for comfort in her darkest hour. When the prayer was concluded they continued to hold hands.

"Grab some clothes," Robin said. "You can't stay here." She walked over to Tiffany's closet and pulled her suitcase down off the shelf. They both began throwing clothes and toiletries haphazardly into her suitcase.

"Tiff, I just want to say I love you, girl, and we will get through this together." Pausing from packing, a thought occurred to Robin. "Don't you think it is strange that you and I have just experienced the most devastating situations in our lives to date at the same time? It's almost like God is trying to get our attention."

Tiffany thought about what Robin was saying for a moment before responding.

"I hope you're right, Robin. I really hope you're right." Tiffany looked around the room one last time. "Let's get out of here."

CHAPTER EIGHTEEN

Josiah lay on his bed, fully clothed looking at the ceiling. He had the top bunk and Keshawn had the bottom. The room was dormitory style with several bunk beds going up and down the length of it on both sides.

The room was sparsely furnished and immaculately cleaned. Josiah loved the lack of clutter and the unspoiled sanctuary the room offered. Josiah lived in clutter and filth all his life. He thought everyone lived that way until he started going over to his Aunt Angie's house to spend the night. He loved going to her place! Everything was clean and in its own place. Her refrigerator was always clean and full of food, and she cooked real food for him whenever he came.

He remembered she use to try and get his mom to clean and to cook for him, but his mom always laughed it off. Looking around at the mess she would tousle his hair and say something like, "We wouldn't know what to do if this place was ever cleaned up would we, buddy." Or, "We like it this way."

She never asked him if he liked it that way because if she had, he might have told her he hated living in chaos. He might have told her living in all the junk made it hard for him to think, and he would have loved it if she had cooked for him sometimes; not every day but just every now and then.

Unfortunately, that was not something his mother believed in. She told him on many occasions that she was a free spirit and didn't like following a whole lot of rules. She believed she should have the freedom to do as she pleased, so he and his mom led a very disorderly life but he loved her no matter what.

As he lay in his bunk bed, he thought about the life he lived now in the group home and the life he lived with his mother. It still hurt him to think that she only came to see him once since he had been removed from his home with her. He knew she was not hindered from seeing him in anyway like Dr. Walters was, but she was just being who she was.

At first the group home was terrifying. He had been pushed, punched, and bullied every day upon arrival until Keshawn chose to be his friend. To this day, he still didn't know why Keshawn had gone from bullying him to defending him, but he thanked God for Keshawn everyday. Keshawn had become the brother he always wanted but never had. He was smart, too. He helped Josiah with his homework and made sure that Josiah stayed on track. When Keshawn accepted the role of big brother to Josiah, it had forced him to walk a different path. Keshawn was always smart but chose, instead, to hide that side of him in exchange for being top dog in the dog pound. Gangster and smart didn't mesh together well but suddenly Keshawn was completing assignments, participating in class, and generally being a role model for the other kids.

His change forced his crew to fall in line so now instead of Keshawn and his crew being sent to the office each day, they had become the school leaders but in a positive way. They had even started a mentoring program for the younger boys that turned out to be wildly successful. The staff had been amazed! They didn't know why Keshawn had changed but it was speculated among the teachers and administrative staff that it had something to do with Josiah, so they continued to attribute it to the "The Josiah Effect."

Josiah just continued to be his same old soft-spoken self. He had an uncanny ability to see the good in people, even when they weren't so good. Josiah loved unconditionally. This was why he always wanted to please people. It had nothing to do with trying to make people like him. Josiah just loved and because he did, everything he touched was changed.

Josiah didn't feel well when he woke up that morning so he didn't go to school. He was now alone in the dorms. His mother was on his mind today. He wondered how she was doing. He wanted her to come and see him but didn't expect it. He thought about his mother and then he thought about Dr. Walters and wished for the hundredth time that he could take Dr. Walters' personality and put it in his mother's body. He was immediately ashamed as he pondered things much too complicated for a 10-year-old to process. Just then, Keshawn came into the dorms carrying a bag.

"What's up? You still feel like you got to throw up?" Keshawn asked, as he opened the bag he had brought with him."

"I feel better," Josiah said.

"I got some soup and crackers Mrs. Dixon told me to bring to you. She gave me a pass for study hall to bring it. I got thirty more minutes."

"Thanks Keshawn! Do you mind picking up my homework assignments?"

"Already did." Keshawn pulled out a trapper keeper and opened it revealing homework assignments that were written down.

"Thanks, Shawn," Josiah said feeling grateful.

As their friendship grew deeper, Josiah shortened Keshawn's name to Shawn, which Keshawn had liked. He later told Josiah that his mother use to call him Shawn and it made him think of her. The two of them had discussed his mother at length on many occasions. Keshawn was very bitter toward her because of his upbringing or lack thereof. Josiah, being who he was, helped Keshawn to see that his mother was ill and hadn't intended to mistreat him, but because of her illness, she hadn't known any better. He pointed out that while during one of her lucid periods, she dropped him off at her mother's knowing he would be safe there.

Keshawn admitted he had never thought of it that way. Josiah also made him see his Uncle Ralph in a different way. He made Keshawn see that his Uncle Ralph loved him. He was just sick like his mother but with a different kind of sickness.

"See Keshawn you are only 12, but already you have had three people in your life who have loved you. Some people go a lifetime and don't get one," Josiah said,

That is what Keshawn loved about Josiah. He had a way of looking at things that was unlike anyone he had ever known. It was hard to believe the kid was only 10. It didn't matter to Keshawn that Josiah was a 10-year-old white kid, as pale as he was dark, but there was something in Josiah that Keshawn instinctively knew he needed. Josiah changed him. He knew since the moment he met him that he was different. The violence, anger, and hatred which had dwelled inside of Keshawn was gone and replaced with patience, understanding, and love.

"You got to get well man, the game is Thursday," Keshawn told him.

"I will be okay by then," said Josiah, sounding tired.

"Okay, I got to get back to class. Is there anything else you want before I go?" Keshawn asked, as he pulled out a bottle of water from his book bag and handed it to Josiah.

"Nah, I'll be okay. I will see you after school," he said, falling back on the pillow as if answering the question had taken all his energy. Josiah closed his eyes.

Keshawn looked at Josiah for a moment with concern etched on his face. "Alright then, see you after school."

Keshawn exited the room but the look of concern never left his face. He didn't like how Josiah looked. He actually looked worse than he had earlier that morning.

"He might need to go to the doctor," he thought to himself. Keshawn's mind went back to the time when he was living alone in his grandmother's apartment after she had been hospitalized. He became extremely ill after eating some half-cooked chicken he tried to cook. He remembered he was sick of eating ho ho's and pop tarts and missed his grandmother's fried chicken, so he decided he would cook his own chicken. The chicken had been in the freezer for a long time since there was no one to cook it. He had taken it out the freezer like his grandmother had done and put it in a bowl of water to unthaw. He emptied his grandmother's old grease can into the skillet as he had seen her do many times and turned the fire on. He got burned putting the chicken in the skillet from hot grease splattering, but somehow had managed to get it in and turn it over. The chicken was brown on the outside but, unknowingly to him, raw on the inside and he ate it.

He became very ill, but there was no one there to help him. After three days of around the clock vomiting and diarrhea, he had gotten so weak he couldn't even stand to go to the toilet. His survival instinct told him he was in danger and needed to get help. He tried to get to the neighbor. He crawled to the front door, but was so weak he couldn't stand up to open it.

He remembered collapsing to the floor and beginning to black out. He knew death was knocking at his door, but he was too tired to stop it from coming in. Right before he blacked out he remembered asking God to help him. He called on the God of his grandmother—the one she always talked and read about. He called out loudly,

"JESUS HELP ME!"

He laid on the floor in front of that door for two days. He could hear the people in the building walking by, he heard the elevator opening and closing but was powerless to call out to anyone, except Jesus.

On day three he woke up and he could tell his fever had broken. He laid there in his own urine and feces, but it was on that day that he knew he was going to live.

On day four he was able to half crawl half walk to the bathroom where he stripped off his clothes and threw himself in the shower and just let the hot water run over his body. He stayed in the shower until the water turned cold.

After putting on clean clothes, he discovered he was starving. He went into the kitchen and grabbed a box of ho ho's and began tearing the wrapper off one but something told him not to eat it. Looking around the kitchen to see what else was available, he saw ramien noodles on the counter and decided to eat those instead. For the next two days he ate ramien noodles until he got his strength back.

Keshawn remembered during that time that he had never felt more alone. It was at that moment that he came to hate his mom and the father he had never known. He knew he had almost died and the saddest thought of all was no one would have known or cared. He became angry and violent after that experience and had remained so until he met Josiah.

Keshawn decided not to go back to class, but to go see Mrs. Dixon to let her know that Josiah was getting worse. Mrs. Dixon was sitting in her office looking over some papers when Keshawn tapped on her door.

"Come in," she said.

Keshawn entered her office and she could tell immediately that he was agitated.

"What's wrong, Keshawn?" She stood up from her chair moving toward Keshawn apprehension on her face. "Are you okay?

"Yes ma'am. I am fine, but Josiah ain't looking too good."

"What do you mean he's not looking too good?

"I just left him and you know how Josiah is, he said he was okay, but he was much weaker than he was this morning when I left for school."

"Let's go take a look," she said, grabbing her jacket out of the closet.

When they arrive to the dorms, Mrs. Dixon immediately walked over to Josiah's bed. Normally, Josiah would have greeted her but when he didn't, she assumed he was sleeping. Reaching the bed she looked at Josiah face and it was beet red. She put her hand on his forehead and it was almost too hot to touch. His breathing was shallow and erratic. Speaking very calmly she said, "Keshawn, go tell Mrs. Rodriguez to call an ambulance."

Keshawn turned and began walking out the door.

"Hurry, Keshawn. Tell them to hurry."

Keshawn began to run as if his life depended on it. When the squad arrived, Josiah's temperature was 106 degrees. He went into convulsions shortly after the medics arrived. Josiah was quickly taken to Nationwide Children's Hospital, where it was determined that he had viral meningitis.

Keshawn was inconsolable and refused to leave the hospital. Mrs. Rodriguez was going to force him to leave until Mrs. Dixon shared the story with her that Keshawn had shared with her about him being alone and ill before he came to the group home. Knowing how protective Keshawn was about Josiah, Mrs. Rodriguez eventually relented and he was allowed to stay at the hospital with Josiah. Josiah hovered on the brink of life and death for several days, going in and out of consciousness, but whenever he would briefly awake, Keshawn was always there. Finally, he woke up one morning and Keshawn could tell he was back.

"Hey, lil bro. It's about time you woke up," said Keshawn, as he approached the bed and began pouring ice in a cup.

"You can only have ice chips for now but I'm guessing you're not really hungry."

"How long have I been sick?" said Josiah, sounding groggy.

"For five days," said Keshawn.

"Dang! We missed the game," said Josiah hoarsely.

"You almost missed a lot of things," responded Keshawn. "You scared the mess out of me. Don't do it again," said Keshawn playfully but you could hear the seriousness of his words under the surface.

"Every time I woke up, Shawn, I saw you either looking at me or asleep in that chair. Have you been here the whole time?"

"You know I wasn't going to leave you man."

"Thanks, Shawn." Tears came to Josiah's eyes.

"Why you crying?" asked Keshawn.

"I always wanted a brother like you and it's like God heard me."

"God did hear you."

"If He did, then why isn't my mother here?" said Josiah. "I asked Him for that, too. Wouldn't they have called her to tell her I was sick?"

"I'm not sure, man, but don't worry, I am here and I will always be here for you."

Josiah began to cry and Keshawn was at a loss. He couldn't stand to see him cry like that. He was always so strong for him and for the rest of the guys. That was why all the guys stood up for him because they knew Josiah had heart.

"Don't cry, Josiah. I'll find a way to get your mother here. Dr. Walters tried to see you but because she wasn't family they wouldn't let her in. She told me to tell you that she would see you soon and that she loved you. She was crying, too."

"I wonder how she found out I was here?" asked Josiah.

"I'm not sure, but she was really upset when they wouldn't let her see you.

Unbeknownst to Josiah, his mother was called and had been at the hospital the entire time. Each time Keshawn left the room to go eat, she would come into the room and pray over her son. She didn't make her presence known to him because he was so very ill and she hadn't wanted to reunite with him under those circumstances. She also still carried a lot of shame concerning the way she had treated him and wasn't sure he would let her back into his life. Patricia continued to hang around in the background, watching and waiting. She was there when Dr. Walters tried to visit. She saw her cry when her visit was refused and was marveled by her bravery. She saw at that moment that Dr. Walters truly loved her son and felt shame for what she had done to separate them. She had risked everything to see Josiah. The lawsuit hadn't stopped Dr. Walters. She had acted more like a mother to Josiah than Patricia ever had. She wished she could have told the nursing staff to let her see Josiah, knowing it was what Josiah would have wanted, but she didn't want to make her presence known. She saw her again later that night in the chapel praying. Patricia asked God what she should do. Up until that time she had been single minded in her request to get Josiah back, but maybe Josiah would be better off without her. She'd said this before but it always came from a selfish place. This time she really wanted to do what was right for Josiah, and if that meant walking away from her son so that he could have a chance at a real family, then she would be willing to do it— But only if God told her to do so. Patricia stayed at the hospital and out of the way as she waited to see how God would lead her.

CHAPTER NINETEEN

Josiah remained in the hospital for several more days where he continued to recover his strength. To say he was the favorite of the entire third floor physicians and nursing staff was an understatement. They had all come to know and love Josiah in his short stay with them and were sincerely sorry to see him go. He was like a ray of sunshine and everyone recognized that he was indeed a very special child. They all knew that he was a ward of the state and lived in the group home. There were even a few who inquired about adopting Josiah, but were told by the state that they were still trying to work things out with his mother. No one could understand how anyone could just leave a child like Josiah.

Gloria Earley was the third shift nurse on Josiah's floor. She was a nurse for over 30 years and has worked on the third floor for 18 of those 30 years. She saw many things in her time there. Some she talked about and some she didn't. Gloria absolutely loved children. In the beginning, she hadn't understood why the good Lord chose not to bless her with any of her own, but later it became apparent that God had a special mission for her and it was right there on that third floor in Children's Hospital in little ole Columbus, Ohio. In her time, she had seen hundreds of children come and go with many going on to become God's angels. She saw her share of good and bad ones, which had surprised her because she believed like most, that all children were innocent, but some children were so damaged and so abused that there remained no more light in them. She prayed for them all but especially the dark ones. Some she had reached while others remained lost to her but she never stopped no matter how discouraging her secret assignment from God became.

Gloria remembered when Josiah had been brought in by squad to the ER. Due to a personnel shortage she had agreed to work a shift in the ER. She hadn't worked the ER in over 20 years, but that day she found herself going into the trauma room to triage the patients and found herself looking at what appeared to be an angel. The child was full of light, more than she had ever seen in anyone before. She almost had to look away. She immediately began to pray. "Holy Spirit guide me." She took the report from the paramedic, while continuing to assess the patient, hooking him up to the machines to monitor his vitals.

Josiah cracked one eye open as she busily moved around his bed. "Hi," he croaked. "Are you an angel?"

The paramedics laughed thinking he was delirious from the fever, but Gloria knew he was like her and could see light in people.

"Hi, yourself. I was going to ask you the same thing." With that, Josiah half-smiled and went right back out and Gloria went back to work.

After he was admitted, Josiah's fever refused to break. Gloria again went to work.

"Holy Spirit, his fever won't break. We've done everything we can do down here, so we gonna need you to do the rest," she continued to pray for Josiah. "I know it is not this child's time, Lord, so just tell me what to do," While on her break, Gloria looked up Josiah's hospital records and saw a prior admission for attempted suicide.

"What are you trying to tell me, Holy Spirit? I don't know what else to do except pray."

She continued to pray, waiting for the Spirit to guide her but heard nothing for days. Josiah wrestled with life and death and still she heard nothing.

Josiah was later placed on her regular rotation and brought to the third floor, which was unusual since the third floor was not for contagious diseases but Gloria later found out there had been a bed shortage and Josiah was placed on her floor right where she could keep an eye on him. She knew who had orchestrated that plan even if they didn't. She was selected as Josiah's dedicated third shift nurse.

One night Gloria had pulled a split shift. While asleep in the nurses' lounge, she dreamt she saw a little boy playing with his mother. The child was beautiful and happy and it was obvious that the mother absolutely loved the child. One day, there was a knock at the door. The mother answered the door to find a man standing on the other side of the door. She disappeared and never came back. The little boy continued to play but worried about his mother and eagerly awaited his mother's return. Gloria looked to see what had happened to his mother but when she saw her again, she had changed. She was dressed promiscuously and she looked drugged up and out of it. The man who knocked on the door in the beginning looked like a regular guy, but now looked dark and sinister. Gloria knew instantly who he was behind the mask which was the man's face. She began to pray for the mother but the harder she prayed the tighter the man held the woman. She had wanted to grab the woman to pull her away from the man, but somehow she was bound and all she could do was pray. She woke up suddenly but remained spooked by the dream

"What are you trying to show me, Holy Spirit?" Gloria sat up and wiped sweat from her brow. Knowing she wouldn't be returning to sleep after that disturbing dream, she decided to get some coffee. While on her way to the cafeteria, she saw a woman coming out of

Josiah's room. She had seen this same woman the night before. She seemed to be almost skulking around the waiting area and always after hours. Gloria was curious who this woman was and why she would be visiting Josiah at this hour of night.

"Hi, my name is Nurse Earley," Gloria said approaching the woman. "I saw you coming out of Josiah's room and I need to make sure you have your visitor's pass."

The woman looked tired and drained of everything but there was something familiar about her but she couldn't quite put her finger on it.

"Yea sure, my name is Patricia Martin," she hesitated. "I am Josiah's aunt." She flashed her visitor's pass and Gloria knew straightway that she was Josiah's mother and not his aunt. While she stood there trying to figure out why the woman would lie about it, the Holy Spirit spoke to her.

"She is the woman in your dream. You need to pray for her."

Gloria looking at her kindly and noting her tiredness, changed tactics.

"I was just going to get some coffee, would you like some?"

Patricia hesitated for only a moment before agreeing to walk to the cafeteria with her to get coffee.

"Buy her some food but do not ask her," the Holy Spirit continued to lead Gloria.

Gloria brought a tray of food over to the table with not only coffee but sandwiches for the both of them.

"I hope you don't mind but I hate to eat alone," Gloria said.

Gloria sat down and began removing food from the tray. The women ate and chatted. Patricia found Gloria easy to talk to. She told Gloria the story of how Josiah had ended up in the group home. She spoke about her sister, "Josiah's mother" very frankly. When Gloria asked her why she always waited until Josiah was asleep to visit him she responded that she didn't want Josiah to ask her any questions about her sister "Josiah's mother."

Gloria listened intently and didn't judge, but waited for the Holy Spirit to give her further directions, but there was none forthcoming. Gloria thought that God was going to have her reveal the fact that she knew that she was Josiah's mother but after the coffee and sandwiches, the woman left. Gloria continued to pray for both Josiah and Patricia Martin.

The next day, it was time for Josiah to leave and return to the group home. The staff decided to throw their favorite patient a goodbye party. Josiah's room was filled with balloons and cards and he smiled so hard you could barely see his eyes. Keshawn was there along with Mrs. Dixon and Mrs. Rodriguez from the group home and plenty of nursing staff and physicians all wanting to say goodbye to this very special little boy.

By now, they all knew Keshawn as well since he had been a mainstay at the hospital while Josiah was ill.

Nurse Earley agreed to work another split shift so that she could be there to say goodbye to her favorite patient, but now the party was over and it was time to roll Josiah downstairs to his waiting vehicle. Nurse Earley rolled a wheelchair into his room where all his things had been packed up.

"Okay, Mr. Charmer, it's time to boot you out of here," said Nurse Earley.

"Okay," said Josiah, as he said his last round of goodbyes to the visiting nurses and doctors. He walked over to the wheelchair and plopped down.

"I can walk down by myself, Nurse Earley. I feel just fine."

"What, and deny me my chance to say my final goodbye? I don't think so young man," she said.

Gloria wheeled Josiah down the hallway toward the elevators to find Mrs. Rodriguez and Keshawn waiting, loaded down with flowers and balloons. Before they reached the elevator, Josiah turned to Nurse Earley and asked if he could give the flowers to the friends he'd made during his stay in the hospital. He referred to other families he had met.

"It's okay with me if it's okay with you, Mrs. Rodriguez," said Nurse Earley.

"Sure, I don't think it will be a problem," she replied.

"Lead the way, Josiah."

Josiah directed her to continue down the hall pass the elevators and they entered into another patient's room. A young girl about 13 years old lay bedridden, while her mother stood at her bedside looking drained and exhausted. Josiah got out of the chair and took a beautiful planter over to the woman.

"Hi, Mrs. Goldstein. How is Sara today?" he asked the woman as if he had known her for a lifetime.

The woman turned her tired face toward Josiah and it was like watching a flower in the desert that comes into the presence of rain. Her face blossomed upon seeing him.

"Josiah," she said his name as if they were old friends. "Aren't you looking well. Don't tell me you're going home. I am truly going to miss you."

She walked up to Josiah and embraced him in a hug. She clung to Josiah for a few seconds as if her life depended on it, as if she was drawing strength from him. She pushed him back but continued to hold his arms.

"I am so glad you stopped to say goodbye. I wanted to thank you for your words of encouragement to me on the horrible day when I first met you. I will never forget them. You were an absolute Godsend that day!"

She kissed Josiah on the cheek and hugged him again. They spoke for a couple of minutes before Josiah got back into his wheelchair and left. They stopped by two more rooms before they headed toward the elevator. As they emerged from the exit doors, the van from the group home was waiting for them. Nurse Earley and Josiah stood facing each other while all the others went to the back of the van to load up all the flowers, balloons, and cards.

"Josiah, it was really a pleasure to get to know you," said Nurse Earley. Lowering her voice conspiratorially, she whispered to Josiah.

"Look, I have to tell you something but you cannot let anyone know I told you this."

Josiah looked into her eyes and waited for her to finish speaking.

"Your mom visited you every night you were here. She always came while you were asleep and stayed all night. I spoke with her one night and she told me she was your aunt. Josiah, she didn't want you to know she was here because she was ashamed of how she treated you. I am telling you this so that you will know that God has heard your prayers and doesn't want you to give up hope. Also, don't worry about the lady doctor either; God said to tell you she will be alright as well."

Gloria said her final goodbyes as Mrs. Rodriguez and Keshawn came around to help Josiah into the minivan. They all said goodbye to Nurse Earley and pulled off. Josiah and Nurse Earley locked eyes, each smiling as the van pulled away from the curb and drove down the street. She didn't know when or how, but she knew that she would see Josiah again.

CHAPTER TWENTY

Life quickly returned to normal at the group home for just about everyone except for Carla Dixon and Maria Rodriguez. They each crossed lines they were not comfortable crossing but both agreed that there was a bigger plan going on beyond what they were able to see. Since then, they had started getting together each morning to pray before starting their day.

Carla's husband, Mark, was a pastor. Each night Carla would come home, and she and Mark would discuss their work day over dinner He would tell her stories about his parishioners' and she would talk about the kids at school. This was their routine and it was almost like white noise after so many years but that was about to change.

Once Carla began telling him stories about Josiah and about "The Josiah Effect," he couldn't wait to get home for his next nightly installment. He became so engrossed in the Josiah stories, he actually asked her if he could meet Josiah.

She had laughed out loud thinking he was joking, but in the midst of laughing she looked at his face and saw he was serious.

"You're not kidding?" she said, looking at him in shock.

"Carla, I don't know what it is about this kid. I have never met him but when you speak about him I feel something on the inside. I don't even know how to describe it. Empathy, sympathy but it pulls at my heart strings. Josiah is a stranger to me yet I find myself not only praying for him but rooting for him! All the stuff you've shared with me about what he has gone through breaks my heart, but it also strengthens my faith."

"That is exactly how I feel as well," said Carla. But as strange as it may sound, he is one of the most resilient people—young or old—I have ever met. He gets one bad break after another but still he smiles, loves, and laughs. I feel honored to have met this child. He makes me look at everything in my life differently. He makes me look at the world with new eyes."

"God has plans for Josiah," said Mark.

"I believe that, and that is why I have gone so far outside of my comfort zone on his behalf. I just know in here," she says pointing at her chest, "that it is the right thing."

"What do you mean? What have you done?" Mark asked, looking dubiously in her direction.

"Remember the therapist I told you about? Dr. Walters?"

"Isn't that the one the lawsuit is about?"

"Yea it is but I think the lawsuit is groundless. I saw them together and what I saw between them is right and true. Josiah needs her and what shocked me was I saw that she needed him as well. I called her when he was admitted to the hospital and when they wouldn't let her see him I called her every day with an update. I knew it was wrong but in my heart, I knew it was right."

"Pheeww, be careful babe. Don't do anything you are going to be sorry about later," Mark said looking concerned.

"See that is the thing with this Josiah Effect, it forces you to do things you wouldn't normally do—to make those hard choices. When the Bible says love thy neighbor as thyself, what does that really mean?" Carla asked.

"In Nazi Germany, the law said you were supposed to turn in anyone of Jewish heritage. When people hid the Jews, where they wrong? Were the people who turned them in right because they obeyed the law? Was Rahab wrong when she hid the spies? According to the law she was wrong but God's law is above the law of man. You're the preacher, but doesn't the Bible say it's better to obey God than man?"

"Yes, but you cannot take that scripture out of context, Carla," replied Mark.

"What do you mean 'take it out of context?" I think that is one of the few scriptures in the Bible which is pretty straight forward." Should I obey any law, rule, or ordinance which goes against what the Bible teaches?"

"Of course not!" said Mark stridently, "But it is a slippery slope when you take it upon yourself to declare something to be above the law of the land or decide the law goes against God's word."

"What do you mean by that?" Carla asked.

Mark could hear the attitude in her voice. "Carla, why are you upset? We are just talking and all I am trying to do is get you to think this thing through clearly. It is easy to see how you can get all caught up in Josiah's life. Shoot, I don't even work there and I want to rescue the child, but baby you are risking your job and your reputation and I have never seen you do this before. I think you are too emotionally involved."

Carla paused, carefully considering her husband's point of view. She knew exactly what he was saying because it wasn't that long ago she had said the same thing to herself. She immediately felt guilty for snapping his head off.

"Honey, I can see why you think that, and believe me I actually had this conversation with myself not that long ago. You know me, I follow the rules. I always have, until now. I don't even know if I can explain it except to say that there is something going on in the realm that is invisible to you—unless God opens your eyes to see it. My part is small but necessary, and I know I am on the right side of this thing, according to Him," she said, pointing upward.

"It took some time and some convincing, but I know I am doing what God wants me to do and it is His job to cover me. If I lose this job then God will provide me with another. I cannot worry about things like that when I know God is working through Josiah to touch the lives of so many people and I believe in the end Josiah will find the love he seeks in this world. God would never ask me to do anything that was morally wrong. That I know for sure."

Mark stared at his wife in open-mouthed silence. He had never heard his wife speak so passionately about anything before. He thought of the scripture Luke 24:32. Jesus had appeared unto two believers on the road to Emmaus and after speaking to them, they said, "Did not our heart burn within us while he talked with us by the way and while he opened to us the scriptures." Mark felt like he had heard the voice of God speaking to him through his wife. He knew in that instant that all the preaching he had done over his pulpit in all the years he had ministered, was not as powerful as the few words his wife had just spoken to him. Deep down he knew why, and the knowing undid him and he began to cry. He discovered something about himself in that instant that he had never known or maybe he had known, but had chosen to ignore it rather than to deal with the truth.

What was the truth? He asked himself this question because he understood that in this instant, in this moment in time, God was calling him out. The God of the universe, the Great Jehovah, the great I AM was calling him out of his lethargy, out of his routine, and out of his traditions and asking him a question. The question brought tears to his eyes because it made him finally acknowledge his own selfishness, his own need to control. How had he come to this place? The question made him look at himself in shame and remorse because he had done what he had sworn he wouldn't do when he had first begun to minister.

He had been young and on fire for God, and had secretly abhorred some of the established preachers' ways of taking God's word and blending it with philosophy or only teaching about one side of God's nature, whether it be God's holiness or God's mercy, or God's judgment. He had always known God loved balance, but what he hadn't known was that those same preachers didn't start out doing that. They, too, had been on fire for God in the beginning, but they become just like Mark had. They bought into the rat race of church tradition, which is the yoke of the Pharisee's. Slowly over time, the true voice of God speaking through the preacher ceased and the preacher began to speak for God, when all the while, God asks the question; When do I get to speak?

No, Mark hadn't preached apostasy or anything that wasn't in the Bible but what he did was silence God as he more and more began to prepare his own messages without the aid of the Holy Spirit. They were good sermons, too; with his educational background in homiletics and hermeneutics, over the years he learned how to stir up the congregation's emotions with the aid of a great choir and a talented praise and worship leader. And with certain inflections in his voice, he saw that they were all technically very, very good, but spiritually they were in error, and he led them to this place.

Now he sat at his dining room table, overwhelmed with a truth he had run from for years, and with God's question reverberating throughout his entire being: WHEN DO I GET TO SPEAK? When does God get to speak? He knew in that instant he needed to repent. He felt as low as the greatest sinner and the shame of what he had been doing pierced him as painfully as the nails which pierced his Savior's hands and feet. Suddenly, it all felt like too much. He tried to pull himself back from the brink. The brink of what he knew not, but he knew if he allowed himself to go over that edge, he would no longer be the Mark he knew. He continued to cry and to wrestle with the truths that assaulted him.

Frantically, he thought to himself, "I am a good man, God. I have never taken the church's money, never touched anyone in that way except my wife. I feed the poor and visit the sick, but God even in all this, I have come up short."

Pastor Mark Dixon had always been a careful man. When he got the call from God to the ministry he knew and understood that he had to walk worthy of that call and he had made it his business to try and do that, but over the years he had seen so many ministries taken down by scandal that he became overly cautious.

He thought about the time when one of his female parishioners came to his office. He was alone. There was no one else was at the church to testify nothing untoward was going on so he insisted upon making an appointment for the woman for the following day. The woman was clearly distraught and he remembered hearing the Spirit telling him to listen to the woman, but he thought it was the devil trying to bring temptation because the woman was young and very beautiful. Everything in him that day told him not to send the woman away, but he did not listened to his inner voice. He had been following his own conscious for so long and not the leading of the Holy Spirit, and he failed to recognize an assignment. He scheduled an appointment for her for the following day and had gone home to his wife proud of the fact that he hadn't given in to temptation. Still, he remembered how the Spirit in him had been grieved and heavy.

It had felt awful. He found out why when he caught the 11 p.m. news. The face of the woman who had come to see him was plastered on his 60 inch television screen. She committed suicide not more than two hours after leaving his office. Her family was interviewed and said she had been distraught ever since the death of her one-month-old daughter from SIDS two weeks earlier. Her mom said she had a mental breakdown.

Mark sat there in stunned silence not believing what he was seeing. The girl had come to him for help and because he was too concerned with thoughts of scandal he turned her away. He thought of this now as he reminisced about the path he had chosen for his life in Christ.

For a long time afterward, Mark was angry with God. He felt like God was trying to get his attention, but deep down he knew he wasn't allowing God to speak to him. He was use to silencing God and doing what he thought was best, but he had never looked at it as disobedience because he had felt he always chose the right thing. His refusal to speak with the woman that night because of the fear of a possible accusation of misconduct led him to think he was being prudent, but in fact, he missed an assignment. He prayed that he had not indirectly been the reason the girl had ended her life.

Carla sat quietly across the table from her husband. After she spoke her mind about Josiah, the Spirit of God had moved over her husband like a rushing mighty wind. She felt the presence of the Holy Spirit as He began to minister to her husband. The tears fell from his eyes, and he looked positively stunned as she spoke to him about following the will of God, even when it superseded the law of the land or her own traditions and habits.

Mark was the most spiritual person she knew and she was confident that God would have her and Mark on the same page when all of this was over. She had no idea that she had just restored a backslider.

CHAPTER TWENTY-ONE

In spite of all the chaos, confusion, awakening, and everything in between that everyone who came into contact with Josiah was experiencing, life went back to its normal rhythm. However, one thing could not be denied; Everywhere Josiah went, and everyone whose life he touched, was somehow slightly different after their encounter with him. Each one experienced something different but somehow they all came away with a feeling of enlightenment or feeling like they had experienced an "ah ha" moment. Paths became clear, hard hearts became tender, closed eyes were opened and a sense of destiny and purpose was either birthed or renewed in everyone he connected with.

Mrs. Goldstein, the mother of the 13-year-old girl that Josiah had gone to say goodbye to before leaving the hospital, was close to a breakdown when Josiah met her in the waiting room one day. They had struck up a conversation. She shared with Josiah that her daughter was dying from leukemia and how hard it was to watch her die a little bit each day. She went on to share with him how close they were and all the things they did together. She had lost her husband in an automobile accident within months of her daughter's birth and she was raising Sara alone.

Josiah just listened, never interrupting, until finally she caught herself rambling.

"I'm sorry, I never go on like this. You probably need to get back to your room," she stammered, slightly embarrassed to expose so much to a stranger much less a child, but he was different somehow.

"No, I like hearing you talk. I was just thinking how lucky Sara is to have a mother like you. It sounds like you make every day special. She will always remember them with a smile. Your stories about her remind me of this one time my Aunt Angie took me to Kings Island. She told me we could stay as long as I wanted, and that I could do whatever I wanted to do. She waited in line with me five different times for over 45 minutes each time, as I rode this rollercoaster called The Beast. She let me have anything I wanted to eat or drink and play as many games as I wanted. It was the most perfect day of my life and I will never forget it because it is burned into my heart. Sara will never forget a minute you two shared because she knows how much you love her. She will always be in your heart in the love you have for her. The same love you have for her, she has for you. She won't forget."

Mrs. Goldstein was surprised by such beautiful words coming out of the mouth of a child. She looked deep into his eyes and they were the most beautiful eyes she had ever seen. They were a beautiful blue-gray and they gazed at her bright and true. There was something like a light that seemed to burn behind his eyes and that something let her know that this was no ordinary child. Without knowing why, she grabbed Josiah's hand and looked intently into his eyes.

"Thank you, Josiah. Thank you for reminding me that one day I will see my daughter again. That each day God gives me to spend with her on this earth is a blessing. Thank you for reminding me of that. I pray right now for you, Josiah. in the name of Jesus, that God blesses you with your heart's desire." She finished the prayer and stood up to leave. "It was truly a pleasure to meet you, Josiah."

"It was nice to meet you, too, Mrs. Goldstein."

This encounter had been one of many that had occurred during Josiah's hospital stay with one thing being shared in each encounter—everyone had come away feeling encouraged and or strengthened.

So Josiah continued to love and to see what God showed him in people, not even realizing who he was or what he was doing, and God continued to use him. Soon it would be Josiah's turn to be encouraged and strengthened.

Meanwhile, Patricia Martin continued to be amazed by how God was closing and opening doors in her life. The more she read about Him the more she came to love Him. It was Saturday afternoon and she sat Indian style on the floor with her back to the couch reading her bible. Her living room was small but it was also bright, sunny, and sparkling clean. This had become her routine. Sometimes her friend, Allison, would come over and they would have breakfast and then study their Bibles, and because neither of them knew enough to really discuss what they had read, after reading they would just talk about the goodness of the Lord and how he continued to show them each day how much He loved them. Patricia was in awe of the love God had for her. It made her realize that she never knew real love, not even from her mother.

Patricia grew up in trailer parks all over Columbus, Ohio. Her mother was too busy to be concerned with the needs of a young daughter, barely paying attention to her so Patricia had quickly learned to fend for herself at an early age. Everyone in the trailer park knew her mother was frequently gone, leaving her young daughter to make it as best she could, so they all rallied to make sure she ate and, for the most part, had what she needed. Of course in every fairy tale there is an ogre and unfortunately life was conspiring to intersect her path with him. His name was Mr. Gilbert. He was an elderly widow and everyone liked him. He was a dumpster diver by day, bringing home what he titled "used treasures" but others called junk. He had a trailer full of magazines and Patricia loved to go over to his place and look through his stack of *Ladies Home Journal, Redbook,* and *LIFE* magazines. She saw a whole other world that didn't include trailer parks or mothers who dressed inappropriately. Everything her mother wore was either too short, too tight, or too revealing but that was how she liked it.

Mr. Gilbert began giving her other types of magazines to read. They had naked people in them. He would give her a stack of magazines and then go to the kitchen, leaving her alone with the magazines but secretly, he spied on her from the kitchen as she guiltily leafed through the pages. Patricia would look back toward the kitchen from time to time as she hurriedly flipped through the pages.

Mr. Gilbert first molested her at the age of nine. She told her mother when she was 11, but her mother either did not believe her or didn't care, so nothing was done. After that, Patricia quietly endured the old man's mishandling of her innocence until she turned 13. She decided to run away to California where everyone was beautiful and there was always sunshine. At least that's what she always saw in the magazines.

She had gotten about a 100 miles from home before her dreams of living in the land of sunshine had come crashing down.

At a truck stop west of Columbus, Ohio, she was brutally beaten and raped, her young body dumped like a piece of garbage on the ground behind a dumpster. The highway patrol found her. Patricia was taken to the hospital where she was treated for fractured ribs, a broken wrist, a punctured lung, and a broken jaw along with several broken bones in her face. They said she was lucky to be alive, but Patricia hadn't been so sure. They knew she was underage, but she refused to tell them where she came from or how to get in contact with her parents and she became a ward of the state. She went on to live in a group home until she was 18. Unfortunately for her, the group home was only slightly better than her mother's home.

After she came of age, she left the home with an air of determination to take life by the horns, but she was ill-equipped to deal with life's challenges so she didn't fare well. She knew how to spot perverts and how to stay clear of them but she didn't know how to plan a better life for herself. She knew only poverty and low living for her entire existence and it was only the magazines that had showed her that there was another life which she desperately craved, but the way to cross that great divide remained an elusive dream to her until she met Jonathan.

She found a job as a maid at the Knights Inn Hotel when she met a handsome stranger staying there. Jonathan had quickly convinced Patricia that he was the man with the plan and not only that, but he was the man of her dreams. She never stopped to ask herself if he was all that he said he was, then why was he staying at a cheap hotel like the Knights Inn, but she had been overtaken by his good looks and boyish charm. Patricia's only experience with the opposite sex was rooted in manipulation and violence.

Sex was something that she shied away from, and affection to her was just a prelude to the awful things that men wanted to do to her. She knew the routine. It starts out as simple kissing and then progresses to rubbing the breasts, then down to the special place between the legs before they hurt you. But Jonathan was different. He told her that he didn't believe in touching a woman who wasn't his wife. He was in his 30s and a very good-looking man. Patricia couldn't believe that he really liked her and when he said he wasn't going to touch her until they got married she fell deeply in love with him. Here was a man who was different than every other man she had ever met.

She continued to work in the hotel and Jonathan continued to live there. Patricia wasn't sure how it happened, but somehow she started paying his weekly hotel bill. It started with him telling her that he was experiencing some hard times financially. She wanted to help but it soon turned into him presenting her with his hotel bill each and every week. Patricia didn't care because they were in love and building a life together.

He explained to her that all his money was going toward their new house he was having built for them once they got married, and she was more than happy to chip in. He described the house to her and it sounded beautiful with two bathrooms. She was about to live her dream life. The life she saw in the magazines.

It wasn't too long before he told her the money wasn't coming quick enough and he had to make the final down payment for the house for $25,000 or lose it. He also told her his mother, who lived in Mississippi, was very sick and he had sent all the money he had to his sister to put on her hospital bill and to pay for her prescriptions. He cried that day. She had never seen a man cry before and didn't actually know they could. She hugged him and told him it would be okay.

"If only I had some savings," he said.

"I have savings," she had volunteered. "You can have it."

"I couldn't ask you for money to help my mother, you don't even know her," he said with despair resonating in his voice.

"She's going to be my mother-in-law one day. I don't mind," she replied.

"I couldn't ask you for your savings," he said humbly.

"You're not asking," she had responded. "I am volunteering. If we are to be one, then we must support each other in good times and bad."

"Yes, I guess you're right," he shot back sounding remarkably well all of a sudden.

Later that day, she had gone to the bank and withdrew all her money she had in the world, except for $1 to keep the account open, and took it back to Jonathan. She laid it before him on the bed like an offering.

Instantly, Jonathan became a new man, no longer seeming sad about his mother. His eyes busily darted back and forth over the room. She noticed then that he was packed up and ready for a trip.

"Jonathan, where are you going?"

"I spoke with my sister while you were gone and it is imperative that I get down to Hattiesburg as quickly as possible. My mother has taken a turn for the worse."

"Oh my God Jonathan, do you need me to go with you? I can ask for a couple of days off and go with you if you like," Patricia offered.

"That won't be necessary, my sweet. If things go wrong then I will need you to come down for the funeral so we will just play this one by ear," he said, as he gathered up the money from the bed.

"What about the house, Jonathan? Will we lose it now?" Patricia asked.

"No, of course not. I will be able to get my hands on some money once I get there because I have some property that I can dispose of, so don't worry about that and I will also give you back your $700. I hate to ask but do you think you could get your hands on any more money? It turns out that momma's bills are higher than expected."

She thought to herself for a moment. She only had $54 in her purse but she needed that to get to work and to eat until she got paid again, but she loved him so much and his mother was very ill, and without giving it a second thought she took the money from her purse and gave it to him. He counted up the money and with a look of disappointment on his face he turned to her and asked, "Is this it?" He could hear the harshness in his own voice and tried to correct it.

"What I mean," he said clearing his throat, "unfortunately this is not enough."

Patricia lowered her head in shame and apologized. "I'm sorry, Jonathan, but that is all I have in the world. I know it's not a lot."

"Do you have any jewelry or antiques or anything that can be sold?" he asked. "I just need to get my hands on some more money. You know I wouldn't ask if it wasn't necessary."

Patricia's face turned red in embarrassment. Jonathan had done so much for her and here he was in need and she was unable to help him. Her old feelings of worthlessness began to assault her and she began to cry. Her low self-esteem prevented her from seeing that

Jonathan had never done anything for her at all, except fill her head with a bunch of unfulfilled promises. She was always the one giving but she was blind to these truths.

Jonathan looked up as he heard a sniffle from her.

"Are you crying?" he asked incredulously. "Why are you crying? I'm the one who should be crying. $754 is not going to get me very far."

Patricia just stared at him. The man who stood before her was not the Jonathan she knew and loved. This Jonathan was mean and cold. His voice didn't even sound the same. Jonathan continued to gather his things together until finally nothing remained in the room. He moved to walk out the door without so much as a backward glance, but Patricia stood to her feet and moved toward him just as he hit the door.

"Can we pray for your mother before you go?" This was the one thing she had learned in the group home that had seemed to give her some comfort.

"You go ahead and pray for her," he said. "I've got to get on the road." He walked out the door and into the hallway toward the elevator.

"What's her name," Patricia shouted down the hallway after him.

He turned around looking at her confusedly. "What?"

"What's her name?"

"Whose name?"

"Your mother's name?"

The elevator door opened right then and he stepped inside.

"Whatever you like," he said as the elevator door closed.

She knew then that she would never see Jonathan again. She laid on his mussed bed, smelling his scent, lamenting the love that was never to be and of course, taking the blame for the failure of the relationship. If she had been different, if she had been more, if she had been less, never even realizing there never had been a relationship at all.

Her relationship with Jonathan set the stage for her future relationships as she continued to pick men who would only use and abuse her. The closest she came to a real relationship was when she met Josiah's father, Josiah Thomas Martin, II. His nickname was J.T. In his own twisted way, he had actually really cared about her but he was also a heroin addict and his lifestyle sucked her into a vortex of drugs and crime.

Patricia had never done heroin before but she pretty much tried everything else. J.T. didn't want her to do heroin, knowing once that door was opened, there was no turning back. He truly did care for her in his own way, he hadn't wanted that life for her.

When Patricia found out she was pregnant, she made up her mind that she and J.T. would walk away from the life of drugs and petty crime for the sake of their child. This proved to be easier said than done. She started her prenatal care at the free clinic while she quit cocaine cold turkey. The weed and various pills she was known to pop from time to time soon followed. She would talk to Josiah in her belly, telling him she loved him, promising him the world.

She tried her best to get J.T. to quit the drugs and to settle down so that he could be a good father to their child, but he either wouldn't or couldn't. The drugs caused him to be violent at times. She was pregnant and felt alone because each day that went by they grew further and further apart. She could no longer be his lookout as he went into stores and stole cigarettes, meat, or anything else that wasn't nailed down. She refused saying she couldn't risk going to jail pregnant. Patricia later found out that he recruited someone else to be his partner in crime, and that was the beginning of the end. Her name was Nikki and like J.T., was a heroin addict. She quickly became the Bonnie to his Clyde, and before too long, J.T. left Patricia.

When Josiah was born there was no one there to celebrate his entrance into this world. No friends, because Patricia had never been able to collect or keep them. No family because she hadn't seen her mother since she was 13 years old and she had never met any of J.T.'s family—only being told his parents lived in Cleveland.

Patricia cried the day Josiah was born. Her spirit was broken and she resisted the child who everyone said was one of the most beautiful babies they had ever seen. She resisted his beautiful eyes that changed from blue to gray, then back from gray to blue, depending on his mood. She loved him but she withheld a part of herself from him because she was tired of being hurt and she swore that she would never be hurt like this again. Josiah looked at his mom with all the love in the world in his newborn eyes. He had enough love to heal her but Patricia was too locked into her own pain to notice. The love in Josiah's eyes was never reflected back by his mother's eyes, so Josiah grew up hungry. He grew up hungry for his mother's love like she had grown up hungry for her own mother's love. Because she was broken, she was destined to break what life gave her to care for. Even as a young child, Josiah always felt the need in her. It was an all-consuming cavernous void that he didn't understand, but spent his entire life trying to fill, never realizing it was never his to fill.

For a time after Josiah was born, J. T. came back to Patricia and tried to be a family, but the drugs would always call him back. By the time Josiah was one, J.T. was out of his life forever and Patricia had sunk back into the abyss.

Growing up, Josiah played with angels that only he could see. It was the angels who rocked him and quieted him when he fretted, because his mother was in the abyss and only God knew where his father was.

CHAPTER TWENTY-TWO

Robin continued to adjust to life without Josiah, but was still quietly making moves to work around the lawsuit. Against the advice of the attorney, she went to see Patricia Martin, hoping to talk some sense into her. She found out that she had moved and no one seemed to know where. Robin was deflated by this curve ball. She was quickly encouraged when she received a call from the school guidance counselor, Carla Dixon. She not only let her know Josiah had been admitted to the hospital, but called her with daily updates after the hospital refused to allow Robin to see Josiah, since she was not a family member.

Robin finally came out and asked Carla why she was helping her, to which Carla responded with a simple, "I don't know," but that she knew it was the right thing to do.

Robin simply thanked her and assured her that she loved Josiah and only wanted the best for him. Carla had responded she knew that and if she had felt any other way she would never have called her. Silently, an alliance was established and the circle around Josiah continued to grow.

The date for the next NBA game was quickly approaching and Robin was as excited as she could be. This was to be an overnight trip which not only included the game but another overnight stay at an indoor water park called Cedar Point's Castaway Bay, followed by breakfast the next morning. The school had engrafted the new mentoring program into the NBA adoption, program allowing each of the older boys to bring the "little brothers" they mentored. The group home was extremely proud of how well the program was going. The program ended up having a two-fold benefit, in that not only did it help with the integration of the new boys into the population, but they also saw the older boys really trying to be examples for their little brothers. Mrs. Dixon and Mrs. Rodriguez couldn't have been more pleased.

Keshawn and Josiah were both excited about the overnight stay and the game. They were on the basketball court playing one-on-one while talking about the trip and making plans. Keshawn jumped over Josiah's head and slam dunked the ball into the cylinder.

"Twenty-one! I win!" he said laughing as he bounced the ball off Josiah's head.

"You just got lucky," Josiah said laughing as he tried in vain to snatch the ball out of Keshawn's hands. They ran down the court like two 6-year-olds, clowning and having fun. Keshawn stopped to catch his breath, bending at the waist and breathing in deeply.

"Hold up, man. Let me catch my breath," Keshawn said, as he continued breathing deeply trying to catch his breath.

"You know, man, I really did get lucky. You are getting better and better. I only beat you by two points and I wasn't even holding back like I use to. Your b-ball game is getting sweet," Keshawn said.

"For real, Shawn?" Josiah said excitedly. "Tell the truth, were you holding back just a little?" Josiah asked excitedly.

"I promise you, I wasn't. When you went on that six-point run you had me kinda shook." Both boys laughed as they walked out the gym. The conversation quickly turned to the upcoming trip.

"Do you think Dr. Walters will be there?" asked Keshawn.

"I don't know for sure, but I know if she isn't there, it will be because someone is stopping her; but I hope she comes. I really miss her."

"Yea, I know you do," said Keshawn. "Just stay positive. Where there's a will there's a way."

"What does that mean?" asked Josiah as he looked at Keshawn with confusion.

"I don't really know. That is what my uncle use to say when I would talk about finding my mother. I think it means not to give up hope."

Josiah thought about this for a moment as he tried to process this concept in his young brain.

"Don't worry about it. Everything is going to work out okay," Keshawn repeated. "You know one of those nurses at the hospital inquired about adopting me. I am supposed to meet her next Sunday."

"What? Who? I mean which one? Did you get her name?"

"Na, not yet but you know I can't leave here until I know that you are okay so we are really going to have pray that Dr. Walters will be able to get custody of you."

"What if she doesn't want to? I mean I wouldn't be mad at her or anything, but Shawn, what if it doesn't work out?" asked Josiah sounding uncertain.

This was one of the few times that Josiah showed his vulnerability. He loved Dr. Walters and didn't doubt that she loved him but there were too many things conspiring against them. She wasn't even allowed to visit him so it was hard for him to conceive that she could actually get custody of him, and that was even if she really wanted to. Then there was the question of his mother.

Nurse Earley told him that his mother was at the hospital every night that he was there, but he never laid eyes on her. He badly wanted to believe what Nurse Earley told him. Once he returned to the group home, he waited for either Mrs. Dixon or Mrs. Rodriguez to pull him out of class and tell him his mother was there to visit him, but it never happened. After a few weeks he quit waiting for her and tried closing his heart to her, but he couldn't because he still missed her. He knew his mother better than anyone and he knew she was gone. She had written him off. The suicide attempt had been too much for her. He had only seen her twice since his suicide attempt and he knew it was that which had run her off. It broke his heart that she left him alone but it was Dr. Walters' love that made him not want to give up entirely.

He suddenly remembered something. Right before he decided he was going to take the pills, the angels came to him and tried to help him resist. He remembered now; they were the same angels that were with him as a young child. They comforted him when he was alone in the dark while his mother would be somewhere getting high with her friends. They protected him from her boyfriends who were involuntary babysitters with no compassion for a crying child. He recognized the angels, but he refused to listen to them. He remembered how sad they were and how they tried to keep him awake until his mother came home and found him.

"Let's stop by Mrs. Dixon's office to see if she needs help with anything," said Keshawn. As the boys walked in the direction of her office, Mrs. Dixon exited her office doors.

"You must be psychic," she said, looking at both of the boys.

"I was just coming to get you, Josiah. I have something I need to speak with you about. Keshawn, can Josiah meet you back at the dorms?"

Josiah's heart began beating quickly and his breath quickened. His mother had finally come. Just when he had given up on her she had finally showed up. For a second he felt pure joy but that was followed by fear. What if she was here to say goodbye? A cold wave of fear rolled over Josiah causing him to freeze.

"Would it be okay if Shawn came with me, Mrs. Dixon?"

She hesitated but only for a moment. "Okay guys, come with me." She took them into her office, shutting the door behind her.

They all took a seat and she turned and looked at Josiah. "Josiah, your mom has contacted us and she has made some decisions about your care."

Josiah was excited and afraid at the same time. Excited because it had been so long since he had seen her and he was hoping that she had decided she wanted to bring him home—Afraid, because what if it was something else? What if she just wanted to say her last goodbye? He didn't think his heart could take another break like that. He had accepted the absence of his mother in his life. He even begun to fantasize about a life with Dr. Walters as his new mother but it never meant he stopped loving his real mother. He just accepted the fact that he would never be able to fill the great void that he always knew was in her.

The room was pregnant with silence. Both Keshawn and Mrs. Dixon waited for him to speak, but he just sat there frozen in place and because he didn't know what to say, he said nothing at all. It felt like they were about to pick the scab off of an old wound so he sat still and silent, waiting for the pain.

"Josiah, did you hear me?" Mrs. Dixon asked looking at him expectantly.

"You okay lil bro?" Keshawn asked him, putting his large hand on Josiah's shoulder encouragingly.

Josiah looked first at Mrs. Dixon and then at Keshawn. He held Keshawn's gaze for several moments drawing strength from him. He knew that whatever was coming, good or bad, Keshawn would be by his side helping him to navigate the waters of uncertainty.

He turned his gaze back to Mrs. Dixon and saw the encouragement in her eyes as well. He knew that she too would stand by his side. He would not be alone so he braced himself and nodded at Mrs. Dixon. She held his gaze for a moment longer before continuing.

"Your mother will be here to see you at 6 p.m."

"But you said that she had made some decisions about my care. What did she decide?"

"She will tell you herself tonight when she comes."

Josiah remained seated for a moment before Keshawn tapped him on the shoulder.

"Let's go, bro."

Carla came from around her desk and kneeled in front of Josiah who remained seated with his head hung down. She put her finger under his chin and lifted his face up until they are eye to eye.

"Josiah, whatever your mother tells you, everything will be okay, I promise you that. I have it on good authority."

Josiah looked at her, his eyes wide and glassy. He leapt out of his seat and threw his arms around her. She hugged his slim frame tightly. She loosened the tight grip he had around her neck and looked him in the eyes.

"Remember, no matter what she says, it will be okay." Taking both Josiah's hand and Keshawn's she began to pray. "Lord, we ask you, God, to intervene in this situation. God, let thy will be done. In Jesus name we pray. Amen." She hugged both boys with tears in her eyes and told them everything was going to work out because she had gotten it on good authority that this was just another step in the plan.

Shortly after the boys left, Maria Rodriguez walked into Carla's office. "I saw Keshawn and Josiah leaving both looking like they had just left a funeral. I take it you told him the news."

"Yea, I did"

"How did he take it?" asked Maria.

"Like you would expect. I am just grateful that he has Keshawn."

"He has more than Keshawn, he has you and me as well," replied Maria.

"I know, I'm just saying," Carla said.

"Carla, you and I have prayed for that child every morning since you drew me into this big plan that you claim God had for his life. You were the one who convinced me that we were doing God's work so I don't want to hear anything that sounds like doubt or wavering coming out of your mouth. Not now! We are in way too deep. No matter what she says to him, we will be here to pick up the pieces. The same way you spoke to me that day when you convinced me to go against everything I knew to be right to follow this "higher calling" as you termed it, is the same conversation you need to have with yourself right now. We have to see this thing through and that means believing that everything that happens is either an orchestrated part of God's plan or it will be converted to fit in His plan. Now what you got to say about that?!"

"Girl, all I got to say is that I feel sorry for your poor husband." You are right, of course," said Carla. "I guess I was just having a moment of weakness. I feel like you just slapped me."

They both laughed. It was a deep cleansing laugh and they both felt better afterwards.

"So did she say what she was going to do?" asked Maria.

"Nope, not even a hint at what direction she was leaning. I am just glad the field trip is this Friday. At least we know Josiah will get to see Dr. Walters which should help if his mother has decided to permanently give up custody rights to Josiah."

"Did you ever stop to think that if she does do that, maybe that is God's plan?" said Maria.

"I'm so confused right now; I don't know what to do," said Carla. "I want to call Dr. Walters to give her a heads up but I don't feel led in my spirit to do that."

"Then don't," said Maria. "So far everything you have done you have been led to do. God will give you direction when it is time," Maria said firmly, as she stood to leave.

"Stick around tonight if you can," said Carla. "I may need you."

"I was already planning to."

Maria exited the room leaving Carla deep in thought. "Well, God," she thought out loud, "I guess the next move is yours." She switched off the lights in her office and left.

CHAPTER TWENTY-THREE

Patricia sat on a barstool with an untouched drink sitting in front of her. It was 3 p.m. on a Wednesday afternoon and here she sat in a bar she had never been in before looking for what, she didn't know—maybe some liquid courage. This was the first time she had been in a bar since the night Jesus changed her life. She was a ball of nerves. Her appointment with Josiah was in a few hours and she was full of trepidation.

She had no idea of how Josiah felt about her but for the first time since he came into the world, she knew how she felt about him. She loved Josiah! It was a revelation on how much. She knew she had treated him deplorably all of his life. It was like God made her sit down and watch a movie of her life with Josiah and it broke her heart. He showed her everything she had done to break his spirit. She saw that Josiah was a special and unique child from the beginning, but she was just too self-absorbed to care.

She could now see that her decision to keep Josiah from his dad was not only a mistake, but a selfish act of revenge. J.T., even with all his problems, loved Josiah. The problem was, he just loved heroin and

Nikki more. She could deal with being second to the heroin because it was that way from the beginning, but to be moved to third after Nikki was more than Patricia could take. She used the excuse that she didn't want Josiah around J.T. until he was clean, but she knew she had been punishing J.T. for not choosing a life with her and his son over heroin and Nikki. For the first three years, she and Josiah moved around, never staying anywhere for too long. After several moves, she was sure that J.T. would never be able to find them and that was okay with her. She never stopped to think if it would be okay with Josiah. Every time Josiah asked her questions about his dad, she became angry, as if his questions were an accusation that she wasn't enough. Eventually, he stopped asking.

She thought about all the men that had streamed through her life after J.T. left. She remembered some really bad times—beatings where Josiah tried to take up for her and being knocked across the room. She repaid Josiah for his heroism by cooking dinner for her abuser and ignoring Josiah for the rest of the night. She never even asked him how he was feeling or if he was okay. Her only concern was for her current lover. She couldn't even remember that loser's name now. There were many, many others with similar stories. She knew Josiah didn't like any of them but that didn't matter. Her male friends either ignored Josiah or were mean to him, but she pretended not to notice.

Then there were the women. At one point, Patricia decided she was done with men and started dating women. She told herself only a woman could understand her pain and treat her the way she deserved to be treated. Surprisingly, she found that there was very little difference between the sexes. In the beginning, the women also pretended to like Josiah, but he quickly became like background noise to them. He was just as invisible to the women as he was to the men, that is, except for Brenda.

Brenda was more of a parent to Josiah than Patricia ever was. Brenda insisted that Josiah be included into their relationship, stating they were a family, but Patricia didn't have a clue how to include him into their relationship since she herself had no real relationship with him. Her interactions with him were awkward and stilted.

Brenda was horrified by the way Patricia treated her son. It was the reason why she left Patricia; she couldn't bear the way she treated him. She told Patricia, with tears in her eyes, that she couldn't even see what a special child her son was. Before leaving, Brenda sat with Josiah in his room and talked to him for a long time then took her bags and left. Josiah was sad after that. He didn't cry because Josiah never cried, but Patricia knew Brenda's leaving had upset him. Periodically, Josiah would receive a letter from Brenda and that always cheered him up. Patricia never read the letters. She never cared to know what they said.

As she considered her history with Josiah, she began to feel discouraged. There was no way to undo all the damage she had done. She felt foolish now for believing it was going to be that easy. What was she thinking? That she would ride in like the white knight and say what? What could she possibly say to him after the way she treated him all these years? Sure she had changed; she didn't drink, smoke, or get high any longer. She also didn't date. She laughed out loud at that. Who was she kidding, no one had ever "dated" her. What she really meant was she didn't have sex anymore. She talked to God everyday and read her bible. Her mind replayed the contrast between her old life and her new life, and conceded that she was not the same. The question remained, would these changes be enough to erase the damage she had done to her son? Her mind went back and forth, back and forth until she wanted to scream. She didn't know what to do. She wanted to bring her son home and try to rebuild their relationship by showing him how much she loved him and how much she changed, but she questioned if that was the right thing to do.

She knew then what she needed to do for Josiah. It was not what she wanted to do, but for the first time in her life, she was going to put him first. He deserved a better mother than the wreck of the one he suffered with all his life.

It warmed her heart to see all the people who cared about Josiah at the hospital. She had seen that they genuinely loved him. It hurt when she lost custody of Josiah and he was placed in the group home, but after her first visit, she saw that it was nothing like the group homes she had lived in. Mrs. Rodriguez and Mrs. Dixon seemed like they were kind and they sincerely cared about the children in their care. She felt comfortable leaving him in their hands, all the while dreaming about the big payoff from her lawsuit against the Burke Center and against Dr. Walters.

There were times she felt a little guilty that Dr. Walters had gotten caught in her web of lies and deceit, but it couldn't be helped at this point. When would she ever have another chance to get the big payoff her lawyer had promised her?

She met the attorney in a bar she had gone to shortly after Josiah's suicide attempt. They struck up a conversation and she, trying to get sympathy to hopefully get him to buy her another drink, began telling him about her troubled son's suicide attempt and how she blamed his therapist because she felt she had turned him against her. The attorney seemed to warm to her quickly after that, not only buying her a drink, but telling her that she could be paid a lot of money for her pain and suffering. From there, things just snowballed until the next thing she knew she was in the midst of a lawsuit against the Burke Center and Dr. Walters.

How had things got so out of control, she asked herself this question over and over again as she sat looking at the untouched drink. She realized in that instant that she had taken from Josiah the one thing in the world that brought him the most joy, and for what? Money? She saw the horror of what she had done as clear as day.

"Oh no!" she mumbled to herself at the revelation of the damage she had done to her own son.

"Oh no!" she said again as she took the shot of liquor and knocked it back in one gulp. The alcohol made a trail of fire all the way down to her belly, but she liked it. It distracted her from the thoughts she was thinking, but not for long.

"Oh no!" This time it came out as a half-sob half-cry of despair. Tapping the bar to indicate she wanted another drink, she took the drink from the bartender as soon as he brought it to her and downed it immediately and asked for another.

After her fourth shot, Patricia began to feel a little better. The thoughts were still there but their power was decreased. The drinks didn't cure her ache, but the sense of raw, overwhelming pain it caused was dulled. She was buzzed and it felt good.

She began singing to the jukebox and snapping her fingers as she ordered another drink. A gentleman who had been sitting at the end of the bar watching her decided to make his move.

"Hi, my name is Michael. Can I buy you another round?"

She looked at the man and saw that he was not attractive, not even a little, but it wasn't like she was going to take him home so why not allow him to buy her a drink.

"Sure," she said.

The man took the seat next to her and beckoned the bartender over and ordered them both another round.

After four more rounds, they were no longer buzzing, but were full-faced drunk! She felt her sexy coming back. She hadn't felt that in a long time. Moving provocatively, she told the stranger she wanted to dance. He was barely able to stand but he pulled her close to him and began to gyrate against her side. Patricia found this extremely funny and began laughing hysterically. They both laughed and danced erratically until he attempted to pull her closer and fell to the floor, bringing Patricia down with him. The bartender came from behind the bar and helped them up. He told them they were cut off and he was calling them a cab.

"Should I call one cab or two?" he asked, looking disgustedly at the drunken and disheveled couple half-leaning, half-sitting at his bar.

Patricia, looking at the unattractive man who now didn't look so unattractive, answered for them both. "One," she replied drunkenly.

The bartender called the cab and helped the driver to load the drunken couple in the backseat.

"I'm married," he said slurring his words. "We can't go to my place."

Patricia gave the cabbie her home address as she gazed blearily at her watch. It was 6:15. She thought she was supposed to be somewhere but she couldn't remember. Her mind was so fuzzy because she was very drunk. "Oh well," she thought. It had been a long time since she had had some fun. Laying her head back on the seat, she promptly fell asleep.

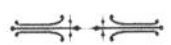

Mrs. Dixon waited in her office with Josiah and Keshawn. Josiah insisted Keshawn accompany him and Mrs. Dixon didn't have the heart to say no. She looked at her watch, noting the time. It was 6:30 and they hadn't heard from Josiah's mother. Josiah chose to dress up for the occasion. He had on his church shoes, pants, and shirt. He wet and brushed his hair, and looked so handsome. Keshawn decided to keep on the same outfit he had worn to school earlier that day.

Both boys were nervous. She could tell by Keshawn's swinging legs and Josiah's losing battle not to bite his nails. Looking at how anxious both boys were, she became angry.

"How dare she!" she thought to herself as she tried to figure out a way to tell Josiah that his mom might not be coming.

"Ummmmm," she said clearing her throat. "Josiah, I think something must have come up. Why don't we just go out and get some ice cream and call it a night. I'm sure she will call to let us know what happened and maybe we can reschedule."

It was as if Josiah was a blow up doll and she had pulled the stopper out. He literally deflated before her eyes. She looked at him with concern before shifting her gaze over to Keshawn. Mentally, she tried to describe the look on Keshawn's face. The only word she could come up with was dangerous. Keshawn looked like he wanted to hurt someone. She hadn't seen that look on his face since he and Josiah had became friends. Instead of focusing on Josiah, she turned her attention to Keshawn.

"Keshawn, are you okay?" She spoke gently not wanting to spook him. He looked like he was in pain. He held his face in a tight grimace and he sat as still as a statue.

"Keshawn?" Mrs. Dixon moved from around her desk and stood before him. She stooped until she was eye level with Keshawn. Placing her hands on his shoulders she stared into his eyes but Keshawn was frozen and could not, or would not move. He held this pose until one lone tear rolled from his eyes. He angrily brushed it away.

"Keshawn, don't worry. It will be alright."

"I'm okay," said Josiah to Keshawn, hoping to calm his temper.

Josiah grabbed Keshawn's arm trying to shake him from his self-induced trance. It was Josiah's words that were Keshawn's undoing. He blinked rapidly trying to forestall the barrage of tears that began falling from both eyes. He looked into Mrs. Dixon's eyes with tears streaming down his cheeks.

"When will she stop hurting him? Please make her stop Mrs. Dixon. Please make her stop."

Keshawn broke down and began crying great hulking sobs. Mrs. Dixon and Josiah tried their best to console him, but Keshawn cried until he was spent. Mrs. Dixon took a handful of tissues from the box on her desk and stuffed them in Keshawn's hands. She and Josiah were crying as well so she went back and got enough tissues for Josiah and herself.

They all sat in silence for a few minutes gathering themselves after the emotional storm they had all just experienced, each a prisoner to their own thoughts.

"Well aren't we a fine threesome," Mrs. Dixon said trying to break the intensity. They looked at each other. All three of them looked like they had lost their favorite toy. Josiah was the first one to smile and it was like the sun coming out after a storm.

"How about that ice cream?" asked Keshawn, his voice sounding gruff with emotion.

Mrs. Dixon gathered both boys in a group hug.

"I promise you, Josiah," she said. "I know it doesn't look like it, but everything is going to be alright. I promise you both that. I don't know how God is going to work all this out, but I know He is. That means you, too, Keshawn."

They all held on to each other, drawing strength from closeness. Suddenly there was a foul smell that permeated the air.

"Josiah!" said Keshawn.

"Sorry," Josiah said, with a sheepish smile.

CHAPTER TWENTY-FOUR

Patricia's hand shook as she tried to light the cigarette hanging from her lips. The cup of coffee felt good in her hand. The warmth of the cup against her skin steadied her, helping her focus. Popping two aspirins into her mouth, she swallowed them dry, not even bothering to wash them down with the coffee. When did she start smoking again, she thought, wondering where the cigarettes had come from. She finally lit the cigarette, closed her eyes, and inhaled deeply.

Her mind was fuzzy from the night before. She remembered bringing the man from the bar to her apartment. They were both sloppy drunk and the drunker he got, the ruder he became. She remembered thinking at first that he was just a lonely older man who had lost his wife, but it turned out that he really did lose a wife, two wives ago. He was currently married and was simply on the prowl for a one night stand. She knew she shouldn't have let him come to her apartment, especially since he was a married man, but she was desperate to continue the good feeling she had and just wanted to party a little. When they got to her apartment, she realized she had made a mistake so she had tried to call him a cab to leave. He got angry and very aggressive. Patricia, familiar with men's anger, and what came next, thought he was going to hurt her. She let him do what he wanted to do and when it was over, he called a cab and left.

Today was the morning after and she was filled with regrets. Regret that she had gone into the bar in the first place. Regret that she had started drinking again after she had been clean and sober for so long. Regret that she had let a stranger pick her up. Yep, this was a morning filled with regrets, but the biggest regret of all was that she let God down. She knew she had. She could feel it. Like a sadness on the inside or a sense of disappointment.

"I need a drink," she thought. She remembered the burning sensation the alcohol made as it went down her throat into her stomach. She remembered how it had made her forget. "Oh no," she thought. "Oh no! I forgot my appointment! Oh my God, I forgot about Josiah." She began to panic. Patricia jumped up frantically searching for her tee-shirt which lay on the floor next to the bed. "I can't believe I forgot the appointment."

She ran pass the mirror and as she did, she caught a glimpse of her reflection and was immediately saddened. She was familiar with the woman in the mirror, but she hadn't seen her in over four months. She looked a mess with her swollen eyes, crazy hair, and puffy features. It was obvious to anyone looking that she had tied one on.

"I can't go see Josiah like this," she thought! "He will think I am still the same. He won't understand that I have changed. "You don't look like you changed right now. You look like good old Patricia, the party girl," the voice in her head raged.

"That woman is gone, I just made a mistake last night. I am a new creature in Christ Jesus."

"Funny how the new creature we just saw in the mirror looks just like the old one," said the voice.

"I don't care what you say Satan, I am a new creature I just made a mistake."

Suddenly, the doorbell rings and interrupts her thoughts. "Who could that be?" she said to herself, grabbing her robe and throwing it on as she went to answer the door. Pulling the door open, she stared in shock at the visitor in her doorway.

It was Ace. He stood in her doorway looking absolutely delicious. She quickly remembered how she looked and began smoothing her hair back.

"Ace, what are you doing here? I haven't seen you in over four months."

"Don't be rude girl, invite me in," he said, pushing his way past her into her living room. "I didn't catch you with company, did I?"

"No, I'm alone," she replied.

"Yea, I figured you would be."

He was still as mean as ever with the snide comments meant to let her know that he knew she was not in his league. She decided she wasn't going to put up with his mess any longer.

"Why are you here Ace? It's obvious that you think you're slumming, so what do you want?"

"Well well, my little Patty Poo is trying to grow a pair," Ace spoke, with an edge in his voice not liking this new Patty. Looking around the room, he noticed that it was actually clean. Patricia had always been a pig for as long as he had known her. "Wow, I can't believe this is the same place. Where are all the ashtrays and beer cans?"

"Thanks for dropping by, Ace, but I have to be somewhere," Patricia spoke, moving toward the door.

"Are you really asking me to leave?" Ace responded incredulously.

"I told you, I have somewhere to be and I am already late."

Ace quickly realized that this is not the same overweight desperate woman that he had left all those months ago. Assessing the situation he decided to change tactics. Grabbing her by the waist he pulled her to him and looked deeply into her eyes. "I missed you," he said looking soulfully into her eyes.

Patricia is thrown off balance by the sudden shift in strategy. Ace was a good looking sexy man, unlike the one she brought home last night, but she decided she wouldn't make it easy for him. If he wanted her, then he was going to have to work for it. She wouldn't be easy like the last time.

"Sure you do," she said. "Remember, you left me."

"I know, baby, but I realize that was a big mistake."

"So what took you so long since you missed me so much?"

"Baby, you know I'm a proud man. I waited and waited for you to call, but you never did. I've just been trying my best to get over you."

What he didn't tell her was that his regular girlfriend, Sidney, had finally gotten tired of his abuse and philandering ways and had kicked him out. Surprisingly, none of his many lady friends offered to let him stay when he ran the same sob story on them, so he was desperate.

"Baby, I'm a new man. I didn't appreciate what I had before, but now I know that you are the woman that I want to be with."

"Ace, quit lying." Her heart pounded as she refused to allow herself to hope that what he was saying was true. She had really been into Ace but he, from the beginning, had treated her like crap. Could she have just misunderstood him? She looked into his eyes as if by looking she could tell whether he spoke truth or lies. But Patricia had always been the kind of person that heard what she wanted to hear and saw what she wanted to see. So again, she allowed herself to be conned, totally forgetting she was a new creature. As Ace began kissing her, she believed that he was telling the truth this time because he had never allowed her to kiss him before. Once Ace realized she had taken the bait, he stopped kissing her long enough to tell her to go fix him some breakfast, as he sat down on her couch with the remote and began flipping through the channels.

Patricia walked back to the kitchen looking dazed and confused. She couldn't believe that Ace had chosen her. She hadn't begged him either. He had finally swallowed his pride and confessed his feelings for her. She was giddy with excitement. "I want to thank you, God, for sending Ace back to me." I'm sorry about bringing that man home last night, but I promise that Ace and I are going to get married and we won't be drinking or smoking anymore," she said silently.

"Make me some coffee, babe," said Ace, who was now sprawled comfortably in her living room.

"Alright sweetie," said Patricia.

And just that quick she forgot about her missed appointment with Josiah, she forgot about the way Ace treated her the last time she saw him, and she forgot about being a new creature. She had always wanted Ace, but a part of her always knew that Ace had never really been serious about her. She couldn't deny that the last time they were together, she believed he was only in it for the money she flashed around. Her thoughts were confirmed when he left her after the money had ran out. But now here he was declaring his love for her. Well, he didn't actually say he loved her, but he did say he made a mistake. What had really let her know this time was different was the kiss. Ace had never let her kiss him before, swearing he was a germophobe, and didn't believe in kissing, so she knew this time was different.

She was as happy as she could be, cooking breakfast for her man. He brought his stuff in from the car, which was a little confusing since she never told him he could stay. But she didn't care—her man was back.

Her nice clean apartment was now a wreck because Ace was a pig. He had only been back for two hours and already he was back to his old self. He had sent her out on a weed run and hadn't offered any money, but she thought since they were going to be living together now, it was okay. What was hers was his and what was his was hers she thought. She knew, even as this thought floated through her brain, that it wasn't really going to be like that.

"It's okay," she thought to herself. "He'll change after we've been together for awhile." As easy as apple pie, Patricia slipped back into the role she was so familiar with which was that of a doormat. She heard him hollering from the living room sofa which he hadn't left since he arrived.

"Doorbell, Patricia!"

"Can you answer the door, I am busy making the pot roast you requested," she yelled back.

"I'm busy, babe. This is the last few minutes of the fourth quarter."

Patricia sighed as she wiped her hands and began moving toward the front door. A little short tempered, she flung the front door open. It was her friend Allison.

"Hey girl, I've been trying to track you down since yesterday. How did it go? Is Josiah here? I would love to meet him." Allison rambled on as she moved inside the apartment without being asked. Since that night they had prayed together, she and Patricia had become best friends. Allison had been granted supervised visiting privileges to see her children and was making progress on her road to recovery, with the end goal being the return of her children. She, unlike Patricia, had found a lovely new church home with a very caring Pastor and first lady, and each day she seemed to grow stronger.

As she walked further into the apartment, she smelled the cigarettes and then the weed. She looked around quizzically. "What's going on in here Sis?" she asked Patricia. As she looked around she finally saw Ace lying on Patricia's couch watching football. She stared at the back of his head and looked from him to Patricia back and forth. "Is that who I think it is?" she asked Patricia.

Patricia was momentarily chagrined as she looked from Allison down to the floor before answering. "Uhh, I think you know Ace right?" "Honey, look who's here. You remember Allison don't you?"

Ace didn't even dignify the question with a turn of his head, but in a distracted, barely audible voice he said, "Uh huh," and continued to watch the game.

Patricia was slightly embarrassed. She began stammering to Allison. "So what's going on girl? Where are you on your way to looking so nice?"

"Don't tell me you forgot," Allison said, staring at her in wide eyed surprise. "Please tell me you didn't forget to pray for me and this job interview today?"

"I'm sorry girl. I forgot all about it, with all this stuff I'm going through trying to get Josiah back."

"Did you tell Josiah?"

"Uh, uh I didn't get a chance to," Patricia stammered.

"What happened? Did they change the meeting time on you?" Allison spoke, sounding furious as she continued to rant.

"They didn't change the meeting time," Patricia said quickly.

That bit of news shut down the full scale tirade that Allison was on.

"Then what happened?"

A pregnant pause filled the air.

"What happened girl? They scheduled a meeting and then just canceled it?" Allison continued to ask. "That's crazy. They can't do that. I am going to give you the number to my legal aid lawyer. She is pretty good. They can't just keep you from seeing him. I know you messed up but you still have rights." Allison started another tirade, but it was quickly quelled by Patricia.

"They didn't cancel it, I missed the appointment."

"Say what?" Allison said in a puzzled tone. "You did what?"

"You heard me, I missed the damn appointment!" Patricia responded with a little more force.

Since they had been friends, Allison had never heard Patricia raise her voice, much less curse at her and she was taken back. She looked closely at her friend and now her eyes were open. She smelled the weed, booze and cigarettes; looking over to the living room she saw two drinks on the coffee table and then she examined her friend. How had she not seen it? Allison had been so wrapped up in the excitement of the job interview and hearing about Patricia's visit with Josiah, she hadn't even noticed that the face of her friend was not right.

"Can you two hold that down, I'm trying to watch the game," said Ace without even turning around to acknowledge their presence. It was like it was his house and they were visitors. She looked at her friend's apartment which always was sunny and peaceful when she came to visit, but today there were shadows everywhere. How had she not seen it?

"Get your coat," Allison said.

"I can't leave now, Allison, I'm about to put a roast in the oven."

"Get your coat now Patricia and I'm not telling you again."

Patricia wasn't sure why, but she quickly moved to do what Allison requested. Before leaving, she walked back into the living room to let Ace know she was leaving.

"Honey I'm going with Allison, but I won't be long." Dead silence was the only response she got. "Honey can you hear me?" she called to Ace again laughing weakly to cover her embarrassment in front of Allison. "Well I guess the game must really be good," she spoke aloud to no one in particular.

Right before the door closed, Ace hollered for Patricia to bring back some more beer. Allison just shook her head.

As the two girls got into Allison's car, the silence between them was thick and heavy. The weather was absolutely beautiful. The sky was a cerulean blue with big white clouds hanging low everywhere.

Allison just stared ahead and drove without saying a word. Patricia rode in silence wondering to herself where her friend was taking her.

Allison pulled up to the curb in front of a church.

"Where are we?" said Patricia. She looked over at Allison and noticed that she had tears rolling down her cheeks.

"What's wrong Ally? Why are you crying?" Patricia looked at her friend with concern.

Allison gripped the steering wheel as if her life depended on it.

"Did something happen with the kids?" Patricia continued to bombard her friend with questions. She didn't have a clue that she was the reason for her friend's distress.

Allison's voice was hollow as she spoke. Her hands never left the steering wheel and she continued to look straight ahead. She spoke so low Patricia had to strain to hear her.

"I just want to know why Patricia? Why? You've been doing so well. What happened with Josiah? You were so excited to tell him the news that you were bringing him home. How do we get from there to missing the appointment?"

Patricia immediately went from concerned friend to a defensive posture. "That is really not any of your business." Patricia responded, folding her arms across her chest.

"How is it none of my business when it is all you and I have prayed about for all these months? Girl, can't you see this is the enemy trying to distract you? You said if God gave Josiah back to you that you would always put God first and then Josiah. How could you let someone like Ace come between you and God?"

"See, I knew you were going to start tripping when you found out Ace and I were back together. You've never liked Ace, but you don't really know him. You need to give him a chance," Patricia pleaded.

"I only know what you told me. Did you forget about the night I came over and you told me everything he had done to you? You remember, we both ended the night giving our lives to Christ? You didn't like him so much that night, but now all of a sudden everything is okay? Pardon me for being a skeptic."

"It's different this time. We're getting married." Patricia knew she was lying, but Allison was making her feel trapped. "I'm going to get Josiah back and we're going to be a family."

"Are you telling me that he actually asked you to marry him? No way! He has to have an agenda. And even if he is serious, do you really think Ace is daddy material? Come on Patricia, use your head."

"Why can't you just be happy for me?" Patricia wailed. "God is finally answering my prayers. I would think you of all people would be happy for me."

"I can't be happy for my friend when I see she's about to make the biggest mistake of her life. You've come so far, Patricia; don't let a buffoon like Ace keep you from reaching your goal."

"He's not a buffoon. You're just jealous because you don't have anybody. I can't believe you're not supporting me in this."

"I can't support you when I believe this is not God's will for your life. Patricia, I know you're lonely, and I'm lonely too, but we both said we would not let anything come before our children. We made a pact, remember? We have grown too close for me to just to let you go over the cliff because if you do, then you will be forcing me to go with you and I know you wouldn't do that and I'm not ready to go over the cliff, so that means you can't go either."

Patricia just sat in the seat staring out the window at the doors of the church, not saying a word. There was a park next door to the church and she could see children playing on the swings and teeter totters. As she stared vacantly out the window, she pondered the words her friend had spoken. "My friend," she thought, as she silently laughed to herself realizing for the first time in her life she actually had a friend. Stretching her hand across the seat, she grasped Allison's hand as she joined in with the tears flowing.

"I messed everything up Ally," Patricia wailed. "They will never give Josiah back to me now," she said sobbing loudly.

"Come on, let's walk over to the park," Allison said, opening her car door.

Patricia got out on her side and they both began walking toward the park. Settling on one of the picnic tables, Allison began to quiz her friend.

"So tell me what happened," said Allison.

"I don't even know. A few hours before the meeting, I remember I began to feel overwhelmed. I thought about all the time that has gone by. I thought about when my son tried to commit suicide, I didn't even go to the hospital to see him. I just couldn't see him like that. I already felt responsible for him being in there. I just felt like he was better off without me."

"I get all that" said Allison. "But Pat, that is the past and you're not that selfish person anymore," she lapsed into her friend's nickname.

"I spoke with you the morning of the appointment and you were counting the hours and the minutes. You were so excited about telling him that he was coming home. What happened that caused you to miss the appointment?"

Patricia hesitated before speaking, as if searching for the words.

"I don't know. I was excited, thinking about what I would say to him. And then out of nowhere, I felt like what's the use. I wondered if he would even want to come home with me. I became so apprehensive, I stopped in a bar downtown. I thought maybe I would just have a drink to calm my nerves. I knew it was wrong. The Holy Spirit kept telling me not to, and I actually made a half-hearted attempt to resist, but I did it anyway. One drink turned into four and then a guy in the bar came over and began buying more. I guess I don't have to tell you how that ended."

"Please tell me you didn't go to his place," Allison interjected.

"No, I didn't," Patricia responded.

"Phewww, that's a relief!" said Allison.

"He came home with me. It turned out he was married, looking for a one night stand. I was drunk and just wanted some company. When he came inside, I think he got the wrong idea. I tried to make him leave but he started getting aggressive. I fought him at first, but then I started feeling like I had brought it all on myself so I just let him do what he wanted to do and then he left."

"What! oh my God. Did he hurt you?" Allison asked, looking at her in horror.

"Only my pride and my spirit," responded Patricia.

"So how did you end up with Ace, of all people?"

"He just showed up on my doorstep this morning. He said he realized that he made a mistake when he let me go."

"Uh, huh, sure," said Allison sarcastically.

"Allison, I know it sounds unbelievable, but I really do believe he means it this time."

"How can you be sure, Pat? You know he is a player. Why would you trust him?"

"He looked me in my eyes and told me he made a mistake and then he did something he has never done before."

"What's that?" asked Allison.

"He kissed me, and he has never let me kiss him before. The entire time we were together, he never let me kiss him. He said he was a germophobe and didn't like kissing. He kissed me, I didn't kiss him."

"Please tell me that you're not using the fact that he kissed you as proof of his sincerity," Allison said in disgust.

"Yes, I am. I believe that was a sign from God that he was sending me Ace to make me happy. It was as if Ace knew how upset I was over missing my appointment with Josiah."

Allison, looking sadly at her friend, saw her in a way she never had before. So much damage she thought to herself. She began to pray silently, asking God to give her the right words to reach Patricia.

"Patricia, I just want you to know that I love you. You have become the sister I never had and it is because of you that I am on this new journey. I owe you my life." As she spoke tears began rolling down her face.

"I wish you could see what I see when I look at you," Allison said. "You are one of the most wonderful, kindest, gentlest people I know and it is an honor to call you my friend." She paused a moment before continuing. "Because I am your friend I must be honest with you. If God was going to send you a man, it wouldn't be anyone like Ace because God doesn't give his children junk or broken things. Someone sent Ace to you alright, but it wasn't God. I believe that the reason you went into that bar yesterday was to set you up for today. Ace doesn't care about you. Look at how he is treating you already. I don't want to hurt your feelings, but he is just using you. Listen to yourself, "he never let me kiss him before." I have seen Ace with my own eyes, tonguing down strippers at that strip club on High Street when you and I use to go out, so I know for a fact that he has no issues with kissing. He just didn't want to kiss you."

Patricia sat in silence as her friend continued speaking.

"Have you even thought about Josiah? How does he fit into all this?"

"Of course I have, why would you ask that? We're going to be a family," Patricia proclaimed.

"Josiah deserves better than this. You told me if you got your son back you were going to be a better mother and you were going to do things differently. I hate to say it Pat, but this kind of looks familiar."

Hot tears burned behind Patricia's eyes, but she refused to let them fall. She was angry with her friend and didn't understand why she just couldn't be supportive. The only reason Patricia could think of was jealousy. She knew Ace was a good-looking man and women just wanted him. That wasn't his fault.

"You're supposed to be my friend, Allison. Why can't you just be happy for me? I know you've been alone like I have for awhile, but God will send you somebody, too."

"Really Pat? Are you serious right now? Do you really think that's what this is about?"

"What else could it be?" Patricia said heatedly. "You and I have grown to be really good friends and I hate that you are letting a man, or a lack of one, come between us," Patricia snidely continued.

Allison sat there in stunned belief just looking at Patricia bewildered. She couldn't believe the words she had just heard coming from her friend's mouth. She was momentarily speechless. She gathered herself to refute her friend's words. Her response was slow, as she searched for the right words to reach her friend. She could now see that things were even worse than she had thought. The Patricia she knew and had come to love had left the building and in her place was the former occupant. The Patricia whose head was proverbially buried in the sand, the one who was so desperate for love and affection, she often settled for scraps and facsimiles. She realized her friend was truly in danger, so she was careful when she spoke.

"First of all Pat, I just want to say again that I love you." Allison purposefully called her by her nickname to remind her friend of their closeness. "I haven't had a real friend for a long time, so having you in my life has been a blessing and I want you to know that I truly treasure our friendship. Now with that being said, I need you to know that my words to you are not motivated by my loneliness or lack of a man in my life."

Allison continued, "You and I are not only friends, but we are sisters in Christ who are sharing a journey. We were each other's support system up until today. I haven't changed, but you seem to have a change of heart. Last night you made a mistake. Instead of repenting and getting back on track, you have done a u-turn and headed back in the direction you told me you hated. Your one desire and passion in this world was Josiah and trying to do right by him. What happened to that desire? It seems that you haven't given Josiah a thought."

"That's a lie," Patricia responded angrily. "That's why I'm doing this. I want Josiah to come home to a real family."

"Now that's the lie," said Allison. "Last night your fear drove you to that bar and one thing led to another and you made mistakes. Can't you see that your judgment has been compromised? You have got to know that this isn't God. This redirection you are taking in your life is not from God. Deep down in your heart, I believe you know this, but you just want to do what you want to do. Would you like to know what comes next? Let me give you a heads up. Josiah gets put on the back burner, again, while you pursue this latest mirage—so poor Josiah gets the shaft yet again."

"Shut up, Allison!" Patricia said, enraged. "How dare she speak to me like that," Patricia thought.

She thought Allison was just being spiteful because of her jealously. Why did she ever think Allison was her friend? Her anger was palpable. She felt like physically striking Allison, but in spite of all the anger and rage in Patricia's mind, she could hear the voice of the Spirit speaking to her.

"Listen, just listen, she is telling the truth."

She tried to use the anger to drown out the voice but it refused to be quenched.

"Listen, just listen."

Patricia began to feel like she was under attack. She wasn't sure if it was from the voice or the words Allison spoke. The voice telling her to listen was overwhelming and this new Allison was making her feel downright uncomfortable.

"How dare she judge me after all the things she has done," Patricia thought. Rage poured through her so strong that she didn't even know herself. She began berating her friend, bringing up her past and all the secret things she had shared with her. She was trying to humiliate Allison in the same like manner she felt humiliated. She spoke so loud that everyone in the park turned in their direction to see what the fuss was all about. Patricia caught her reflection in Allison's glasses and did not like what she saw. She looked positively demonic, with her mouth in a twisted snarl and her eyes piercing with anger.

Then she noticed Allison's expression of hurt. She had wounded her friend, a death blow more hurtful than a physical wound. Patricia became silent as a mute, intently watching her friend as she absorbed the blunt force of the words she had wielded.

Allison looked like she had been physically abused. Her already pale skin was ghostly white as she sat frozen to her seat without saying a word. It was her eyes that told Patricia that she had went too far.

"Allison, I'm sorry," Patricia said as she came to herself. "You know I didn't mean any of it. I don't know what came over me."

Patricia stumbled over her apology, realizing she had really hurt Allison with the words she had spoken. She hadn't meant to bring up those things that Allison had shared with her because she knew how painful they were to her. She felt like Allison backed her into a corner and the only way out was to attack. For those brief moments she had forgotten that Allison was her friend. She had forgotten that beside God and Josiah, Allison was the only one in this world who truly loved her. For those brief moments, Allison had become the enemy and she was in a fight to the death, so she went for the jugular. From the look in Allison's eyes, she had won, but now she regretted it. Allison just sat there like she was in shock. Finally, Patricia quit talking, resulting in several minutes of awkward silence until Allison stood up on shaky legs.

"I've got to go," Allison commented, still stunned. "I'll drop you off."

Patricia didn't know what else to say. She looked at her friend with uncertainty.

"Are you going to be okay, Allison?" You seem out of it," she said.

Patricia now spoke to her friend out of concern and fear. She knew what she said had gone far beyond a spat between two best friends; and she couldn't imagine what the repercussions might be.

Allison didn't respond, but instead began moving in the direction of her car while Patricia followed. She drove Patricia home without a word.

CHAPTER TWENTY-FIVE

Robin, Tiffany, Amera, and Jo were all together the Saturday before the kids NBA game scheduled for the following Monday. There were only two more remaining games after this one and Robin was sad to think she would not be able to see Josiah for a while. But the situation with Josiah was truly teaching her to let go and let God. Even though the thought of not seeing Josiah for a while made her sad, she now had a peace about things that she didn't have before.

This Saturday, however, found the ladies experiencing a day of pure decadence. Robin wanted to say thank you to her three best friends for all that they had done for her, so she had arranged a day of indulgence that they would not soon forget. Problems would not be on the agenda today for any of them. Today was to be a worry-free day of indulgence as they all enjoy massages, manicures, and pedicures, compliments of Robin.

Robin was doing everything at her home. They all had their individual massage beds, each with their own masseuse. Lunch was being prepared by Urban Chef Catering and was scheduled to be served after their massages. Once lunch was completed, nail technicians would be coming to do their manicures and pedicures. Needless to say, they were experiencing pure bliss. They were all so relaxed that the customary chitter-chatter, which was their normal, was remarkably missing for once.

"Sis, this couldn't have been more on time," said Jo, being the first to break the silence.

"The last three weeks of the tour was a beast. I just wanted to come home. I was so stressed, girl, I fired Cliff four times." All the ladies busted into hysterical laughter.

The relationship the girls shared with Cliff was not really employer-employee, although, that was how it began. Cliff provided security for both girls when they were on tour, but he had become so much more. They simply loved him like a father and he loved them and treated them as if they were his daughters. Their relationship had been strengthened when they had realized they all served the risen Savior and were serious about doing the will of the Father. Cliff's family had expanded to include Robin and now Tiffany.

Both Robin and Tiffany had been in church all their lives, but the church had not truly been in them, even though they were both good moral people. Amera and Jo helped Robin to find her way to the truth inside of her. The situation with Josiah had been a turning point in Robin's life. She had always been able, through hard work and tenacity, to accomplish whatever she purposed in her heart to do, that was until Josiah came into her life. She found she was ill-equipped to deal with the emotional baggage that loving Josiah had unleashed. She, too, as a child loved parents who were too selfish to see the precious gift she offered them, so she understood the pain that Josiah experienced. She thought she had gotten over that chapter of her life, but Josiah stirred up emotions and memories long forgotten. Once they surfaced, she was forced to deal with them in order to fight her way through the depression she suffered from losing Josiah. It was in this place that she truly met God—in her shattered place. She cried out to the God she thought she knew, but found out she didn't—the God that her grandmother called on and prayed to on her behalf. She had learned the only way out was through Him. She loved God today in a way she had never known she could. Once she got it together, she helped Tiffany to find her way; so now here they all were together, experiencing God in new ways. Amera discovered that the more she loved the more her capacity to love was increased. Jo learned to trust the leading of the Holy Spirit even when she didn't understand or know where it was leading. Robin discovered that God was sovereign and she may not ever know or understand why she ended up with a mother like Carmen and a father who didn't love her enough to tough it out, but God loved her and that was enough. Tiffany learned forgiveness. She struggled and wrestled with this concept in the beginning because of the wound her husband had left on her soul. Robin shared the story of her childhood with Tiffany, telling her how she had carried a spirit of unforgiveness with her since that time. She told Tiffany she first had to acknowledge it was there. Then she had to accept that forgiveness was really not about the other person, but about your own well-being and your relationship with the Father. After that, she was free to forgive and move on. She realized her grandmother had known all along that she was in bondage, but she also knew that God would deliver her granddaughter in the fullness of time.

So here they were all together. The four of them were as close as sisters. They were one for all and all for one. They each basked in God's love for them and felt so blessed. As their massages came to an end, each was reluctant to move, not wanting to dispel the tranquility they were all experiencing.

A tinkling bell sounded, alerting them that lunch was ready, breaking the laissez-faire spell that the massages had cast over the ladies.

The girls each got up and grabbed their personalized white terry cloth robe with their name engraved on it. Robin thought of everything. They began moving toward the kitchen instead of the more formal dining room. The table in the kitchen was beautifully set and the servers were lined up in anticipation of the ladies arrival. As soon as the ladies sat down, a mimosa was placed before them. An entire buffet was set up on the oversized kitchen island with everything you could think of to eat. Even though the kitchen had been set up buffet style, the servers remained to refresh, refill, or provide any other services they may have desired.

"I can't believe you did all this for us, Robin," Tiffany said, in a soft voice. She was in awe of what her friend had done for them. It was such a beautiful gesture.

"Everything is so perfect, like a dream. I feel like Cinderella at the ball," said Jo.

"We love you, Robin," said Amera.

"Yes, we do," seconded Tiffany.

"Me three," said Jo.

"I love you all, too," said Robin. "I am just so glad that God put all of you in my life. You all know what this last year has been like for me. I didn't know how I was going to make it, but God got me through. He did by sending me three angels, three sisters. I am a better person, a better therapist, a better Christian, and a better friend because of what you all have sown in my life. Words are inadequate to express what you all mean to me." Robin took a sip of her mimosa before continuing.

"The only person missing is Simone, but I got in on pretty good authority that she got a better offer. Tiffany looked quizzically around the table at the smirking faces of Robin, Amera, and Jo.

"What?" she said. "What do you all know that I obviously don't?" Tiffany asked.

"Simone and Cliff are having their own lunch today so she couldn't attend," said Robin.

"No way!" exclaimed Tiffany.

"Don't tell me you missed that, Tiffany? All that awkwardness, them trying not to look at each other. I thought it was hysterical.

You know how Cliff tries to play his cards close to the vest, but Miss Simone had him shook from day one," said Jo, laughing out loud.

The table erupted in laughter as each of the girls began to talk about how they knew and what they had observed. Needless to say, it was the most perfect day but, Robin still had a few tricks up her sleeve. She told the girls after their manicures and pedicures to get dressed because they were going on a road trip.

"Where are we going?" said Amera.

"None of your business nosey," responded Robin.

"You have to tell me so I will know how to dress," Amera shot back.

The other girls joined Amera and began trying to get Robin to tell them where they were going and Robin adamantly refused but she did give them a little tip.

"If you're smart, you will wear shoes that you can walk in and that is all I am saying."

With that she turned and exited the room smiling mischievously as she headed for the bedrooms with three in tow.

A white stretch hummer limousine pulled up to Robin's house 45 minutes later. She heard Tiffany's squeal first and then the excited comments of both Jo and Amera followed. As she began her descent down the stairs, three pairs of eyes turned to look at her. They each looked like little kids on Christmas—eyes filled with excitement and big kool aid smiles plastered on their faces.

"Come on, Robin, tell us where we're going," said Amera.

"Yea, Robin, inquiring minds want to know," Jo chimed in.

"At least give us a clue, Robin," said Tiffany, thinking she could get Robin to reveal the truth since she had never been good at guessing game. She always gave it away.

"You know I never could play those dumb guessing games. I always gave it away."

Both Amera and Jo looked at Tiffany with respect and appreciation.

"Good one, Tiff! I just gleaned a piece of useful information," said Jo, as she climbed into the limo.

One at a time, the rest of the girls entered the limo to find it well stocked with snacks and drinks.

"How far are we going? You've got enough snacks to feed an army," said Tiffany.

"Don't worry about that, just figure out whether we are going to watch a movie first or listen to music." Robin pulled up Pandora radio on the limousine's computer, and before they could ask any more questions, the car was filled with the sounds of old skool music.

"I remember this, even though it was before my time. My mom use to jam to this," Jo said, popping her fingers and singing the lyrics to Car Wash, a 1976 classic by Rose Royce. She was quickly joined by Robin, then Amera and Tiffany completed their quartet. The girls rode down the highway singing, laughing, snacking, and having the best time ever. The car began to slow down and the girls looked through the tinted window and saw they were entering what appeared to be a mall.

"Where are we? What time is it? How long have we been riding?" Tiffany asked three questions in quick succession.

"Wow! I can't believe we have been riding for over three hours," Amera said, looking at her watch.

"This is almost like a scavenger hunt. I'm having so much fun!" Jo said, reaching over and hugging Robin. "Thanks, sis. You truly don't know how much I needed this."

"I may not have known, but God did," Robin responded, as the other girls joined in and made it a group hug. They each took a moment to thank God for His mercy and just to savor the moment, knowing Robin was the instrument used, but it was their Father who orchestrated this entire day and it made them all feel special.

"Anyone feel up to shopping?" Robin asked, although she already knew the answer.

"Can I at least ask what city and state we are in," said Jo?

"I guess I can at least tell you that without spoiling anything. You are in Indianapolis, Indiana," said Robin.

"If this day gets any better, I won't be able to take it," Jo replied. "I love the River Walk."

The girls were deposited in front of the Ralph Lauren store.

"Okay, we only have two hours," Robin said to the girls, as they begin eyeing all the delicious stores the outdoor mall was offering. "Do we want to stay together, pair up, or individually shop?"

"You know our motto, all for one and one for all. We stay together. Everybody pick their favorite store and we will hit them in order," said Jo.

"Yea, that's a good idea, Jo," said Amera.

"And if we still have time left over then we will just go by majority rule," said Tiffany.

"That's okay with me," said Robin.

"Wait a minute, why do we only have two hours?" asked Jo, looking at Robin suspiciously.

"You'll just have to wait and see," said Robin, with an impish look on her face.

The girls hit the stores at a feverish pace. Their limo driver insisted upon following them so he would be able to return the bags to the car rather than have the ladies carry them around.

They had a perfectly lovely time shopping and kibitzing throughout the mall, until Robin looked at her watch and beckoned to the limo driver. He turned abruptly and headed back to retrieve the car. The ladies had given up on trying to find out what was next and instead were just following directions, allowing the surprise to continue to unfold. They knew something else was up because Robin insisted upon purchasing them each a really nice dress and shoes, as if they were all going out to a nice dinner.

After a brief ride, the door opens to find the ladies at the entrance of the Conrad Hotel, a beautiful luxury hotel in downtown Indianapolis. As they entered the lobby, the concierge walks up to Robin greeting her and her party.

"Hello, Dr. Walters. You and your lovely friends are most welcome." He signaled for the bellhop as he inquired about their luggage.

"We only have shopping bags, but we do have quite a few," Robin stated.

"We have prepared the penthouse for you and your party. Follow me, please," the concierge instructed. The penthouse was over 4,000 square feet of pure unadulterated luxury. The ladies were blown away.

"Robin, I am not trying to get in your business, but girl are you really rolling like this? I mean if I count up what you spent so far today, I just feel like I want to chip in or something," Amera said nervously.

Robin laughed out loud. She walked over to Amera and hugged her tightly. She released her from the hug, but kept her hands on both of her shoulders as she looked into her eyes.

"You know I love you right?" Robin said.

"I love you, too, Robin, but I just want to make sure you are okay."

"Amera trust me, I am fine. Now, we only have 45 minutes to get ready.

"Forty-five minutes again?" all the girls bellowed in unison.

"Quit fussing, ladies, and find a bed and a bathroom and make yourselves beautiful. The night is just starting."

"Oh my goodness, you mean there's more?" Jo asked quizzically.

"Just a little bit more," Robin responded.

The girls began to chant. "Robin is the best! Robin is the best! Robin is the best!"

Robin laughed hysterically falling back on the couch holding her stomach, unable to speak because she was laughing so hard. The girls all piled on top of her, tickling her until her face turned red and she began gasping for air.

"Let her up before we smother her to death," Tiffany said laughing.

The girls each head in different directions, looking to claim both a bed and a bathroom. Exactly 42 minutes later, the ladies were made up and ready as they met in the living room. Each of them was exquisite in their own right, but they were not just beautiful in both face and body but they each had a beauty which came from within. They stood grouped together complimenting each other. Before going down to dinner, they grasped hands and Jo led them in prayer.

"Father God, we come before You with a spirit of joy and thankfulness. We realize that today is a gift from daddy and we are in awe of You, Father, and the love You have for us. God, that love is returned from each of our hearts. God, we love You with everything that we are or ever hope to be because we understand that there is no life outside of You. We cannot breathe without You, God. Keep us bound together in love and unity, God, and keep our spiritual ears open, always to Your call and Your leading. We bow down before You, God, because You are so awesome. In Jesus name we pray."

Amens were echoed around the room. The ladies took a second to pull themselves together after Jo's awesome prayer. The entire day had been special from beginning to end and it wasn't over yet.

"Ready ladies?" asked Robin.

"Check," said Jo.

"Check two," said Tiffany.

"Check three," said Amera.

The ladies exited the room talking, laughing, ready for what's next. They caused a stir as they entered the lobby. Everyone was wondering who they were, whispering, commenting on how striking they all looked and they did all look lovely. Several people recognized Jo and Amera and asked for autographs.

The limo driver, who was waiting at the entrance of the lobby, saw the ladies coming. He escorted them out the door to the waiting vehicle, opening the door for them. After safely ensconcing the ladies in the limo, he drove them to a posh looking restaurant. The place was stacked with people waiting to be seated, but the limo driver escorted them to the front of the line. The maître d' smiled at Robin, acknowledging her and her party.

"Good evening, Dr. Walters. We have your table ready."

The hostess walked them to a beautiful table overlooking the water and seated them. Once they were seated, a waiter approached the table to offer suggestions from the wine list. Robin ordered a bottle of her favorite wine, and she and the girls looked around at the beauty and ambiance of the restaurant. Floor-to-ceiling windows overlooked the river with the night lights twinkling in the distance. It was breathtaking.

"Wow! This is beautiful," said Amera. "Jo and I have travelled all over the world and I can truly say we have been in some beautiful places, but I tell you, this ranks up there." Amera added looking around the beautiful restaurant.

"It is my absolute favorite restaurant in Indy. I love it here!" said Robin.

"I remember when you brought me here for my birthday," said Tiffany.

"I hate to break the mood, but we have exactly 90 minutes to enjoy our meals and then we're off to the races again."

The girls all groaned. "There is absolutely no way you've got something else planned. What's next? Are we flying to Dubai tonight? Or maybe Miami?" said Jo sarcastically, with a smile.

"I hope not, at least not before I get your name," a voice out of nowhere chimed in. They all turned to find a tall chocolate gentleman standing by Jo's side, with the most beautiful smile. He extended his hand to Jo as he introduced himself.

"My name is Marcus Cantrell. I saw you and your friends when you were being seated and I couldn't help but notice how uniquely beautiful each of you are. Are you models?" he asked.

"Thank you, Mr. Cantrell, for your lovely compliment, but no, we are not models," Jo responded.

"Please, call me Marcus," he said, in a voice that sent shivers down Jo's spine.

Every pair of eyes at the table watched in rapt fascination as the conversation unfolded before their eyes. It was obvious that he had eyes for no one but Jo. It was like he was in a trance and, shockingly, Jo seemed to be caught up in the same trance. It was like they were the only two people in the room. Robin smiled to herself and decided to give her girl a break.

"Marcus, would you like to join us for a glass of wine?" Robin asked.

Marcus, for a moment, was unresponsive as he and Jo continued to gaze into each other's eyes. Realizing a question had been addressed toward him, turned to Robin with his absolutely charming smile and politely declined. He pointed toward a table just one removed from where they were sitting and, Father in heaven, if there were not three of the finest men sitting there all staring at the interaction between Marcus and the girls. As Robin looked back over to the table she noticed that one of them was the absolute spitting image of Marcus. Robin's mouth dropped. She couldn't even fake it.

Marcus, being use to this reaction, spoke directly to Robin.

"I know, it's startling. He is my twin and he was too scared to come over, so just like always, he put me up to it. But please know that I would have come anyway," he said, turning his eyes back toward Jo.

"Ladies, over there to the left of my twin is my best friend and pastor, Jason Bell; and to the right, my business partner and other best friend, Charles Moore. My twin's name is Nico. We are all reputable businessmen in good standing within the community. I don't want to interrupt your meal, but could we possibly share dessert or coffee with you ladies after you finish your meal?"

All the ladies sat in complete silence. They were so caught up in the across-the-table stare down that they didn't hear anything Marcus said.

"My friends seem to be struck speechless at the moment," said Jo. "This is definitely a first." Marcus and Jo both chuckled. "So I will just answer for us all and say sure, that would be nice."

She and Marcus smiled at each other, reluctant to let it go. Marcus was the first to break the spell. Shaking his head, he said his goodbyes making a hesitant exit. After he left the table there was total silence.

Clearing her throat, Robin asked, "What was that? I feel like I just got ambushed. Who was that man? I mean who are they?"

The other girls looked just as dazed as Robin. Jo looked around the table at her sister-friends and saw they had all been affected the same way.

"What is this, God?" Jo thought, as she quickly said a silent prayer to herself. What she didn't know was that each of her girls had done the same thing. And what the ladies didn't know was that the men had done the exact same thing.

Dinner was excellent, but the tension at the table was as thick as a pea soup. As good as dinner was, they were all anxious for dessert. As soon as the waiter brought the dessert menus and began serving coffee, the four gentlemen got up from their table and began moving in their direction. They were all tall. Each one was well over six feet. They each had lean and fit bodies; Jason was slightly heavier than the other three, but not by much. You could see in the cut of the very expensive tailored suits each one of them wore, that they all had muscular physiques.

The ladies shifted their seats to allow the waiters to place chairs in strategic locations next to each of them. Each of the gentlemen knew exactly where they wanted to sit and it was exactly where each of the ladies wanted them to sit. They went around the table making formal introductions. Robin looked around the table at all the men. Except for Marcus and Nico, they all looked different, but they were all fine. Charles had a lighter complexion than the other three, and the most beautiful hazel colored eyes; Jason was cocoa brown and the twins, rich dark chocolate. It was obvious they were professional or at the least made a good living. Marcus and Nico were identical, except Marcus was slightly leaner than Nico. Marcus declared he was the older by two minutes. The twins laughed, cracking jokes, making bible references to Jacob and Esau. When the ladies responded, knowing the biblical story and how they strived against each other, both brothers were momentarily taken back. The twins looked at each other nonverbally communicating as only twins can.

"Can I ask you a question, Robin?" asked Nico.

"Sure," replied Robin, looking at him inquiringly.

"Are you saved? I am only asking because you know the back-story for the twin reference we were joking about. I don't mean to throw a wet blanket on the party, but I was just curious."

"Yes, I'm saved. We all are," Robin revealed.

It was as if God had breathed on them all. Something in the atmosphere shifted. Marcus, looked directly into Jo's beautiful almond-shaped eyes and said, "And we all are, too."

Tiffany, who was sitting beside Charles, smiled and he smiled back. Amera was sitting next to Jason. And he smiled back at her as well. It was as if each couple were in their own world as they tried to find out as much as they could about each other in the small amount of time they were allotted. Marcus and Jo only had eyes for each other and they didn't even try or pretend they were linked into the group. Suddenly, Jason's voice penetrated through the personal cocoons each couple had woven.

"You have got to be kidding me! Hey Marcus, do you know who you are talking to?" Jason asked. "Remember that CD we were listening to on the way here?"

Marcus, not wanting to appear rude, briefly turned his attention away from his beautiful companion.

"You mean the same one you have been playing in your car for the last two months? I love it too, man, but you done wore the grooves down on that thing. What about it?" Marcus asked. Without waiting for an answer, he turned his attention back to Jo.

Jason, realizing he had lost Marcus, laughed knowing he would find out soon enough who he was speaking to.

The more Marcus and Jo talked, the more he was blown away by her beauty. She was simply beautiful, both inside and out. "She's got to have a man," Marcus thought. Saying a silent prayer, again, he asked God to keep him.

"God, if this is not of you," Marcus prayed, "then please help me because I just met this woman, but I feel like I love her already. I feel like she was made just for me." He was overwhelmed by what he was feeling for this woman he had known for less than two hours.

Nothing like this had ever happened to him before. Marcus felt out of his element. Marcus was a mature, responsible adult male who ruled his heart and body well. He and his brother were surgeons and they each made a great living. In addition to being a surgeon, he and his friend, Charles, owned a computer consulting firm and it was doing very well. He was blessed with both looks and finances and if that wasn't enough of a lethal combination, he and his brother were raised by a single mother and knew not to mistreat women. His mother had ingrained that into both of her sons. Marcus was the quiet twin, while his brother was the free spirit. They each knew how to treat a lady and how not to entertain a woman who wasn't a lady. They dated, but they never misled or misused women. Their mama didn't play that. So now, at the ripe old age of 34, he had finally met the girl of his dreams.

Marcus became intoxicated each time he looked into Jo's beautiful eyes. He had never known a woman more beautiful. Her long black hair curled around her face, framing it perfectly. Her high cheekbones and straight nose spoke of American Native heritage, but her eyes were the killer. They were almond-shaped and the color of honey. He could look into her eyes all day. As beautiful as she was physically, she had a light which emanated from within that absolutely intoxicated him. He didn't understand what was going on between them, but when he looked into her beautiful golden eyes, he knew she was experiencing the same thing and was as confused by it as he was. Her eyes mirrored his thoughts. He had to know. He felt like he had a fever. Again, looking deeply into her eyes and finding the safety there that he needed, he asked her, "Am I crazy? I feel like, like—" Marcus began stumbling over his words.

Jo reached across the table and grabbed his hand and held it for a moment, feeling in him the same fear and uncertainty she was feeling. The five words she spoke were exactly what he needed to hear.

"I know. I'm afraid, too." she said breathlessly.

They sat there with her hand over his and continued to stare at one another.

"This is God," he said. "This is the Father."

"I know," she replied again.

They smiled across the table at each other knowing now that what they were both experiencing individually was the Father's blessing, and an answer to a private prayer that each of them had prayed many years before. All around them conversations flowed freely. Everyone laughed and enjoyed each other's company, but the two of them just sat in silence, overwhelmed by God's love. Marcus looked at her and marveled at the gift God had given him, because he knew she was to be his wife. She stared back at him and saw the God in him and relaxed and daydreamed of brown babies who looked just like their daddy. A lone tear slipped down her cheek. Marcus took his finger and wiped it away.

"Are you sad, love?" He knew the term was forward, but felt no discomfort in using it. He now knew that she was privy to everything that was going on between them because God had revealed it to them both.

"Not sad at all; just overwhelmed at the way God loves us."

He knew exactly what she was talking about. They were truly on one accord. They sat there until the restaurant closed and then they all walked along the River Walk. All four couples held hands. No one going too far because they all had figured out on their own that this night had been ordained. When it was time for them to separate, there was a palpable sadness that permeated the atmosphere. It was bittersweet. Only Marcus and Jo knew for certain that God was joining them, but the rest only hoped that the relationships they were forming that night would be significant for each of them.

Back at the hotel the girls were undressing getting ready for bed. They were all a little sober and wrapped in their own thoughts. Tiffany broke the silence, and when she spoke, it sounded like she was going to cry.

"Is it just me or did something special happen tonight?" Tears rolled down her face, but she continued. "I don't even know what to call it or how to describe it. I mean, what I felt tonight was so beautiful. I've never felt a connection with any man like that before. I barely know him, but we connected in a place that was sincere. I thought when my marriage ended that I would never love again, but I can see myself loving that man. I am embarrassed to say it because I just met him, but I feel God in this. Please tell me I'm not the only one," Tiffany added. They all gathered around Tiffany, hugging her and patting her back.

"You're not alone, Tiff. I felt it, too," said Robin sheepishly. "I had four front-row tickets for us to see Fred Hammond, Marvin Sapp, and Kiki Sheard, and I just forgot all about them once we met the guys. Like you, I was embarrassed because I had just met him, but I could feel that he was feeling the same way. It was awkward. Like the elephant in the room. We acted like we didn't know it was there, but I knew and I am pretty sure he knew, too."

"I am so glad to hear you all say this," said Amera. "I thought I was in an episode of the *Twilight Zone*. Isn't it amazing how we met them at the same time? What if he doesn't call?" Amera said, sounding worried.

As soon as the words passed her lips, her purse began to vibrate. She reached inside her purse and pulled out her cell phone. "Who could be calling me this late? It must be Cliff. I hope everything is alright," said Amera.

Suddenly the sound of another cell phone could be heard ringing. This time it was Jo's. Robin caught a glimpse of Jo walking back to her bedroom to take the call. The look on her face was indescribable. The closest Robin could come to describing it was rapturous. Only Robin and Tiffany remained in the room. They knew who it was that had called Jo and Amera. They looked at their cell phones, still and silent, lying on the coffee table before them.

"I'm happy for Amera and Jo," said Tiffany, trying to sound upbeat. "I really hope it works out for them." She had been sure that Charles had felt the same thing she had but, no matter.

"Hey girl, I am going to bed," she told Robin. As she stood, Tiffany reached down to grab her cell phone off the table when the awkward silence was broken by ringing. It was Robin's cell phone. Robin's face lit up with a smile as big as Texas. Answering her phone, she turned and whispered to Tiffany.

"You're next."

Tiffany turned to go to her bedroom and right before she reached her bedroom door, her phone finally rang. Breathing a sigh of relief, she answered.

"What took you so long?" she said laughing.

They each went to their rooms that night as happy as a kid on the last day of school.

CHAPTER TWENTY-SIX

Carla Dixon tried to reign in the excitement of the boys who were practically bouncing off the walls. It was a bright and beautiful spring day in April and the boys were all simply beside themselves.

The NBA had chartered a bus to drive the boys to Chicago for the last game of the regular season. It was utter chaos in the parking lot of the school as the boys all carrying comforters, pillows, and backpacks tried to line up without much success. After the game, they would spend the night at a hotel and the following day they would all be going to Six Flags. To say that they were all excited was an understatement. They were absolutely ecstatic! Mrs. Dixon and Mrs. Rodriguez, along with Cliff and Greg Fisher, the basketball coach, tried to get the boys aboard the bus.

Every seat on the bus was assigned. Once the boys boarded and went to their assigned seats, they found a genuine NBA jersey, hand-signed with the number of their NBA big brother. As if that wasn't enough, there was a second jersey for each boy with his own last name on the back with his favorite player's number. The bus was fully loaded with individual gaming systems and DVD players with a wide assortment of movies and every snack they could dream of. Many of the boys came from backgrounds where not only did they not have nice clothes, but many didn't have enough food to eat so this was truly over the top for them.

Since the implementation of the new mentoring program, the school had gained national attention as a model program for group home foster care. Several young boys had come into the school much like Keshawn, with an attitude and a chip on their shoulder. Others had come barely speaking and withdrawn, but the mentoring program had drawn the best from each of them. The program's success was based on the theory of replication. The more mature boys, who were the mentors, simply understood their young counterparts. They knew the fears, the anger, the hurt they were experiencing because they too experienced the same emotions when they first entered the system. Once the new boys knew they were in a safe environment, they began to open up to their mentors. The program mentored collectively and individually, but the heart of the program was based around the spirits of Josiah and Keshawn. Once they had converted their own inner circle, they all committed to making sure that every boy who came into their school would not be subjected to bullying or intimidation of any kind. They treated all the new boys like they would like to have been treated when they arrived. The program worked wonders! The boys were happy. This did not go unnoticed by the school, Mrs. Rodriguez or Mrs. Dixon. They still met each morning—rain or shine—before school was in session to pray over the school, the faculty, and the students. They even prayed over the curriculum. Mrs. Dixon headed up the mentoring program, but there were several volunteer counselors who requested to be a part of the program because it was reaping results far beyond anyone's expectations. A sponsorship with an NBA team was just the icing on the cake. It just didn't get any better than that.

It was slightly overcast but the temperature was unseasonably warm. Carla Dixon mopped the perspiration from her forehead as she marked the names off her list for each boy that boarded the bus. Thank God the bus was a chilly 67 degrees.

Finally the bus was fully loaded and the boys sufficiently settled down enough for Cliff, who agreed to chaperone, to say a prayer of protection before they got started on the road. As soon as Cliff said "Amen" the boys let out a loud whoop and the bus was on its way.

The further west they drove the darker the sky became. The bus driver was an older black man named Joseph. Cliff sat in the first seat closest to him and noticed the change in his countenance as he continued to drive.

"What's wrong, Joseph?" asked Cliff.

"I don't like these clouds," Joseph said. "I been driving for over 30 years and the last time I saw clouds that looked like these, we drove right into Hurricane Hugo. I got that same feeling now as I had back then. Something ain't right."

"Turn on your weather radio," said Cliff.

"Already on. So far they are saying just severe thunderstorm warning but I can feel it in my bones. Something ain't right," repeated Joseph.

"How soon before we stop for lunch?" Cliff asked.

"About an hour and 10 minutes," Joseph replied.

"Are you a praying man, Joseph?" Cliff said, looking at Joseph intently.

"Absolutely! Been saved for 30 years next month and I am already with you."

Forty-five minutes later, Maria came to the front to speak with Joseph and Cliff.

"I don't want to alarm anyone but it is looking positively scary outside."

By now, the sun had completely gone away and the wind had picked up. The cars on the freeway struggled to stay in control.

"Joseph has on his weather radio, but so far they are only saying severe thunderstorm warnings," Cliff said to Maria, trying to sound calmer than he actually felt.

"I'm not trying to cause a panic, but in my spirit I think it's going to be a little more than a thunderstorm," she said looking directly into Cliff's eyes.

Cliff didn't even try to soothe things once he realized she was a believer too.

"Yea, Joseph and I both are getting the same message. We are trying to make it to our lunch stop which will be at a mall; we should be able to find protection there. Keep the kids calm. Don't let them see you being nervous," warned Cliff.

"I won't. How much longer until we get to our stop?" she asked.

"About 25 more minutes, I've had to slow down because of the wind," said Joseph.

"Well if you see somewhere to stop before that feel free to make a judgment call," Maria added.

"Okay, will do," Joseph said, never taking his eyes off the road.

You could see the tension in his shoulders and Maria knew that Joseph was well aware of the potential danger that threatened them all. As she walked back to her seat, she caught the eyes of Carla and Greg. They each looked at her with the same question in their eyes. She returned the look to each of them that said keep it together so they both wiped the worried looks off their faces and plastered on fake smiles much like the one that Maria wore as she walked back to her seat next to Carla. So far the boys seemed oblivious to the weather as they watched movies and played video games but a few were starting to look out the window.

"Oooooo, look how dark it's getting outside. It's not even night time. Why is it so dark outside, Mr. Fisher?" asked one of the younger boys.

"It's just about to rain that's all," said Greg. "How do you like that movie, Raymond?" he asked to distract the boy from his train of thought.

Suddenly there was loud tapping as if someone was throwing rocks at the bus. "Look! It's hailing outside," said one of the boys.

Golf ball-sized hail began pelting the bus. The noise was deafening. It felt like they were in the middle of a combat zone and they were receiving fire. Now the weather had everyone's attention. With the hail came rain so hard and heavy it was impossible to see anything from the windows. Maria got up and began to move toward the front. Keshawn and Josiah stopped her as she was walking by.

"Do you need us to do anything?" they both asked.

"Just stay calm; if they see you two are calm they will follow your lead," said Maria.

"Okay," said Keshawn.

Josiah merely shook his head affirming and they reached across the aisle to two of the older mentors and told them what Mrs. Rodriguez had said.

The sounds of fear were starting to be heard above the sounds of the hail bombarding the bus, so Keshawn, Josiah, and the two older mentors began to speak to all the other boys.

"Let's play a game," Keshawn said, capturing the boys' attention.

"That's a good idea," said one of the older mentors. As they corralled the other boys' attention, Maria spoke to Cliff and Joseph.

"I don't think we are going to make it to that mall," she spoke quietly, yet openly to both men.

"There is now a tornado warning and it is not far from here; it is moving in our direction. Because of the rain and the traffic we will not be able to outrun it so our best bet is to pull over under an overpass, but we've had open highway for a while now," Joseph said, sounding like the veteran he was, while Cliff remained silent.

"If we don't find an overpass then what can we do?" Maria asked. Cliff could hear the fear in her voice.

"We pray, Maria. We pray for God's mercy because right now our backs are against the wall," Cliff answered. Just as he spoke these words to Maria, the entire back end of the bus was lifted like a pair of hands had picked it up. Pandemonium broke out as all the kids on the bus began to scream in terror.

CHAPTER TWENTY-SEVEN

Patricia sat on her small balcony inhaling deeply from a Newport cigarette. She was forced to smoke on the balcony because she smoked menthol cigarettes and Ace couldn't tolerate the smell of menthol cigarettes. She found it interesting that he had no problem with the smell of the Camels he chained smoked as well as the weed, which was his constant companion.

In the beginning, Patricia had tried to tell Ace she didn't drink, smoke, or get high anymore, but it became increasingly more difficult to resist the temptation of these lures with him constantly having them around. Her futile attempts to resist went in one ear and out the other while Ace continued to be what he was—a first-class jerk. Eventually she broke down and started smoking cigarettes again. The weed came next, and of course, what is a good joint without a cold one; so now she was back to doing everything that God had delivered her from.

She was in a contemplative mood today as she thought about the last eight weeks of her life. "Wow," she thought. "What a difference a day makes. How did I go from doing so well and trying to get Josiah back, to running behind a man who could care less about me?"

Yes, she finally admitted it to herself—Ace had not changed. He was only with her because his "real" girlfriend threw him out. She had gotten the scoop from the club she had started frequenting again. Everyone knew Ace had used up all his free passes with everybody and no one had been willing to give him another chance. Everyone who knew Ace had been burned by him at least once. Why hadn't she seen it? Everyone else had. Allison had tried to tell her he was using her, but Patricia accused her of being jealous and said some really mean and nasty things to her.

Patricia really missed Allison. She often wondered how she was doing and tried calling her, but Allison wouldn't return any of her calls, except the first one when Allison told her that she forgave her, but until she got herself together they would no longer be fellowshipping. She also promised to pray for Patricia every day and then quietly hung up the phone. Patricia cried that night and proceeded to get very, very drunk.

She was lonely and starving for intimacy so she decided to try and seduce Ace, who hadn't touched her since the first day he walked back into her life. Ace was absolutely disgusted by her drunkenness and her attempt to seduce him and forced her to sleep on her couch. That was more than four weeks ago and he still insisted she sleep on the couch while he slept in her queen-sized bed. Every time she tried to say something about their sleeping arrangement, Ace would bring up that humiliating night as if he was afraid of her so she would just drop it.

That didn't stop Ace from expecting her to cook for him and to make sure he had enough money for cigarettes and weed. Supporting his habits caused her to be late on her rent for the first time in a very long time. Her landlord told her if she continued to stay current on her rent, he would write her a credit reference which would help her establish her credit. She threw that out the window just to make sure Ace got his weed.

Ace was not good to be around when he wasn't high. Heck, who was she kidding—Ace was never good to be around, but it got worse if he ran out of weed. As she sat there and looked clinically at her life and her relationship with Ace, she saw clearly for the first time. If she had only gotten back on track that next day after she messed up, she would probably have Josiah back by now, but she hadn't. Instead, she allowed Ace to enter her world and drag her deeper into darkness, and now she was surrounded by it. Before, she was so blind to the darkness, but now she was marveled by the fact she saw darkness everywhere. Every corner of her apartment was filled with it. She remembered when her place was full of light. "Where did that light go?" she asked herself, as she slid the glass door open, leaving the balcony and entering back into her apartment. It looked like a pigsty.

Everywhere she looked she saw trash, beer bottles, and overflowing ashtrays. Looking at her coffee table, she noticed the Bible that hadn't been touched for more than eight weeks. Moving towards the coffee table she gasped in horror. As she looked closer she saw Ace's weed and bong on top of her Bible. At that moment she saw it for what it was. A sign or a statement from the enemy showing evil had triumphed over good. As she looked on the sight with horror, she backed away and said repeatedly, "God forgive me. God forgive me." She continued to say it over and over until she backed into the door of her apartment. Grabbing the handle quickly she turned and ran out the door as if the devil was after her.

Running down the street like a crazy woman, she realized she had left her purse, she had no jacket, and she still had on her house shoes. As she tried to calm down, her mind replayed the events of the last eight weeks and she could clearly see the trap the enemy had set for her and how easily she had fallen for it. She now understood how she had only offered token resistance, not resisting unto the blood as the Bible instructed. Now she completely understood why Allison was so upset. Allison recognized the trap and tried to help by reminding her of their mutual promise to God, but Patricia turned on her like a rabid dog, instead of remembering the relationship they had forged through the fire. How could she have been so stupid! How could she have been so blind?

When she told Ace she was going to get Josiah back and wanted them to become a family, he said he wanted to wait so they would have a chance to get to know each other before they introduced a kid in the mix. Patricia continued to put off seeing Josiah and didn't even have the decency to call and explain what happened. She received official looking letters from the county after that. She ignored them by telling herself when she and Ace got married, that would make everything okay. She felt like crying because she had been so foolish. It all hit her like a movie. She could see clearly all the bad decisions and poor choices she had been making for the last eight weeks. She had given up her child and her only friend for what? For Ace?

"Oh my God, what have I done?" she cried to the heavens above.

As if on cue, the heavens opened with torrential rains driving her to seek shelter. She had no idea where she was until she saw the bakery on the corner, then she knew she was close to Allison's house. Moving quickly, she headed in that direction, praying to God that her friend would be kinder than she had been to her.

CHAPTER TWENTY-EIGHT

Love was in the air! Robin, Jo, Amera, and Tiffany couldn't have been happier. Relationships for all the girls had formed quickly, and all were spiritually grounded. The guys were all located in Indianapolis except for Charles, Marcus' business partner, who lived in Chicago.

All the couples, except Jo and Marcus, were still feeling each other out and comfortable in the undeclared zone. However, from day one, Marcus and Jo only had eyes for one another, and both declared that they would be married, but no date was set yet.

Although they all only met a couple of months before, they each knew without a shadow of a doubt that it was God who had brought them together. Amera and Jo lived in Atlanta, but now spent most of their time with Robin in Columbus when they weren't on tour. The guys and girls alternated the three hour drive from Columbus to Indianapolis or vice versa each weekend with Charles flying in from Chicago.

They loved hanging out with each other. They played scrabble, monopoly, spades, bid-whist, laughing it up like they were teenagers, but that was not all they did. Marcus and Jo seemed to be the more mature couple, so they often led the group in Bible study and wonderful discussions of God's goodness, grace, and mercy. On Sundays, they all went to Robin's church. When they were in Indianapolis, they all went to Jason's church and found the congregation there to be very nice.

What they all shared was unique and they thanked God for the gift He had given them in each other. Even the way they paired up without knowing each other was perfect. Robin and Nico's personalities balanced each other perfectly and their worldly experiences, or lack thereof, aligned as well. They both dated and experimented in college, but each had quickly decided they would wait for marriage. Marcus and Jo were both virgins—they were serious about their walk with God. Amera had been in two long-term relationships before finding God, and though she was not a virgin, once she re-committed to God, she ended that part of her lifestyle. She was kind, gracious and outgoing. Jason being a church pastor, often thought she would make a lovely first lady, but for now he was content with just getting to know her. Tiffany's feelings for Charles overwhelmed her in the beginning and left her in an emotional tizzy. Her experience with her marriage made Tiffany something she had never been before and that was afraid. Although God healed Tiffany from the wound her husband had inflicted with his infidelity and homosexuality, Tiffany was still showing residual symptoms, but Charles was completely understanding and patient. Only God knew how all these relationships would work out.

At first Tiffany was too ashamed to share the deep dark secret of why her marriage ended, and Charles never pushed or cajoled her. Instead, he waited for her to show him how far he could go with his questions. As he looked at her with big brown eyes so full of love, she could see he genuinely enjoyed being with her and was content with whatever she gave him. His patience gave her the courage to finally open up, leading her to share with him the heartbreak of her failed marriage. He held her gently in his arms as she relived the horror of the discovery in her marriage. He rejoiced with her as she went on to tell him how that same heartbreak turned into joy when it led to her finding God. Charles assured her that he would never hurt her in that way, and that they could go as fast or as slow as she liked because he already knew what he wanted and he was more than willing to wait for her to catch up. She looked deeply into his eyes, seeing the truth there that she needed to quiet her frightened heart. As he held her gaze, she decided to trust again. Leaning into him, she held onto his waist, drawing strength from him as he held her gently.

This weekend, the girls were going to Chicago to the last NBA game of the regular season. They were all going to fly out the day before the game and stay at the same hotel as their boyfriends. Robin was excited to see Josiah again. Although she hadn't seen him for some time, Carla Dixon had continued to call her with updates on his status.

Carla didn't tell her, however, that the state moved to take permanent custody of Josiah after his mother failed to show up for any of their scheduled appointments and never returned their phone calls or responded to any of the letters they sent requesting that she contact them. For a while, Josiah was very upset but had quickly adjusted. After all, he was use to his mother falling off the grid. On the surface, Keshawn appeared to be okay, but she sensed some anger simmering under the surface, however, she truly believed both boys were going to be okay. The Josiah Carla talked about with Robin was a much stronger version of the one Robin had previously counseled in therapy. She hoped she contributed in some way to his new-found strength. Whatever the impetus, Robin knew the true source was God. After she cried with Josiah in that hospital room, she knew the Josiah that emerged the next day was different. He was stronger. Josiah accepted the fact that no matter how much he loved his mother, he couldn't change her. He was left with two options, he could hate her or love her as she was. He chose the latter and because of that, God started the healing process. Josiah, although just a child, was faced with a very adult situation; but because of the type of child he was, he chose to love and forgive instead of hate and that choice freed him. She knew that he still hoped his mother would change, but he accepted that no matter how much he loved her, she would not change until she was ready.

Robin thanked God for the group home and for Carla Dixon. She knew that Josiah was in good hands and that the people at the home genuinely loved him. When she spoke with him at the games she could tell that he missed her but she could also tell that he was happy, loved, and cared for. He blossomed under the combination of these ingredients. Knowing this took away the desperation she felt when she was prohibited from seeing him. She imagined all types of horrors that could occur in the group home, but leave it to God to have him placed in the one group home where he was able to thrive and grow. It was almost a year since Josiah first came to the group home, but it still seemed like yesterday to her.

It appeared the lawsuit might be settled soon and she would be free to see Josiah again. She couldn't wait. Robin decided that if the state took permanent custody of Josiah, she would pursue adoption. She didn't know how he would feel about that, but if he was okay with it then Josiah would be her son. She would spend every penny she had to make that happen. She shared the story of Josiah and her love for him with Nico, who instead of telling her she was crazy, looked at her with love in his eyes and told her he would help her in any way he could. She was going to introduce the two of them at the game. He also mentioned that he, Marcus, Charles and Jason would love to speak with the school to see if they could help with their mentoring program. Robin closed her eyes and thanked God once again for sending her this extraordinary man.

She felt comfort knowing that everything she experienced that past year—starting from the day she read Josiah's letter—had all been a part of God's plan to help her to see how holding onto the past hurts that her mother and father had done to her was holding her hostage. Josiah was the catalyst that helped her to see beyond her own pain to the self-inflicted bondage she had been nursing for years. God's patience with her helped Robin to realize the wall she placed between them. God helped her tear it down. All He was waiting for was for her to say she didn't want it there anymore. She experienced life anew ever since. God sent Amera, Cliff, and Jo to help her on her journey and look how that turned out.

As a result, Cliff and Simone met and their relationship was beautiful to behold. They set the example that all the girls looked up to. The two of them loved God so deeply and it was apparent in everything that they did. They often didn't need to speak, but communicated on a spiritual level that was a joy to experience. When they were together, the Holy Spirit would often shadow them, making them appear as if they were glowing. God was moving in their little family. All the ladies were in relationships and not one of them needed to settle. They each had strong Christian brothers who were all healthy, wealthy, and wise, but they weren't giving any more than what they were receiving because Robin knew that all the guys were getting what the Bible referenced. *Proverbs 31:10: " Who can find a virtuous woman? For her price is far above rubies."* Robin knew her character and that of her friends, and knew that they all strived to be the woman mentioned in that particular scripture. When they each made that a priority, God sent them men after His own heart that recognized and appreciated their value.

The ladies loaded their luggage in Jo's Range Rover to head out to the airport. They were all excited and chattering away like magpies. As Robin went back into the house to lock up and set the alarm, her cell phone vibrated. Smiling to herself, she cheerily answered the phone, thinking it was Nico calling to see if they had left yet.

"Somebody is a little impatient," she said, sounding like a teenage girl waiting on her boyfriend to call.

"Excuse me? May I speak with Dr. Walters?" a no-nonsense voice said on the other end of the line.

"I'm sorry, this is Dr. Walters."

"Dr. Walters, this is Gloria Earley and I am a charge nurse at Children's Hospital. The answering service advised that you are the covering physician for Dr. Lakeland."

"Actually I am not her covering for this weekend, Dr.Gupta is," replied Robin.

"Dr. Gupta was in a car accident earlier today. Dr. Walker is listed as Dr. Gupta's covering, but he is not answering any of his pages and we have a situation which needs to be addressed now."

"What's going on?" said Robin.

The horn outside began blaring and Robin looked at her watch. They needed to leave now if they were to make it to the airport on time.

"There seems to be a problem with the dosage amount Dr. Lakeland prescribed for one of her patients."

"What do you mean a problem with the dosage amount prescribed? Who is questioning the amount prescribed by the patient's physician?"

"I am," said Nurse Earley.

The horn blared again, this time a little more impatiently.

"Tell me in as few words as possible, Nurse Earley, what exactly is going on."

"Dr. Lakeland has prescribed 2 to 5 mg Haldol every four hours."

"That is a standard administration of Haldol. What's the problem?"

"It is for a 12-year-old who weighs about 70 pounds."

Robin gasped before answering. "Has the medication been administered?" she asked, with fear in her voice.

"No, it hasn't. I refused to administer it until I found a doctor who could make me believe that this was not a mistake."

"Thank God!" said Robin, relief evident in her voice.

As she spoke, the door opened and Jo walked in with a look on her face that said "get your butt out to the car this instant" but upon seeing Robin's face, she quickly changed it to a look of concern. Robin put her finger up to indicate to Jo to give her a minute and spoke to Nurse Earley again.

"You were absolutely correct not to administer such a high dosage of that medication to a 12-year-old who only weighs 70 pounds. It would have more than likely killed the patient. Give me a number where I can call you back directly in a couple of minutes. I have to finish something here."

She wrote down the number and quickly disconnected the call.

"I am so sorry but an emergency just popped up and I am going to have to go to the hospital."

"I'll go tell the girls. We can try and catch a later flight," Jo responded moving towards the door.

"No need for all of us to suffer because I chose to be a doctor instead of an interior decorator," said Robin, smiling woefully. "You guys go on and I will catch a red eye and meet you there."

Jo protested, but Robin refused to allow her to change the plans for all the girls. She pushed her out the door and waved to the girls before calling Nurse Earley back.

By the time Robin resolved the crisis at the hospital all the flights from Columbus to Chicago were done for the day. She was left with no other choice but to fly out in the morning, but when she looked at the flight times she saw that there wasn't a flight that would get her there even close to game time. She decided she would get some sleep and get up in the pre-dawn hours and drive to Chicago.

Her phone rang just then and it was the girls and the guys calling to see where she was. She told them what happened and what the new plan was, and they all agreed to go to breakfast when she arrived. Nico offered to drive down to get her and bring her back, but she refused, telling him she didn't want him all cranky at the game from no sleep tomorrow. They laughed because they all knew Nico's temperament was the opposite of cranky and no one had ever known him to be in a bad mood.

Robin woke up at 4 a.m. and was on the road by 4:30. Instead of music, she decided to listen to a book on CD. She had no idea that her phone charger had a short in the wire and her phone never charged the night before. Within an hour of being on the road, her phone died and because she didn't have on the radio she didn't get any of the warnings about the weather. She drove down the road as happy as she could be, thinking about Josiah and Nico and how good it would be for them all to be together. So engrossed in her thoughts, she failed to notice it was after 8 a.m. and instead of getting lighter outside, it was getting darker.

CHAPTER TWENTY-NINE

By the time Patricia reached Allison's house she was soaked through and through. She had run out the house with no coat and only wearing house shoes. The rain had long ago destroyed her house shoes, leaving them casualties along the side of the road, and by the time she reached Allison's house they were gone. She stood at Allison's door barefoot, black mascara running down her face, and her blonde hair wet and bedraggled looking plastered to her head. Patricia looked positively frightening!

She banged on Allison's door like the FBI. A few moments later, a cute little girl who looked to be about five years old answered the door. She stared at Patricia with a fearful look on her face and Patricia immediately thought about how she must look to the little girl. She tried to lull the child into a state of calm by speaking softly to her.

"Hi," she said in a soft voice, "Is your mom home?"

The little girl just stood there staring at the scary-looking lady, not sure what to do. Patricia tried again to ease the child's fears.

"I'm a friend of your mother. Is she home?" Patricia repeated.

The little girl screamed at the top of her lungs, "Mommy!"

Within seconds, Allison came running into the entryway with a towel on her head and a look of surprise on her face. The look dissipated as she recognized the woman who stood in her doorway. She took her daughter's hand and pulled her close, hugging her as she admonished her about opening the door while she was in the shower; she then told her go watch SpongeBob with her brother. The little girl cheerfully walked away, content that all was well and whoever the scary woman was, mommy would handle.

Turning to face Patricia, Allison's face settled into hard lines. Patricia stood expectantly in the doorway with a hopeful look on her face, but as she looked into Allison's eyes that hope began to fade. They stood there looking at each other, neither speaking. Patricia was the first to break the awkward silence.

"Allison, may I come in for a moment? I know I look a mess, but I can explain everything. It is raining cats and dogs out here, please let me come in."

At that moment, the rain changed to golf-ball size hail. Allison, looking at the hail stepped back opening the door wide enough for Patricia to enter, but she never said a word.

"Thank you, Ally. I know I don't deserve this but…"

Before she could finish, Allison interrupted her. "Don't call me Ally! You can't call me that. The only person to ever call me that was my friend, Patricia, and I can see by looking at you that she is gone. Don't you ever call me that again." She spoke with so much emotion in her voice it was hard to tell whether she was angry or hurt.

"Why are you here?" she asked Patricia.

Patricia hesitated before speaking. She wasn't sure why she had come here. She'd just responded to the voice within her and it directed her to go to Allison's.

"I'm not sure why I am here, I just know that I had to see you," Patricia replied.

"What's wrong? Did lover boy rough you up again?" Allison mocked.

"No nothing like that. I just, I don't know, I just felt like if I..." her voice trailed off.

"It's funny how you are at a loss for words now, but the last time we were together you certainly had no problem getting your words out then. You remember when you shouted out for the world to hear my deepest darkest secrets." You certainly had no problem finding your words that day," Allison blurted at her.

Allison referred to the last time they saw each other when Patricia said all those mean and hurtful things to her. The words she spoke that day had deeply wounded Allison and brought about their separation. Unfortunately, for Patricia, that was the day she needed Allison the most. Patricia had already stumbled and lost her way and needed someone who truly loved her to guide her out of the darkness and back on the right path. The enemy knew that Allison wouldn't have stopped until she got Patricia back on course, so he brought division—in the form of Ace—between them. After that it had been easy. Patricia isolated herself from the one friend who could have helped her. Patricia rejected the only light in her life and chose to follow after Ace. The consequences were staggering. She was suffering as a result and so was Josiah.

"I see you got your kids," Patricia said. "Is it permanent or temporary?"

Allison's face softened for a moment and her eyes glistened with tears.

"It's permanent as long as I finish the assigned parenting classes and continue doing therapy for the next year," Allison replied.

For a moment, both of their faces glowed with happiness.

"I am so happy for you, Ally—I mean, Allison," Patricia said, shifting nervously from foot to foot as silence filled the air. Patricia thought, "I need to say the words."

"I just want you to know that you were right and I was wrong."

"About what?" Allison asked, looking at Patricia with a guarded look on her face.

"About everything," she said pausing. "About everything." With that, Patricia broke down as she repeated the phrase "about everything" and sobbed as if her heart was broken. Allison gathered Patricia in her arms, hugged her and told her everything was going to be alright as she walked her over to the couch.

After getting Patricia seated with a box of tissues, she went into her kitchen and made a pot of tea, returning with the pot, two cups, sugar and lemon. Patricia, though still upset, had calmed down sufficiently enough to have a real conversation.

"Ally, I mean, Allison."

"You can call me Ally, Pat. Go ahead with what you wanted to say."

Smiling gratefully, Patricia continued. "Ally, the first thing I want to say to you is that I am so sorry for what I said to you that day. I know you remember what I said so I am not going to repeat it because it hurts me every time I think about it, so I can only imagine what it does when you remember it. I can't undo what I've done, but I would like a chance to make it up to you because I realize that you were family to me. You were my sister in every way that counted. You and I were on this amazing journey together, growing and learning to love God more every day. I have never experienced anything like that ever in my life," she paused and took a sip of her tea.

"Everything you said about Ace was 100 percent correct. I was already down from the night before and the enemy knew I was compromised and it was a perfect time to send Ace to my door. The thing is, I was really over Ace. When he came to my door, I was indifferent, but the longer I let him stand there and talk to me, the more I started to listen. I should have shut the door as soon as I saw him, but I stood there and let the enemy seduce me like I had done the night before, when I went into that bar and took that drink. All I had to do was repent and get right back on track, but instead, I allowed myself to get pulled deeper into darkness. I knew after a couple of weeks with Ace that I had been duped by the enemy, but it was like I was on a merry-go-round and I couldn't get off, so I just went through the motions. I watched myself be humiliated and degraded by a man that no one else wanted, but me, because they all knew he was a bum. I feel so stupid."

"I ain't trying to make you feel worse but, girl, you were pretty stupid," Allison said, with a smirk in her voice.

"Thanks a lot, Ally, just what I needed to hear." Patricia took the throw pillow off the couch and threw it at her friend.

"No you didn't!" said Allison. She grabbed a pillow of her own and bashed Patricia over the head with it before running with Patricia in hot pursuit. The girls had a pillow fight of mammoth proportions with Allison's son and daughters eventually coming out to join in the melee. As the five of them fell to the floor giggling, Ally slowly got up from the floor.

"You need a shower," she said moving down the hall toward the linen closet. Throwing a towel and wash cloth to Patricia, she went into the bathroom and turned on the water.

"Take a shower and wash your hair because you smell like a wet dog."

"You really know how to kick a girl when she's down," Patricia commented.

"Whatever!" said Allison, moving toward the kitchen. "When you're finished, I will introduce you to the kids."

Thirty minutes later, Patricia sat at Allison's kitchen table with her and the children, heads lowered as they said grace. Allison made hotdogs, french-fries, and pork & beans which she said were the kids' absolute favorite meal. Patricia thought her children were beautiful and she noted they seemed well adjusted. Thank God for her mother who had been caring for the children and reared them with good old-fashion values. The children were polite and well mannered. Patricia thought to herself how lucky Allison was to have her dream come true. She was once on the verge of having her own dreams come true, but one little misstep led her on another path and now she wasn't sure if she would ever see Josiah again. She wished she could go back and do the last two months over again, but it was too late for that.

Allison put the kids down for a nap while Patricia cleaned up the kitchen. She thought about all the times that she and Allison had sat at this same table, praising God and talking about the day when God would reunite them with their children. It was Patricia who got Allison to question the life she was living and to give her life over to Christ, but it was Allison who became the faithful and patient one, waiting for God to move. Patricia looked at where Allison was and where she herself was and became ashamed of how she had let the enemy trick her. She knew in that instant that she was done with Ace and living life out of the will of God. She kneeled at the chair she and Allison had kneeled at so many times before and went before the throne of grace. She asked God for forgiveness and strength to make the U-turn she knew needed to be done without delay.

When she opened her eyes, she saw Allison kneeling at the chair across from her praying in earnest. She didn't hear her return to the kitchen because she was so deep in the Spirit as God cleansed and restored her back into fellowship. She quietly waited until Allison's prayer ended and their eyes locked.

"I'm back home," Patricia said.

"I know. Welcome home, sis." They hugged and gave God the glory for restoration.

CHAPTER THIRTY

The only word to describe what was happening on the bus was chaos. A funnel cloud had formed and came down right in the pathway of the bus. It was like a scene straight out of the *Wizard of Oz*. The bus had been caught up in the vortex of the tornado and flung over a hundred yards away landing in a cornfield upside down. Carla Dixon tried to be heard over the sound of the wind howling outside, mingled with the screams of the frightened children.

"Quiet children, I need to know who's hurt and who's okay? I know you're scared but please try to focus on the sound of my voice," Carla calmly spoke to the children. They were all strapped in, but they hung upside down like bats.

"Maria!" she called out trying to ascertain the status of her friend and the school's principal. She could hear the sobs of some of the boys while others were deathly silent. She decided to do roll call starting with the adults.

The wind outside of the bus still continued to howl like a wild banshee which didn't help to lessen the children's fears. Sobbing could still be heard but the cacophony was slowly quieting down.

"Cliff, can you hear me?" There was silence for about 15 seconds before she called his name again. "Cliff!" she called louder this time, but still no response. She began to panic a little in her mind, but she knew she couldn't let the children know how frightened she was. One last time she called out Cliff's name. She thought she heard something.

"Quiet children! Cliff can you hear me?"

Suddenly she heard a voice barely above a whisper.

"I'm here," Cliff said but he didn't sound too good. She could hear the pain in his voice.

"Cliff, is the bus driver okay?" she asked.

"Not sure, unconscious I think," Cliff struggled to speak. "Joseph!" he called the bus driver's name several times until finally Carla heard a groggy response.

"I'm alive," said Joseph sounding weak, but okay.

"Greg!" Carla called out to the basketball coach, who responded immediately, and sounded alert.

"I'm here, but it looks like we got some injuries back here. I am going to unbuckle myself and take the hit and then I will come to you first Carla and help you and then we can start from the back and move forward helping everyone to get free. The bus is upside down so I am not sure how we are going to get out."

Carla wasn't listening. Maria still had not responded. Calling in earnest, she tried to locate her friend.

"Maria!" pausing briefly, she called again. "Maria!"

She remembered then that Maria hadn't been strapped in but had walked to the front of the bus to tell Joseph to pull over just when the tornado had hit. "Oh my God!" she said aloud. Frantically, she began to call Maria's name, until she heard Cliff's voice telling her to calm down because the children were beginning to respond to her hysteria.

"I can't find Maria," she cried. "I can't find Maria!"

Greg became the voice of reason at that point, taking control he spoke in a voice loud enough for Cliff who was in the front to hear.

"I am unbuckling my seatbelt now," Greg said. A loud thud could be heard as he fell from his seat to the roof of the upside-down bus.

"I'm okay," he said a few seconds later. He began moving toward Carla's seat which was a few rows ahead of his. He had to stoop in some places and crawl in others because the bus had been crushed when it was flung into the sky and thrown to earth with force strong enough to kill everyone on board. Greg just hoped they would not have any casualties, but looking at the damage he was not too hopeful. The wind finally began to die down as he reached Carla's seat. The seat next to hers was empty. Maria sat in that seat and now she was somewhere unresponsive. He said a silent prayer as he unbuckled Carla and caught her weight as she plummeted out of her seat.

"Thank you, Greg," she said hugging him briefly. "Before we unbuckle the children, let's get Cliff and Joseph loose and maybe we will see Maria since she was up that way when it happened." They crawled toward the front of the bus, the sounds of crying children all around them.

"Mrs. Dixon, I can get myself out and then I can help get the rest of the boys out," Keshawn said as she and Coach Fisher passed by. She looked up at him and his face was covered in blood. She gasped.

"Keshawn are you okay? Where are you bleeding from?" she asked.

"I hit my head when we were being tossed around. I saw stars for a minute, but I think I am okay. Josiah is unconscious. I need to get him out of this seat hanging upside down," he spoke as he unsnapped his belt. By hanging onto the belt he avoided being thrown to the floor. After he was free, he unsnapped Josiah's belt catching his limp body like it was a feather. He laid him on the floor and patted his face trying to get him to wake up, but to no avail.

"Keshawn, stay with Josiah and don't unsnap any of the other boys because we need to make sure they don't have any back or neck injuries before we release them. We will be back." She and Coach Fisher continued moving toward the front of the bus, praying all the while that they would find everyone banged up, but okay.

When they got to the first row, both Cliff and Joseph were conscious but still hanging upside down. Joseph's face was covered in blood but he looked alert. He looked bad but he appeared to be in better shape than Cliff, who had slipped into unconsciousness and was covered in blood. They decided to release Joseph first. This turned out to be a good idea because as they looked at Cliff, they realized they had forgotten how big he was. They came up with a plan to get Cliff down with the least amount of wear and tear on his body.

"Okay Carla, you unsnap the buckle while Joseph and I try to catch him and give him a soft landing as much as we can," Greg suggested. Cliff mumbled gibberish as he slipped in and out of consciousness. Cliff mumbled again and Joseph was able to understand part of what he was saying.

"Pocket. He said the word pocket. He wants something out of his pocket." Joseph excitedly began patting his pockets. He felt something and tried to stick his hand in his pocket.

"Let's get him down first," said Greg.

"No!" Cliff could barely speak, but he had mustered all his strength to say no so they knew it was important. "Pocket," he repeated. Joseph slid his hand into Cliff's pocket and removed a pendant, holding it before Cliff's eyes.

"Is this what you wanted?" Joseph asked, holding it up for Cliff to see.

"Yes." Cliff's voice was growing weaker by the second. "Push," the word was barely legible but Joseph held his ear close to Cliff's mouth and heard what he said.

"You want me to push it?" Joseph asked.

He looked at the pendant, unsure of what to push as he turned the pendant over and over in his hands looking for a button to push.

"Cliff, I don't see anything to push on here," Joseph said with confusion. "Are you sure this is what you were talking about?" As he spoke, he continued to turn the pendant over in his hand.

"Push!" Cliff spoke again stronger this time, but the effort almost made him pass out again.

Joseph just began pushing the pendant, not really knowing what he was doing, but when he pushed on the small diamond in the center, there was a click and a light was illuminated inside the small pendant.

"I did it!" he exclaimed. "What's it for?" he asked Cliff as they began to get him down. Cliff had exhausted himself and could barely speak, but before passing out he spoke one word.

"Calvary."

Within five minutes of the pendant being clicked, sirens could be heard in the distance, five more minutes later the rotors of helicopter wings could be heard. The storm had passed and sunshine could now be seen outside. Fire trucks and rescue workers were everywhere swarming the outside of the bus trying to determine how they would get everyone out without further injury.

Three hours later, everyone had finally been removed from the bus. Carla sat in the back of an ambulance getting her injuries attended to as she watched the squads leave carrying the wounded. Cliff, who was considered critical, had been airlifted as soon as the rescue team arrived. Spencer, a 12-year-old, was the most seriously injured with possible back and neck injuries. Josiah had been taken away as well, diagnosed with a mild concussion, but they insisted on taking him in for observation. They had not found Maria's body anywhere. They surmised when the front windshield had been blown out by the force of the gale, she was sucked out and into the actual storm. The prognosis was not good. Carla couldn't stop crying. It was hard to believe her friend was gone.

Of course, it didn't take long for the media to arrive. News reporters were everywhere, sticking microphones in the children's faces, playing the story up for all it was worth. She looked and saw a news crew standing around the back of another emergency vehicle trying to speak to one of the boys and she couldn't take it anymore. Carla marched over to the emergency vehicle, pushing her way pass the news crew and cameramen, shielding the frightened looking boy.

"You people ought to be ashamed of yourselves. These are children who have just experienced the most traumatic moment of their lives and you don't have the common decency to give them some peace."

She pulled the little boy name Simon close to her holding him tight She could feel his small body trembling. Instead of feeling ashamed, the news crew tried to get a quote from her, but she wouldn't have any of it. Shooing them away, she grabbed Simon's hand and began moving toward the relief tent which had been erected for the survivors.

Thinking of the dear friend she had lost, she allowed silent tears to roll down her face. She asked God why He took her friend just when they were starting to know Him in a real way. "Sometimes, God, I just don't understand," she thought. "Help me to understand this." She moved into the relief tent where the rest of the boys were. Looking around, she saw many of them drinking hot chocolate and talking to relief workers, but others were laying on the cots with bandages, neck and leg braces, or crutches for accompaniments. She thought to herself, God your word says in Romans 8:28 *"And we know that all things work together for good to them that love God, to them who are the called according to his purpose."* "Show me your purpose here, God, because right now all I see is pain."

CHAPTER THIRTY-ONE

As the audiobook reached its climax, Robin pushed the eject button on her car's CD player. Robin decided to listen to the radio instead of another CD, so she scanned for a strong signal. She had noticed the weather changing for the last hour and was starting to feel a little concerned as she felt her car constantly battling the wind to stay within her lane as she drove down the highway.

"It looks like I am riding into a storm," she said to herself. She looked and saw absolute blackness ahead and became a little concerned. "I hope I can drive through that thing," she continued. "It looks pretty bad up there." Suddenly, a deluge of rain began coming down in sheets. Robin couldn't see ahead or behind her. She went from being concerned to being afraid.

Robin began praying at that moment. Trying to stay calm, she reasoned with herself. "If I stop," she thought, "then anyone can run into the back of me because if I can't see them they certainly can't see me. Putting on her flashers she slowed down to a crawl. The big black mass was much closer now than just a few moments ago. Robin began to feel uneasy. She hit her OnStar voice activation and instructed her

Bluetooth to call Amera, but got no response. Frustrated, she picked up her phone and without taking her eyes off the road, she hit one on her speed dial and put the phone to her ear, but heard nothing. Looking briefly at her phone, she saw that it was dead.

"Shoot! Think, Robin, think, what to do, what to do?" These were her thoughts, as the menacing black cloud moved closer. There was nowhere to really pull off on the side where she would have felt safe. She knew that if a truck came along she would be a gonner. A moment of sheer panic began to rise in Robin's chest and just when she began to feel overwhelmed with fear, a small and comforting voice said to her, *"Be still."* Robin didn't want to listen to the voice, because the mass of darkness was coming and it was moving directly toward her with seemingly malevolent intent. She heard the voice again. *"Be still."*

Although she was worried someone would ram her from behind, she did as the voice commanded knowing instinctively that it was God. Slamming on her breaks she came to a complete stop and just stared at the black mass moving toward her. It was then that she noticed that the black mass did have a shape.

"Oh my God! Oh my God! It's a funnel! It's a funnel cloud!"

Momentarily, she forgot that she had just heard the Lord tell her to be still. Placing her car in reverse, she threw her arm over the seat so she could turn her body to see behind her as she began driving in reverse.

"Be still and know that I am God."

The calm clear voice she heard overcame voices of panic screaming in her head. Turning back around she confirmed that it was definitely a funnel cloud and it was absolutely headed straight at her and would be upon her in less than a minute.

"God, I know this is your voice but I don't know why you are telling me to stay when I see danger coming my way. It doesn't make sense to me, God, but I am going to trust you. If this is not your voice, God, and I have allowed the enemy to fool me, then forgive me and receive my spirit into your hands."

Robin closed her eyes and began to pray. She thought of Amera, Jo, Tiffany, and Jason. "What a shame," she thought, "that Nico had real promise." Robin prepared to die and her soul was at rest. She decided to open her eyes and stare death in its black ugly face because she remembered the scripture, "*Death where is your sting? Grave where is your victory?*" Robin quoted the scripture as the massive black cloud overtook her car and hurled her up into the midst of the funnel. As her car spun around, she banged her head against the door and that was the last thing she remembered.

⟜⟝

Robin cracked her eye open and the light was so bright it hurt her eyes. She was disoriented for a few moments. Trying to synchronize her mind and body, she suddenly remembered being caught in the storm.

"Oh my God, the tornado," she thought to herself. "This must be the light that everyone talked about when they died." She cracked her other eye open and felt a pounding in her head. "You would think," she thought to herself, "if I am already dead, it would be impossible for me to get a headache, but my head is killing me." She giggled softly to herself.

"My head is killing me—now that is really funny," Robin thought to herself, still disoriented. She was amazed by death. She thought it felt the same as being alive, except for the light.

"I wonder if I will get use to the light in time?" she continued. She tried again to open her eyes and again the light was blindingly brilliant, but she really wanted to see where she was, so she forced them open. She was unable to process what she saw. She saw a pillow of white before her and thought it might a cloud. As she studied her surroundings, she began to make out what she was seeing. Out of her peripheral, she saw green. She appeared to be surrounded by foliage, but something was not quite right. Squinting her eyes, she examined the white object that appeared to have become one with her body and discovered it was not a cloud at all, but an airbag. As reality dawned, she slowly rotated her head to the left and then to the right. She was in her car and pinned against the seat by the airbag.

She felt foolish thinking she had died. In every account of a near death experience she had ever read about, they all said that there was a bright light. The bright light she saw was merely sunlight peeking through. What was confusing was the green foliage all around her. Taking a moment, she thanked God for sparing her life as she slowly began gathering her faculties. She ascertained from the pull of gravity that her car was face down. Being unable to maneuver because of the airbag, she found the button on the side of the seat and slowly let her seat back. Unsnapping her seat belt, she wiggled her way into the back seat. As she looked around, she could see that the green foliage appeared to be pine needles. Looking out the window she saw tree branches and it was then that she realized her car was stuck in a tree.

"Oh my God!" she thought to herself, as she realized that her car was wedged upside down in a pine tree. There was glass from the shattered windows everywhere. Not knowing how high up in the tree the car was, or how secure, she manipulated her body toward the back windshield, which was gone now and slowly climbed out onto the trunk of the car. She grabbed hold of the body of the tree as she inched her way onto one of the tree's branches. As she sat on the branch looking at her car, she again thanked God for deliverance. Her car looked like an accordion. Looking at her car, she knew there was no way she could have possibly survived had it not been for the mercies of God.

"Thank You, God!" she cried, looking up toward heaven. There were many broken branches above her. She could see the path the car had taken down the tree's trunk, being stopped at a V-shape of branches in the tree. The car was now solidly wedged within that V and she now sat safely within the embrace of the tree's uninjured branches. Reluctantly, she looked down to see how far from the ground she was and was pleasantly surprised to find she was only about 20 to 30 feet off the ground.

She was too high to jump, but examining the branches below she could see a path that would get her to approximately 10 feet from the ground and that jump she was willing to risk. "I may get a sprained or broken ankle, but at least I will be on the ground."

"Shoot!" she mumbled to herself, thinking she should have tried to get her phone and purse before exiting the car, but remembered the phone was dead. She had thrown it on the passenger seat right before the storm hit so there was no telling where it was. She looked out to see if she could tell where she was, but all she could see in front of her were more trees. Hugging the tree trunk with all her might, she twisted her body around to see behind her and it was then that she saw the devastation the storm had left in its wake. There appeared to be an open field beyond the trees, but debris and cars littered it everywhere. Through the cover of the trees, she could see the sunlight as bright and beautiful as it could be. It was like the sun was doing its best to deny the savagery of the storm that just happened minutes before.

She began to make her way down the tree. "It's a good thing I was a tomboy when I was a kid," she said out loud, as if she was having a conversation with someone. As she reached the lowest branch that might tolerate her weight, she looked down to see how much further she had to go. She had underestimated the remaining distance between her lofty perch and the ground which was where she wanted to be. It was more like 15 feet remaining instead of the 10 she had guessed, and she wasn't sure if she was up to the challenge. She looked at the remaining branches and none of them looked like they were able to bear her weight and Robin didn't have the courage to jump either. A decision needed to be made.

Slowly, she placed her foot on one of the frailer branches below, holding tightly to the stronger branch above. Swinging her alternate leg to another frail branch below, she hesitantly put her weight on the branch and surprisingly it held. Holding onto the trunk of the tree like it was an old friend she hadn't seen in years, she slowly slipped her one leg down searching for the next branch below. Suddenly, she felt the strength of the first frail branch she had connected with beginning to fail. She quickly tried to find the perch she had just left to search for a new branch, but as she felt the one branch breaking that was holding all her weight, she panicked and tried to reach the thicker branch above, but she missed and began to plummet to the ground.

She hit the ground on her behind with a loud thump. The impact caused her to bounce up in the air before finally landing on the ground to stay. The fall knocked the wind out of her and for a moment, she lay on the ground in silence as she tried to catch her breath. Slowly, she raised up to a sitting position. As luck would have it, she didn't appear to be seriously injured and everything seemed to be in one piece. Her butt hurt like the dickens, and she was positive she would be black and blue for days, but she was okay. She slowly stood to her feet, glad to discover she was none the worse for wear minus her sore tush.

Robin had no idea where she was or how far the storm had taken her. God was with her in that moment and He was still with her now.

"Who gets caught up into a funnel cloud and walks away with just a bump on the head?" she asked herself, as she replayed the moments before she had been taken up into the storm. She remembered God's voice telling her to be still, all the while battling her natural inclination to run. She finally gave in to the voice of the Spirit believing it was her day to die. God had other plans, and here she stood. Talk about peace in the middle of the storm. What she had just been through gave that saying a whole new meaning. She marveled at the awesome power that God displayed for her that day. Not just the power of the storm, but the power of life over death.

Robin had to find her way out of the forest. All around her, trees were uprooted and flung in various directions. As she reached the edge of the tree line, she could see the highway in the distance. Cars were upturned, overturned, and smashed up; people were milling about everywhere, many of them walking around like zombies in shock. Robin began moving toward the highway. Sirens could be heard in the distance so she knew help was on the way. As she drew closer to the highway, debris was everywhere. She walked past a row of seats that appeared to have been ripped from a mini-van. As she passed, she gave it a cursory glance.

As she angled her way around the obstacle, she stopped and slowly turned back around to observe the row of seats. She thought she heard someone. She stopped moving, standing silent listening to see if what she heard would come again.

"Help," a faint voice could be heard ever so slightly.

Robin held perfectly still as she tried to determine from where the sound originated.

"Help," she now clearly heard the voice—a hoarse croak, a plea of desperation.

Looking around, she could see no one within hearing range of where she was. Turning in a full circle she tried to determine where the voice could possibly be coming from. She strained to find the source of the cry. Her eyes dropped to the row of seats which was the only thing close to her that marred the landscape. She saw what appeared to be the tips of someone's fingers, but she wasn't sure because they were covered in mud. Moving closer to the row of seats to examine the anomaly, she saw one finger lift itself in the air, as if it was asking for permission to speak.

Robin ran over to the seats and dropped to her knees in the mud and grabbed the finger which immediately closed around her fingers. Disengaging her finger, she flipped the row of seats backward, uncovering a woman who was covered from head to toe in mud. Immediately, Robin began to examine her trying to find out the woman's condition. The woman was unable to fully speak and was having trouble breathing. Robin, being a doctor, was able to deduce that the woman's medical condition was serious, if not critical.

Taking her shirt off, which she had worn over a tank, she wiped the woman's face and removed mud from her mouth and nostrils to help with her breathing. She knew this woman needed help right now or she wouldn't make it. She leaned over and spoke directly into the woman's ear. She saw that they, too, were filled with mud so she wiped them out before speaking.

"You're banged up pretty good. I'm going to go try and find help for you. I will be right back."

The woman's hand grasped Robin's as she tried to tell her something.

"Tell Liffyue," her words trailed off sounding garbled and confused. She was unable to get the sentence out, but she continued to hold onto Robin's hand.

"Tell who?" Robin asked, trying to get her to finish the sentence, but she had used the last little bit of strength she had to call out. She was happy someone was with her. She hadn't wanted to die alone.

"Tell," the woman repeated, but no more came out as she drifted into unconsciousness.

Robin felt for a pulse and it was faint and erratic. She knew if she didn't get help for her within the next few minutes this woman would die. Jumping to her feet she began to run, making it to the highway in record time. All around her was chaos. All around her were the sounds of children crying. She could see frightened parents trying to soothe their even more frightened children, while other parents held still small lifeless bodies in their arms as they wept inconsolably. Robin continued to run. Her instinct was to stop and help others, but she knew that time was of the essence so she ran as hard and as fast as she could toward the sound of the sirens. Ahead, she could see the lights of the first paramedic truck parked with many more still moving toward the position of the first one. Out of breath and gasping for air, she fell upon the first paramedic as he was removing his medical kit from the back. He turned around and caught her as she collapsed in his arms.

"Are you alright ma'am?" he queried. "Are you injured?"

She could barely catch her breath to tell him he needed to follow her. He patiently waited as she took precious few seconds to catch her breath before telling him the situation.

"There's a lady who will die if we don't get to her immediately. Let me show you where she is. I think she may have a pneumothorax."

His eyes widened momentarily as he noted the use of the medical terminology. "Are you a doctor?"

"Yes, but a psychiatrist."

"Where is she?"

"Follow me," she directed.

He whistled for his partner who was coordinating with another paramedic and they took off in a sprint. As they reached the woman, they begin triaging her by first trying to wake her up, but she wouldn't revive. Unbuttoning her shirt, they listened for a heartbeat.

"Good call on the pneumothorax," one paramedic said.

His partner immediately began to pull out the instruments to put in a chest tube. They scrubbed the surrounding area free of the mud which had caked her entire body and made an incision under her breast by inserting the tube into the incision until it reach the lung. The woman emitted a small gasp once the tube hit home. Quickly, they finished triaging the woman and got her ready for transport. Instead of returning to the squad to get the gurney, they chose to transport her on the row of seats. All three of them gently maneuvered the woman's body as smoothly as possible onto the seat. Upon the count of three, they worked in tandem to lift the seat and carry her as quickly and gently as possible to the squad. As they reached the highway, several men rushed over to assist in carrying the woman. The paramedics continued to try and stabilize her for transport to the hospital. The first paramedic came out to give Robin an update.

"With a little luck and a whole lot of prayer, you may have just saved that woman's life," he said, as he examined the small cut on the side of Robin's head from where she hit the window in her car.

It had bled quite a bit, but Robin hadn't even noticed or cared as she extracted herself from the car and then from the tree. Looking around at all the dead and wounded, she shuddered to think what could have happened.

"I can help you with the second thing," she responded.

"The second thing?" he had forgotten his words that quick as he had begun cleaning and bandaging Robin's head.

"The prayer," she said, "I can definitely help you with the prayer."

He smiled, looking into her eyes. The look acknowledged she and the woman were both lucky to be alive.

"There's a relief tent about a mile and a quarter down the highway. You can hitch a ride with us. She's going to need to be airlifted. We've already called ahead," he said.

Robin got into the front with the driver while the other paramedic rode in back with the patient, monitoring her vitals. They arrived at the relief tent headquarters. There were tents set up everywhere. Medical personnel scrambled around frantically carrying bags of blood and medical equipment. Several yards away, to the left of the tents, there was an area where a medical transport helicopter sat waiting for their patient to be loaded before lifting off. The paramedics loaded the woman onto the chopper and the door quickly shut and the helicopter immediately lifted off. The paramedics began moving back in Robin's direction. Robin's paramedic friend told her where to go.

"There is a relief tent straight through there about thirty yards down," he pointed. "It will have a sign that will say Red Cross. Go there and register so everyone who may be looking for you can know you are alright."

"Oh no!" she exclaimed. "I haven't even thought about that. My friends are probably looking for me. Do you have a cell phone I can use real quick? I promise it will just take a second."

"Towers are down so my phone doesn't have a signal but the relief tent will probably have some. Good Luck!" he said moving toward the staging area for medical personnel.

Robin called out after him. "I don't even know your name," Robin said.

He turned back toward her but continued moving away from her.

"Alfred," he called out. "Alfred Preston." Giving her a small salute, he looked up just as another helicopter came into view.

"Bye Alfred," Robin whispered, as she watched him load another patient onto the helicopter. "Thank you." Her voice was barely above a whisper. It was if all the emotion from the day had caught up to her and she was suddenly overwhelmed. She looked around at the chaos the storm had caused and yet here she stood unharmed, except for a slight bump on the head. When she considered where her car was, and where she had woke up to find herself only minutes before, it all just became too much. She dropped to the ground right where she stood and cried for the loss of life as well as the preservation of life. A gentleman came over to her and for a minute he just stood listening to her release. Finally, when she began to slow down he dropped to the ground in a spot next to her and placed his arm around her.

"It's okay," he spoke so softly she could barely make out the words, but she felt a spirit of comfort behind the words. "It's okay," he repeated. He sat there with her for more than 20 minutes just comforting her. As Robin pulled herself together, she hugged the gentleman and thanked him for just being there. Standing up, she began moving in the direction of the Red Cross relief tent.

Entering the tent, she went to the table that said registration and gave them her name and contact information. They referenced her name against the names they had been given of people on the outside who were looking for loved ones and her name was not on it. They told her that all the cell towers were down for now, but they were being worked on and they would be notified as soon as service was restored. The registration lady was kind and gentle as she spoke to Robin, noting the tears that streaked her face. Reaching down to the floor beside her, she dug out a container of baby wipes. She held it out to Robin telling her where the food was located. Robin was grateful for the woman's kindness. She removed several of the wipes and as best she could, she wiped her face, hands, and neck where the blood trail went. She had only seen it after she had taken off her shirt to wipe the injured woman's face. She thought about the woman and wondered if she survived. She prayed she would make it.

After thanking the woman for her help, she moved in the direction of the food tent. Gratefully, she accepted the cup of coffee that was offered as soon as she entered the tent. She slowly made her way toward the back of the long food line in the makeshift cafeteria. She grabbed a tray placing her coffee on it as she went down the line accepting the spaghetti and salad the line workers were dishing out. She noted the smile that each worker gave her as she moved down the line. A smile that said more than words ever could. She felt the bond of love that often forms after tragedies; an understanding of shared humanity. Taking her tray she surveyed the tent looking for an open seat. Most of the tables were full, but toward the back of the tent she spied a table where a lone woman sat. The woman had her back to Robin so she didn't see her approach. Walking around the table to sit opposite of her, she gently placed her tray of food on the table. Robin attempted to make eye contact with the stranger to greet her, but before she could speak a word, she opened her mouth in shock. She stared at the woman whose mouth was also open in shock. It was Carla Dixon.

"Mrs. Dixon?"

"Dr. Walters?"

They stared at one another from across the table. Robin was the first to break the silence.

"Mrs. Dixon, are you alright?

"I am fine, Dr. Walters, how are you?" Carla asked.

"I was supposed to fly in yesterday, but I got an emergency at the last minute so I decided to drive up early this morning. Did you drive up by yourself?" Robin asked.

I rode on the bus with the kids," Carla replied.

Robin went into full blown panic mode. "Please tell me that the bus didn't get caught in the storm. Please tell me I am panicking for nothing. The kids are already in Chicago safe and sound, right?"

As she stared into Carla's eyes she knew without her having to say a word that they too had been caught in the storm.

"Josiah! Is Josiah alright?" Robin asked.

She thought then of the parents she had passed on the highway. Some had carried dead children in their arms. She dropped to the seat as if her legs refused to bear her weight any longer.

"Oh my God, Oh my God," Robin began hyperventilating.

"Robin, Josiah is alright," Carla said. "I'm sorry, I didn't mean to make you think something was wrong with him. He's been taken to one of the local hospitals for observation. He has a mild concussion." Carla eyes misted over. "I was thinking about my friend, Maria. She was the school's principal. When the storm hit, she was sucked out the window and we don't even know where her body is."

Robin pulled herself together. The relief that washed over her after finding out that Josiah was alright was palpable; now here was a woman whom she couldn't really call a friend because she only knew her name and where she worked, but this woman had done more for her than her own mother had. She tried to return the favor. She moved around the table and sat next to Carla and tried to comfort her.

"So if they haven't found her body, why are you assuming she is dead?" Robin asked bluntly.

"She was sucked out of the bus into the actual storm. There is no way she could have survived that." Carla was holding on by a thread, but now that thread was broken and she said what she had been afraid to think.

"I know God is sovereign but this doesn't seem right to me. Why would He take Maria? She and I were just starting to get to know Him on a deeper level."

She looked at Robin and Robin saw pain so raw and deep it made her want to cry. She hugged Carla and told her not to give up hope. She told Carla the story of how she, too, was caught in the storm and how her car landed in a tree, but through it all, God had protected her.

As she finished sharing her story, Carla began to look a little more hopeful.

"Wow! That is quite a story," remarked Carla.

"Yea, I know, and someday I'm going to laugh about it, but not today."

The woman she had found crossed her mind at that moment and she knew she needed to pray for her.

"When I got out of that tree, I found a woman who was close to death. I ran and got help for her, but I'm still not sure if she will make it; I feel the Spirit telling me to pray for her. Will you pray with me, Carla?"

Carla agreed, and right there at the table the ladies held hands and began to pray.

"Do you know her name?" said Carla.

"No, I don't," said Robin. "But God does."

They went before the throne unaware of how long they prayed or who heard them. When the prayer came to a close, and they opened their eyes, everyone in the tent had stopped eating and joined the prayer. They all stood around Carla and Robin encircling them within a circle of hands. Amens could be heard all around as the prayer ended. Everyone began to hug one another regardless of whether they knew each other or not. Some people were crying while others were encouraging, but everyone said they felt better after the prayer.

"I'm sorry, God, about what I said earlier," said Carla. "I hope Maria is somewhere at another relief tent drinking coffee waiting for cell phone service like I am; but if she isn't, God, then I must accept that you and you alone know what is best and I trust you even when I don't understand."

Carla Dixon spoke to God from her heart as she prayed in her mind for her friend's survival.

CHAPTER THIRTY-TWO

Robin wanted to find out what hospital Josiah was taken to, but as soon as she reached the tents exit, a horrible thought hit her. Cliff? Where was Cliff? He had agreed to chaperone the boys. Oh no, she thought. Please don't let Cliff be on that bus. Please God. Doing an about face, Robin marched back to the table where she had been sitting with Carla.

"Excuse me, Carla," said Robin.

Carla looked up and met Robin's eyes, but didn't speak.

"Was Cliff DeVault on that bus with you all?" Robin asked.

Carla's eyes flooded with tears. She closed her eyes and dropped her head.

"Please Carla, Cliff is a very good friend of mine and I know he was going to chaperone, but I'm not sure if he was taking his own transportation down or whether he chose to ride the bus."

"Yes," Carla responded weakly.

"Yes what?" said Robin, feeling the same fear she felt when Carla told her about Josiah, but this time there was no quick explanation to keep her from thinking the worse. Just more tears.

"Please tell me Cliff is alright," said Robin.

Carla was in a daze and Robin noticed she wasn't right. Maybe Carla was in shock, Robin thought. She should have seen the signs earlier, but she had been too focused on her own stuff.

"Carla, don't move, I'm going to get you some help." She walked out of the tent and returned within minutes with a paramedic. They both looked at Carla with concern.

"Carla, this is Michael and he is a paramedic. He's going to take a look at you," said Robin.

In a matter of minutes Carla's condition had degraded dramatically. She was almost unresponsive. Two more paramedics entered the tent wheeling a gurney in with them. They waited while Michael took Carla's pulse and blood pressure and shined a flashlight in her eyes. He immediately beckoned for the other two paramedics to bring the gurney. As they loaded Carla onto the gurney, Michael took a moment to speak with Robin.

"She has a blown pupil. It looks like a possible brain bleed." He asked Robin several more questions about Carla and her behavior when Robin first encountered her. Robin answered his questions and then asked him if it would be okay if she asked Carla about her friend. Michael told her yes, but he doubted if she would be responsive and cautioned her to be brief. Robin walked over to the gurney where medical attendants were putting an IV into Carla's arm. Robin was amazed at how Carla now seemed to be only a shell of the woman she had just spoken with only minutes before. She prayed for Carla right then and there, but she had to find out if Cliff was alright.

"Carla, I'm not sure if you can hear me, but if you can, I only need you to nod your head. Is Cliff alright?"

For several seconds Carla did nothing but lay there and look out into space as tears rolled down her cheeks. She shook her head no. Robin's heart felt like it had been ripped from her chest.

"Carla, are you saying Cliff is not alright? Are you saying Cliff is hurt?" More tears and then a nod to indicate affirmative. Robin fell back as if she had been pushed. She stumbled out of the tent running back to registration. A small line had formed, but Robin ignored everyone in the line running back to the older lady who had been so kind to her before.

"Please, please, you've got to help me. I just learned my friend was in the storm and he was hurt. I need to know how bad he was hurt and where they took him." The nice lady asked the woman that Robin cut in front of if it was okay for her to help Robin first. She told her of course and moved back allowing Robin to take her place in the line. Robin was frantic as she waited for the lady to get the book down from the filing cabinet behind her.

"What's his name, sweetie?" she asked to Robin.

"Clifford DeVault."

She ran her fingers down the line of names until finally her finger stopped on line number 48. Line 48 was highlighted.

"It looks like he was life-flighted to Loyola University Medical Center."

"Life flighted? What do you mean life-flighted? What was the nature of his injuries?"

Robin's voice was harsh and this woman didn't deserve her tone.

"I'm sorry, ma'am. Cliff is like my dad and I just found out that he was on the bus with the kid..." Robin's voice trailed off as she absorbed the shock of the latest news. She knew as a physician that if he had to be life-flighted, then he was in pretty bad shape.

"Can you check one more name for me?" she asked, her voice sounding hollow. "The name is Josiah Martin."

The lady began again to run her finger down the page full of names turning to the second page before finding what she sought.

"I have a Thomas Josiah Martin III. Would he be who you are looking for?"

"Yes!" said Robin excitedly. "Can you tell me his condition?"

"I don't know his condition but it does say he was transported to Shriners Hospital for Children for observation. The more serious cases were highlighted and his is not, so I think he may be okay."

Robin wanted to go to Josiah, but she knew that Cliff was the priority. She needed her girls so badly right now. She knew by now they were somewhere trying to find her and Cliff, but there was no cell service; she couldn't immediately update them on the circumstances. She had no idea of how she was going to get to Cliff, but if she had to walk then that's what she would do. Coming up with a plan, she addressed the women who continued looking through her book.

"You have been so helpful. I really appreciate all that you have done, but can I ask you one more favor?" she said, looking pleadingly at the woman.

"Sure," she replied.

"I need to get a message to Josiah. He doesn't have any parents who will know where he is. My name is Dr. Robin Walters and he is my patient." Robin flubbed just a little. Tell him that I am here and I will be coming to see about him and not to worry."

The lady wrote everything down that she said and promised to get someone to get the message to him. Robin thanked her profusely and turned to exit but before she could leave, the woman spoke.

"Wait a minute please. It looks like there is a number to call for anyone inquiring about Cliff Devault."

"That will be good if the phone service ever come back online."

"Actually," she said, "I don't know who your friend is, but it says here that anyone inquiring about Mr. Clifford DeVault should be referred directly to the Deputy Director of Operations."

Reaching into her drawer she pulled out a green ID badge and gave it to Robin.

"Go to the tent directly behind this one. When they see your ID badge they will know what to do."

Robin followed the instructions the woman gave and when she flashed the green ID badge, they immediately took her to the office of the Deputy Director of Operations. The DDO looked harried and exhausted. He was talking to the governor on a satellite phone, giving him updates on the status of the relief operation. He quietly put up one finger to indicate to her to take a seat and he would be with her momentarily. He quickly finished his conversation and made a couple of notes on a pad before turning to her.

"How can I help you?" he said brusquely.

"I'm not sure. When I asked about my friend, the lady in registration gave me this badge and told me to come see you."

He looked at her curiously, "Who is your friend?"

"Clifford DeVault." It was like she had said a magic word because he immediately began to defer to her.

"I am sorry Mrs…?"

"It's doctor. Dr. Robin Walters."

"I am sorry, Dr. Walters. The president called the governor and advised him that we are to do everything in our power to make Mr. DeVault as comfortable as possible and to facilitate any family or friends who may inquire as to his well-being. I can have one of my men drive you over to Loyola Medical Center. We were recently updated that he had made it through the surgery okay but he lost so much blood that it is touch and go right now. They say the next 24 hours will tell the story but be assured we are doing everything in our power to make sure he survives and that is coming from the very top."

Robin sat in stunned silence as the words echoed through her mind. Surgery? Survive? Twenty-four hours? She felt like she needed to throw up. She looked at the DDO, who, in turn, had stopped talking and was staring at her with a concerned look on his face.

"Are you alright, Dr. Walters?" He hesitated while waiting for her to respond.

"I had no idea that he was that badly injured. Would it be possible for me to use your phone?"

"Sure," he said, handing her the phone. "I'll give you some privacy. Take as long as you like."

She dialed Jo's number knowing at a time like this they would all be together. Jo answered on the first ring.

"Hello?"

"Jo, it's me, Robin."

"Oh my God, Robin, where are you? Are you okay? We've been worried out of our minds."

"I'm alright, but I have some bad news. The children's bus was caught in the storm and there were several injuries."

Jo gasped, "Is Josiah okay?"

"Josiah is fine, but Cliff has been seriously injured." Robin could feel the shock and fear travel through the phone. Jo went totally silent. Robin thought they had been disconnected.

"Hello, Hello? Jo, are you there?"

"Robin?" Marcus took over the call. "Where are you? We are coming to get you."

Robin began crying like a little girl because that was how she felt. This day felt like it would never end.

"I've got to get to Cliff, Marcus. He's alone and he needs us," Robin spoke between tears.

"Robin, I need you to do me a favor," Marcus said. "I am going to get Nico. He has been in his room praying for over four hours. I want to let him know you are on the phone but don't let him hear you crying. I'm afraid he might do something stupid. He knew before the storm hit that something wasn't right. We teased him until finally he went into his room and has been there on his knees praying for you. Find out where you are while I take the phone to him. Jo, Amera, and Tiffany are all crying right now, but they are okay. We will be there to get you ASAP. By the way, whose phone is this? The number is showing blocked."

"I am in the disaster staging area, but I have no idea where this is or if there are more than one. Right now I am in the Deputy Director of Operations tent, and this is his phone, if that will help. Cliff is at Loyola Medical Center. The DDO said he will have someone take me to Loyola so that is where I will be. Can you guys get there?"

"We will meet you there," said Marcus, "but first I will let you speak with Nico, but only for a second because I need to speak with the DDO."

"Please, Marcus, hurry. I need my family," she started tearing up again.

"Don't worry, sis, we will be there shortly," he assured her.

Nico took over the line and it was so good to hear his voice. His voice was full of emotion. She heard relief, fear, worry, but mostly she heard love in his voice, and even though they had not spoken the words to each other, she knew in that instant that he loved her and she him. He told her to hold on, they were on the way and right before handing the phone back to his twin he told her what she had been waiting to hear. "I love you Robin."

"I love you, too, Nico."

Marcus hopped back on the phone and he told her to get the DDO on the line, which she did. Within minutes, she was being transported by jeep to Loyola University Medical Center compliments of the DDO. It appeared that not only did Cliff have clout, but the guys did as well. An hour later, the jeep came to a halt in front of the hospital. Nico, Marcus, Charles, Jason, Jo, Amera, and Tiffany all came running out to the jeep practically pulling her out of the seat as they pulled her into the biggest group hug she had ever experienced. There wasn't a dry eye to be found anywhere. Robin collapsed in Nico's arms glad to lean into his strength because she felt like she was at the end of hers. He pulled her in and supported her as they went to ICU where Cliff was fighting for his life.

Nico and Marcus presented their identification and spoke with the charge nurse. She updated them on Cliff's condition and informed them that they all could not go back to see him at the same time. She asked the girls what their relation was to the patient. Without so much as a blink of an eye, "Daughters," they said in unison. She looked at them sympathetically.

"Would you all like some coffee?" she inquired.

"Why don't you all get some coffee while Nico and I check on Cliff," Marcus suggested. "Then we can rotate and go in two at a time."

Everyone, except Marcus and Nico, began moving toward the family waiting room.

"Oh no," said Jo.

"Please don't say that," said Robin. "I can't deal with one more thing happening today."

"Somebody has got to tell Simone," said Jo.

They were all silent for a moment. "I will tell her," said Jo.

"No, that's okay," said Robin, "I will tell her." She sounded weary to the bone.

"Let's all tell her," said Tiffany, taking out her cell phone. They called Simone, who already knew something was wrong, but upon learning that Cliff was seriously injured in the bus crash, she went stone cold silent. Several seconds of silence went by before Simone quietly responded.

"I'm on my way," was all she said.

"Simone, you can't get through yet and I am not sure if there are any flights coming in either."

"I said I am on my way and if that means I will have to walk there then so be it, but I will be there today!" she snapped at them but they knew she didn't mean it.

Robin suddenly remembered the phone number the lady in the registration tent gave to her for anyone inquiring about Cliff. Robin got on the phone and gave Simone the number.

"I will call you guys back once I have a plan together," said Simone and abruptly hung up the phone.

At that moment, Marcus and Nico walked back into the waiting room looking very sober. They got coffee before everyone formed their chairs in a circle so Marcus and Nico could update everyone at the same time.

"It's pretty bad," Marcus said. "Cliff was impaled by an object that blew in through the windshield of the bus. It really wasn't that big of an object but the force of the wind gave it momentum and the angle that it went in nicked his heart. They say they lost him on the table twice. His vitals are weak, but his will is strong. I'm putting my money on Cliff. Between God's will and Cliff's willpower and our prayers, I think Cliff will make it."

The girls were all shocked into silence. The guys each sat by his lady offering love and support. The sound of Tiffany's cell phone broke the silence. It was Simone. She told them, when she called the number, they asked her who she was calling about. After she gave them Cliff's name, she was put on hold for several seconds before someone came on the line and told her they would have to a call her back. She said a few minutes later a man called her and introduced himself as Ralph Quinn, the head of White House security. He had advised Simone he was empowered to assist in making sure Cliff DeVault had everything he needed, no matter how large or small the request. She told Mr. Quinn that she was Cliff's fiancée and she needed to get to him, but the roads leading into Chicago were closed and no more flights were leaving Columbus to Chicago that day. Mr. Quinn assured her that was not a problem and asked her if she wanted to drive herself to the airport or did she want him to send a car for her. Simone knew she was too upset to drive and told Mr. Quinn that being picked up might be safer. He informed her he could have a car to her location in 30 minutes. She would be flown to Chicago via military hop.

They were all relieved to hear this and asked what time she would arrive so that they could pick her up. She told them that wouldn't be necessary because Mr. Quinn made all the transportation arrangements for both air and ground.

"See you shortly," she said and hung up the phone.

CHAPTER THIRTY-THREE

Patricia was so happy to have Allison back in her life, but as good as that felt, it couldn't compare to being back in right relationship with God. Allison agreed to go with Patricia to pack up all of Ace's things.

Allison dropped her kids off at her mother's house. She told them she would be back to get them in a couple of hours. Their eyes got as big as saucers at the thought of her leaving them because they remembered the last time she had dropped them off at their grandmother's house, she didn't come back. She could see the fear in their eyes. She gathered her babies into her arms and pulled them to her, assuring them that this time would not be like the last time. She really was coming back.

"Have fun with your grandma and I will be back to get you in two hours." She showed them where the hands on the clock would be when she returned and they seemed somewhat pacified after that.

Patricia and Allison pull up in front of her apartment. Patricia had butterflies in her stomach and just hoped Ace was gone so she could pack up his stuff without interference, but she was not to be that lucky. When she opened the door to her apartment, she found Ace where she always found him—on her couch playing video games. He didn't even turn to acknowledge her presence, but instead demanded she get him a beer from the fridge. She gathered her courage.

"Ace, we need to talk," she said calmly.

"About what?" he asked without taking his eyes off the TV.

"Could you turn off that game for a moment so we can have a conversation?" she said, slightly louder this time.

"It's going to have to wait," he said. "I'm working on my high score. Fix me something to eat. Where's my beer?" She was amazed that she had actually endured this level of selfishness for so long. Allison walked over to the television set and unplugged it.

"There you go, Pat," she said. "Now do what we came here to do." She stood there, arms folded, waiting for Ace to say something to her about the unplugged television set, but he caught a glimpse of the look in her eyes and decided to pick his battles. He knew what this was. Girl power. He laughed inside. He laughed because he knew Allison had gotten Patricia all worked up, but he knew all he had to do was tell her he wanted to really be with her and her stupid son and she would be like putty in his hands. He was going to forbid her to see Allison once he smoothed this over, he thought to himself. How dare she come over here and try to mess up his happy home. He would deal with her later, but for now, his focus was on getting the horse back into the barn. He decided to change tactics.

"What's wrong, Patricia? Did something happen today to get you upset?" he said, in a conciliatory tone.

Taking his eyes off the darkened television screen, he tried to look soulfully into her eyes but she was just so dang ugly, he thought to himself, that he decided to look at her forehead instead. He laughed to himself as he envisioned ugly Patricia with a bag over her face. Bringing himself back to the present, he tried to pretend to be the understanding boyfriend for Allison's sake. If he could just get her to leave he could get full control back. Patricia was trying to buck because her friend had gotten her all pumped up, but as soon as he got Allison out, he was going to punish Patricia. He couldn't wait until her friend left.

"Patricia, you either tell him or I am leaving. I didn't bring my kids out into this storm so that you could sit here and try to find a nice way to tell lover boy you're done. Just say it or I am leaving."

"Patricia, I think we need to talk alone," said Ace. "This is my home, too, and your friend is making me feel uncomfortable. Could you ask her to leave?" he said with a pleading look on his face, but Patricia wasn't buying it this time.

"No, Ace, I won't be asking her to leave but I am asking you to leave. I can help you pack if you like or you can do it yourself, but you have exactly 30 minutes to get your stuff and leave."

She could see the steam rise off Ace as he digested the words she said to him. In an instant, Ace's countenance changed and something rose up in him that was dark and ugly. Patricia stepped back in fear but Allison, who had also seen the switch, stepped forward, unafraid of the demon that now was controlling Ace.

"Get your Bible, Patricia," she said forcefully, never taking her eyes off of Ace's face.

"Good thing I brought my oil," she said, removing a bottle of blessed oil from her jacket pocket. "Come here, Patricia," she commanded. Not once did she remove her eyes from Ace, who rose up as if he meant to attack Patricia, but stood motionless as Allison anointed both Patricia and herself with the oil she had brought. She told Patricia what scripture to go to in her Bible and as she began to recite the scripture from heart, Patricia began reading it right along with her. They could both see when the demon left Ace. His face changed.

"You've got 20 minutes now," said Patricia sternly.

Ace began gathering his things, all the while swearing and cursing. Finally, the door slammed with a loud bang and just like that, the Ace chapter in her life was officially over.

"Wow Allison! How did you learn to do that? You were totally in control."

"I was never in control. I told the Holy Spirit we needed help with this one and He just took over and worked through me. I had nothing to do with that, except I got out of the way and allowed the Holy Spirit to work through me."

"But how did you even know to do that? We got saved at the same time but it seems like you are so much more advanced than I am."

"That's because I go to church and am under good leadership. Truthfully speaking, I was always afraid something like this would happen to you after you kept refusing to go to church once we got saved. I prayed everyday that you wouldn't fall into temptation, but God told me that was a wasted prayer. We all will be tempted from time to time. We pray to yield not to temptation, but we also go to church to learn tactics and warfare to fight the enemy. The Bible says to forsake not the assembling of yourselves together. God has a purpose for church. You see how faithful God has been. I have my children back and you're going to get Josiah back as well.

Together, Patricia and Allison began cleaning up her apartment and returned it to the pristine order that Patricia had learned to love before hooking back up with Ace. As Patricia picked up McDonalds wrappers off the coffee table, she saw her cell phone. The light that indicated missed calls was blinking furiously.

"Looks like someone has been trying to call me but I can't imagine who," said Patricia. "I don't have any friends besides you." She picked up her phone and listened to her voicemail. As each message played, a look of fear came over her face. Allison looked on in concern as Patricia listened to five different voicemails all about the same thing. Hanging up the phone, she turned to Allison with a look of shock on her face.

"Josiah has been in an accident and was admitted to a hospital outside of Chicago."

"Chicago? Why would they admit him in a hospital so far away?" Allison asked.

"They were on a field trip going to Chicago to see a basketball game and the bus got caught in a tornado."

"Tornado? When? Where? Turn the television on."

Patricia turned on the television and changed the station to CNN. Images of the storm's damage flashed across the screen. It looked like a nuclear bomb had been dropped in the area.

"They didn't say how he was injured or how bad it was but they did say he was not on the critical list. They're driving another bus down to pick everyone up and parents are allowed to go. The bus is leaving from the school at two. I've got an hour and fifteen minutes to get myself cleaned up and over to the school."

"Go take a shower and change your clothes. Do you have money to travel with?"

"A little, but I don't think we have to pay to ride down there.

I will run to the bank as well. You just get ready."

"Thank you, Ally. I love you so much."

"I know, now hurry. I will be right back." Allison rushed out the door to run the errands. The first place she went was to her mother's house. She let the kids know where she is going, told them when she would be back and gave them the time. They looked a little more relaxed this time as she rushed back out the door. She swung by the bank and returned to Patricia's apartment. She heard the blow dryer going in the bathroom. "I'm back," she hollered, as she finished cleaning the living room.

Patricia came out of the room after about 15 minutes packed and ready to go. Allison slipped her a hundred dollar bill and told her if she ran out of money to give her a call. They jumped in Allison's car and headed for the school. The bus was just about finished loading when she arrived. Patricia jumped out of the car and rushed over to the line and ran to where a woman was checking everyone's identification. She gave the woman her name and Josiah's name and showed her ID. After they cross referenced her name with the list of children, she was cleared to board the bus. Patricia moved toward the bus but before boarding, she turned to her friend and blew her a kiss, mouthing the words thank you.

CHAPTER THIRTY-FOUR

Simone sat on the side of Cliff's bed with her head resting on his arm. She had been that way since she arrived at the hospital. She prayed, briefly slept, woke up, and prayed some more. The only time she left his side was to go to the restroom. Amera, Jo, and the guys remained at the hospital as well. Only Robin left and that was to visit Josiah. She informed them that Josiah was doing fine and Carla Dixon was also improving and getting stronger after an emergency surgery to stop the bleeding in her brain. They had lost one child. A 10-year-old boy named Dallas. He hadn't been at the group home very long, and had just accepted Christ as his Savior the Sunday prior to the trip. They all knew that hadn't been a coincidence.

When she walked into Josiah's room, the look on his face said everything she needed to hear. He hugged her so long that Keshawn, who was buried in the corner all stretched out in his sleeping chair, was forced to tell Josiah to let her go so she could breathe. They all laughed. Robin went over to Keshawn and hugged him just as long, telling him how relieved she was that they were both alright.

The boys recounted the story of how the bus had been picked up and tossed, and how they hung upside down like bats before they were rescued. She told them she could do them one better and shared her story of how her car had actually been caught up in the funnel cloud and taken somewhere and dumped in a tree and how she had to climb down the tree to safety. They all laughed when she shared the story of how she had thought she was in heaven because she saw the bright light, only to find the bright light was really sunshine, and what she took for a cloud was her deployed airbag. They laughed so hard that the nurse came in with a stern look, telling them to settle down, looking sharply at Robin.

"Are you the boy's mother? She asked looking over at Keshawn.

Robin knew that the nurse assumed that because she was black and Keshawn was black that her connection must be to him.

"No, I'm his mother," she said nodding her head in Josiah's direction. The boys hid the smiles on their faces. This nurse had been mean since the day they arrived. She refused to allow Keshawn to stay with Josiah, but was overruled by the charge nurse who stated it was okay due to the extreme nature of the circumstances. The children were without parents so if they felt more comfortable with each other, then small allowances would, could, and should be made, she said. She hadn't liked that at all, so she ignored Keshawn whenever she came into the room to monitor Josiah's vitals, and they ignored her. But now she had again overstepped her authority and Robin feeling a little ornery thought she would have some fun with her. Robin asked if she could see Josiah's chart.

"I'm sorry, only physicians can see the charts," she said with an attitude.

"My name is Dr. Robin Giselle Walters. Would you like to see my credentials?" Thank God she had gotten her purse back the day before. The National Guard found her purse while getting her car out of the tree. She handed her credentials to the nurse for her review. Feeling satisfied, the nurse handed them back to Robin.

"Now I would like to see his chart please."

Realizing she had made another error, the nurse quickly changed her tone of voice to a more deferential one.

"I'm sorry, Dr. Walters. I had no idea that Josiah's mom was a physician. Here's the chart. Let me know if I can do anything else for you," she said, as she backed out of the room.

"Can you bring the boys some juice and cookies?"

"Sure, I'll send the aid in with them right away."

"Can you get them? I want to ask you a couple of questions when you get back."

"Sure, Dr. Walters. I'll get them now and come right back," she said, hurrying out the room.

Nurse Berger had been fired from her last three jobs because of her poor attitude. She had only been at this hospital for a little over a month, but there were already three complaints against her. She couldn't afford to lose another job so she quickly adjusted her attitude and went to get the juice and cookies.

"Wow!" said Keshawn, "That was awesome." He looked at her with amazement on his face.

"One thing I hate is a bully," Robin said passionately.

She went through Josiah's charts examining both his and Keshawn's cuts and abrasions. She asked them both a series of questions to see if they were still experiencing symptoms of concussions and both boys seemed fine.

"Who's in charge of you boys?

"Coach is," said Keshawn.

"Where is he?"

"He said he wasn't leaving until someone got here from the school to relieve him so he should be around the hospital somewhere," Keshawn said.

"Are you guy's hungry?"

They both spoke in the affirmative.

"The cafeteria has a Wendy's. How about burgers?" she asked.

"That sounds great!" said Josiah.

"Doubles for everyone?" Robin offered.

Keshawn said yes, but Josiah quickly interrupted telling Robin that Keshawn was just being polite and that he really wanted a triple. Keshawn threw his pillow at Josiah and both boys cracked up.

She took their drink orders and headed out to the cafeteria where she found a haggard looking Greg Fisher, the school's basketball coach. He sat at a table drinking coffee with an older black gentleman. He looked up when she stopped at his table and waited for a lull in the conversation between the two men.

"Are you Coach Fisher?" she asked.

"Yes I am, is something wrong?" he said quickly and stood to his feet.

"No, everything is fine," she assured him. "I am Dr. Robin Walters. I just came from seeing Josiah and Keshawn."

"Are they okay?" he asked, fear changing his look from haggard to terrified.

"Yes they're fine. I am from Columbus as well. I was driving down to go to the game with the kids, but I, too, got caught in the storm."

Just the mention of the storm brought fear back into Greg Fisher's eyes. He took a minute before speaking. "That storm," he replied, "I don't know if I will ever be the same again."

"Give it to God, Coach Fisher. He is the only one who is able to heal you from something like this," said Robin.

This comment brought an interested look from the older gentlemen.

"I was just telling him the same thing," said the man. "When I saw that we couldn't outrun the storm, I began praying like I have never prayed before in my life. Me and Cliff..."

"You were with Cliff?" Robin said looking at the older man curiously.

"He sat right up front with me and let me tell you we were both praying. You know Cliff?" he asked Robin. Both men looked at her with curiosity.

"Yes, he's like a father to me," Robin said.

Both men became excited. "Where is he?" asked Coach Fisher. "We haven't been able to find out where they transported him because they went hush hush after the military helicopter came down and took him away."

"I tell you, it was the dangest thing," said the elderly gentleman. "He told us to push this pendant he had in his pocket and after we did within minutes there were squads, helicopters, and medical personnel everywhere. Lives were saved due to that quick response. I don't know who Cliff is or what that thing was, but he saved our lives." Both men concur as they gave Robin details of the accident and how things went down. Robin told them where Cliff was and informed them of his condition.

"That man got too much God in him to die. I believe he is going to be okay, but I am going to find a ride to the hospital so I can check on him," said the elderly gentleman.

"Me too," said Coach Fisher. Then he remembered he had to wait for reinforcements and in that instant, school personnel began streaming into the cafeteria looking for him. They all gathered around him hugging him, glad to see he was unharmed and sat down for a debriefing as Robin quietly slipped away.

She picked up the boys orders and hurried back to the room, but as she opened the door, she got the shock of her life. Patricia Martin sat on the side of Josiah's bed beaming like a brand new penny. Robin was momentarily speechless. She knew that Josiah hadn't seen his mother in over a year, so she wondered how she had found out about what happened to Josiah. But that didn't matter right now. She needed to know how her being here had affected Josiah, but one look at Josiah's face answered that question. She had never ever seen Josiah look like he did in that instant. There was a light that shone out of Josiah that Robin could only associate with the word angelic. This child was happy, but it was so much more. He was ecstatic, but it was more than that. She searched her brain looking for the right word and then it came to her. Josiah looked complete, he looked whole and happy. The edges of sadness which always remained hidden in the corners of his being were gone and all that remained was light. This was Josiah's letter to God being answered. She knew right then and there that the mother who sat beside Josiah right then was not the same Patricia Martin she had met more than a year before. She could see the light which came out of her as well. She stood in the doorway, looking at the two of them as they beamed at each other, knowing a new beginning had started right there in that room.

One part of her was happy because she loved Josiah with a love that was real and true; the other part of her felt her heart rip in half as she accepted that Josiah was not to be her son, and the thought of that devastated her. She stood frozen like a statue in the doorway with a Wendy's carrier full of drinks and her hands filled with bags of burgers and fries.

Keshawn was the only one who saw her open the door and because he knew all the pieces to the puzzle, he knew what Dr. Walters was experiencing and his young heart ached for her.

"Hey Dr. Walters, I was about to come and look for you the very next time my stomach growled. I am starving," he said.

Both Josiah and Patricia turned to acknowledge Robin; each of their faces on high beam.

"Look Dr. Walters, my mom is here!" Robin had truly never seen him happier.

She knew that Josiah had no idea of how this was affecting her but she was surprised to see that Patricia did know. She could tell by the sympathetic look in her eyes. She knew the pain Robin was in and she knew why, but instead of using that information to further injure her, she stood up and walked over to Robin.

"Let me help you with those bags," Patricia said as she took the food out of her hands and divided the burger and fries between the boys.

"I'll get another chair," she said, starting to walk out the room but Robin told her she was fine and didn't need a chair. She looked at both the boys happily eating and a tear slipped down her cheek.

It was at that point that Patricia Martin grabbed Robin and hugged her as if her life depended on it. Now both women were crying over the unspoken words that lay between them, that could not be voiced within hearing range of the children.

"Can we walk?" Patricia asked, wiping her face.

"Yes, I would like that," responded Robin.

They told the boys they were going to walk back to Wendy's to get frosties. This was greeted with a loud yell of approval as they left the room. An orderly passed by and Patricia asked him where they could find a good place to talk. The orderly suggested the solarium and pointed in the direction it was located. Robin was still in shock so she just followed along. They stopped at a stand and bought coffee before reaching the solarium. Upon arriving, they found seating in an area that looked like a Brazilian rainforest. The place was beautiful and peaceful, a perfect place to talk.

"I have a lot I need to say to you Dr. Walters, the first of which is I'm sorry. I'm not even sure how the lawsuit got started. I had a stupid conversation in a bar with a man one night and the next day he was telling me we were both going to be rich. I was desperate for money at that time, so I just turned a blind eye to the truth. I can't tell you how sorry I am that I allowed that to happen."

"You are the best thing that ever happened to Josiah and I know that this is going to sound crazy, but I think God put you in Josiah's life to be more than his doctor."

Robin's eyes widened at this comment, but she just continued to listen.

"I know you love Josiah. I saw you at the hospital when you tried to see him and they wouldn't let you. I was there every night, but I didn't want anyone to see me because I was too ashamed. Again, it was all about me. All of Josiah's life I never even acknowledged his needs because I was too self-absorbed."

Robin's eyes widened, but she said nothing. This was definitely not the same woman she had met.

"There is a lot more I need to say to you, but I just wanted you to know that I see Josiah now, and I realize I never really saw him before. What a beautiful child he is inside and out, and I never even saw it but you did and so do I now. I am telling you this because I am going to get Josiah back and I don't care what I have to do to make that happen. You deserve to know this because not only do you love him, but you have stood in the gap for him when I, his own mother, was nowhere to be found."

Tears began streaming down Patricia's face as she spoke. "What I did to both you and Josiah was shameful, but I promise I am going to make it up to both of you. I will be dropping the lawsuit. You can see Josiah whenever you like and if it is okay with you, I would like for you and I to get to know each other better, since I am going to need you as I move forward into this new life God has planned for me."

There it was! The words she needed to hear. That was why she had looked so different, talked, and acted different. Somewhere along the way, Patricia Martin had met the Father. They continued talking before returning to Wendy's to get the boys frosties.

When they got back to the room Josiah still had that goofy grin pasted on his face and it must have been contagious because now Keshawn was wearing the same grin.

Both she and Patricia sat on one side of Josiah's bed while Keshawn sat on the other as they compared storm stories. Josiah looked from Dr. Walters back to his mother and it was plain to see that he couldn't have been any happier. Patricia suggested that they pray a prayer of thanksgiving before Robin left. She had advised them she needed to get back to Cliff who wasn't doing well. Before leaving she told them the news she had gotten about Carla Dixon. She was recuperating after her surgery.

As she left Josiah's room and headed toward the garage, she thought about all the things that had happened in the year since she had met Josiah and knew that God hadn't brought her into Josiah's life at all, but instead, He had brought Josiah into hers. Her relationship with Josiah brought her face-to-face with her anger toward God because of what her parents had done. She hadn't even known it was there. Because of Josiah, her relationship with the girls, including Tiffany, had deepened, being forged in the fire along with everything she suffered, bringing her closer not only to them but to God as well. She experienced a father's love not only from God, but from Cliff as well as a mother's love from Simone. She knew God brought her and Nico together, but only after she had come face-to-face with her own demons and made things right with the Father.

Now she was free to love with her whole heart and she realized that she did love Nico with everything she had. They had a lot to talk about. Now here they were, finally, God was answering Josiah's prayer. She had thought that God was going to give Josiah to her and she would be the answer to his prayer, but she realized she would only have been a substitute. She saw that now. Josiah would have been happy with her, but his prayer to have his own mother love him would have gone unanswered like hers had been as a child when she had asked God to bring Carmen back. Through all of this, she had learned that God works in mysterious ways. She knew now how lucky she was to have a grandmother who loved her and raised her to love and fear God. If her own mother had raised her, she shuddered to think how she would have turned out. God always knows best. She knew that the course she had set for her life was about to change, but she also knew that as long as she allowed God to lead and guide her, even when disappointment came, she could handle it, because He could.

The ride back to the hospital seemed long, but for some reason her spirit felt uplifted. Even with tragedy all around, she knew that God's hand was orchestrating a perfect ending to everything they all had suffered.

CHAPTER THIRTY-FIVE

After three days in a coma, Cliff awakened in the middle of the night. He saw Simone's lovely hair lying on the covers of his bed. She had fallen asleep again in prayer at his side. It took all the strength that Cliff had in him to will his hand to place it on top of hers. When she awoke and felt his hand on top of hers, she looked to see if he was awake but was disappointed to find his eyes as they had been since the day she arrived— closed. He was still lost in a world she was not privy to, but she knew somehow he had come out of it long enough to place his hand on top of hers. She began to talk to him, trying to coax him from the dream world which was trying to hold him. She spoke to him about her love for him, and how surprised she was to find him at her age, and what joy he had brought to her life. She told him how she found pleasure in the simplest things they did like walking in the park, reading their bibles, and praying together. She told him she has never been happier in her life than she is when she's with him. She pleaded with Cliff to come back to her, telling him they were just beginning and that she needed him on this side with her to face life challenges as well as to enjoy life's victories.

She talked to him like he was awake and listening. All the things she wanted to say to him but had been too afraid to speak, she said them that day. She poured out her heart until she felt a very slight squeeze from his hand. It happened only once and it was ever so slight, but she knew she felt it. Feeling encouraged by this promising gesture, she continued to talk. She told him about the girls, that they were all okay. She told him about the kids, mentioning that Josiah and Keshawn were both doing fine.

As she continued speaking to Cliff, the girls and the guys came in pairs to speak to Cliff as well. The girls were strong, for the most part, but they all broke down at some point. They each had a pair of strong shoulders to lean on and Simone was happy about that.

At around 4 o'clock that afternoon, Cliff opened his eyes for the second time. He blearily looked around the room, trying to make out who was there. He already knew Simone was at his bedside and had been for a long time. He had heard her songs, prayers, and revelations. It was her voice he followed to find his way back home.

He grasped her hand feeling its warmth, reveling in it. Simone looked up and found him staring at her. The smile she gave him was the most beautiful thing he had ever seen. He thanked God in that instant for allowing him to see it again, because he knew it had been touch and go for him. He wanted to spend whatever time he had left in this world, in the company of this woman. He loved her with a love so deep it had pulled him back to this world, because he was not ready to leave her. He could have gone on to his eternal rest because he had seen it and it was beautiful, but he didn't want to leave her and God, in His infinite mercy, had obliged him. No words were necessary between them. They both knew.

The doctors all fussed over Cliff, surprised by his vitals and clarity of mind. They were cautiously optimistic that he would have a full recovery. Cliff was transferred from ICU to a regular room after all his doctors had checked him and found him doing remarkably well. The hospital received a call from White House security and they were treating Cliff like he was some kind of V.I.P. They were all joking about it, as all the girls and their guys were together in Cliff's private suite. They were trying to find out who Cliff really was and why he warranted such treatment. Simone recalled the story of how desperate she was to find a way to Chicago, and had called the number Robin gave her in the hopes of getting some direction but instead got first-class royal treatment. She was whisked from her front door all the way to Cliff's bedside.

They were all laughing when a news story on CNN caught Robin's eye. The television was on but the sound was down. Showing on the television screen was a picture of a woman with a phone number to call if anyone had seen her. Robin silenced everyone turning the sound up. The woman was a principal of a school in Columbus, Ohio, and on a field trip with the children when their bus got caught in the storm. It was speculated that the woman was pulled through the windshield of the bus when it was caught in the eye of the storm. The news anchor went on to give the woman's name and a contact number for missing victims of the storm. Robin dialed the number immediately.

"Hi my name is Dr. Robin Walters and I have some information on the missing school principal from Columbus, Ohio." Robin was passed through to another line and a female's voice came on the line. Robin shared with her the story of how and where she had found the woman, and that due to her injuries, she had to be air lifted somewhere, but she wasn't sure where. Every single local hospital had received patients so the search was broad.

"She was treated in the field for a pneumothorax," Robin remembered.

"Now that may just be the piece we need to narrow the search. Would you like me to call you when we find her?" said the news anchor.

"Yes, please do," Robin repeated her name and title, and offered Nico's cell phone as the best way to reach her.

As Robin hung up the phone she remembered something else.

"Maria Rodriguez!" she said excitedly. "Her name is Maria Rodriguez!"

Everyone waited for Robin to explain her interest in the news story and what she meant when she kept saying Maria Rodriguez's name. Robin's mind was travelling at the speed of sound. Maria Rodriguez was the friend that Carla Dixon was so upset about. She had mentioned her by name right before she had her episode. Robin remembered that Carla was transported to Northwestern Memorial Hospital.

"Nico, I need to get to Northwest Memorial Hospital like right now."

"Okay, let's go," he said and grabbed his jacket off the chair.

"What's going on, Robin? Can you tell us anything before you leave?" Simone said, sounding like a concerned mother.

"Carla Dixon is a counselor at Josiah's school who has been keeping me posted about Josiah throughout this lawsuit. I told you the last time I saw her, she was distraught over the loss of her friend. Well that's her friend's picture on the news. She is the principal of Josiah's school, but get this, she is the woman I found under those seats right after the storm. Remember, the one I ran and got the paramedics for?"

"Wow! Talk about a coincidence," said Amera. "We should go with you."

"Thanks, but that won't be necessary. I just want to let her know the good news."

"What if it isn't good news? Shouldn't you try to find out what happened to Maria before you run up there and tell Carla something positive and get her hopes up only for someone to have to tell her later she didn't make it," Simone was always the voice of reason; what she said made sense.

"Without any ID, she would have been admitted as a Jane Doe. We need to find out where they took her but how?" Robin thought out loud, considering the obstacles that blocked her path.

"Wait!" she cried. "What if I knew the name of the paramedic which transported her I'm not even sure why, but I asked him his name right before they put her on the helicopter."

"Now we know why," said Marcus. "What was his name?"

"Alfred Preston," she said.

Marcus and Nico went to work immediately, using their titles as physicians to help them navigate through the red tape. Exactly 13 minutes later, Nico hung up his phone with news to share.

"I've got it!" he said. Nico had gotten the name of the paramedic, the firehouse he worked at with their phone number, along with Alfred Preston's personal cell number. Robin began by calling the house number and got no answer so she figured they must have been out on a run. She thought she would call his cell and leave a voicemail, but was surprised when he picked up the phone.

"Hey Alfred, this is Dr. Walters. You may not remember me, but I was the one who found the woman under the car seat."

"I remember you, Dr. Walters, how are you? Is there something I can help you with?" he said politely.

"Well actually there is. Someone is trying to locate the woman we helped that day, but I wasn't sure where she was taken after she was airlifted. I know that day was pretty hectic, but if you could remember that would be great."

"You're talking about the woman with the pneumothorax right?"

"Right," responded Robin.

"She was transported to Loyola. The first wave of critical care patients all went there."

"Are you sure?" asked Robin.

"Positive," he said.

"Thank you so much, Alfred! I really appreciate this."

"Glad I was able to help."

Robin quickly hung up the phone and excitedly told everyone what she learned. Maria Rodriguez was in the same hospital Cliff had been recovering in. Nico called the hospital administration and quickly found out she was on the third floor. Everyone started to exit the room, except Simone, who once again was the voice of reason.

"All of you don't need to go. Robin and Nico you two go see how the woman is doing and if she is doing okay then go ahead and let Carla Dixon know her friend is alright. We will wait here until we hear from you." Cliff continued to sleep soundly, breathing normally, as the rest of the group settled down to wait until Nico and Robin returned.

Robin and Nico stepped off the elevator onto the third floor, looking for room 336. The door was slightly open as they entered the room to find Maria Rodriguez sitting up in her bed awake but strapped to a heart monitor staring out the window.

"Hi Maria," said Robin.

She slowly turned her head in their direction and looked them up and down.

"That's my name?" she asked. "It's been right on the tip of my tongue all this time but I couldn't remember it to save my life. They say I have a concussion and my memory will come back once I get into familiar settings, but I don't mind admitting it's a little scary not knowing what you have been doing for the last however many years of your life. If you don't mind me asking, what is your name? You obviously know me, but I apologize because I cannot remember either of you but you seem a little familiar," she said this looking directly at Robin.

"I was the one who found you under a row of minivan seats. I ran and got help," Robin explained.

"I remember you now. The Angel who wiped my face."

"Yes that was me. Do you remember that you are a principal of a school? You have a friend who is very worried about you named Carla Dixon. Does any of this ring a bell?"

"No, not really," she said, "but I do hear children's laughter a lot in my dreams."

"We are not going to stay. This is my friend, Dr. Cantrell." Robin thought about asking Maria to allow Nico to take a look at her, but felt that might have been too invasive since she had no memory.

"I am going to let your family and friends know where you are, so they should be swarming you shortly. Nice to meet you," she said shaking her hand.

They left the room and Robin quickly called the news anchor back and gave her the room number for family and friends. She told her that Maria was experiencing amnesia. The news anchor said she would inform the school and the family.

Robin and Nico left to go see Carla Dixon, who had been admitted to Northwestern Memorial. Carla was surrounded by family and friends as she sat in her bed with a bandaged head. She looked strong and vibrant, not at all like someone who had brain surgery two days before.

"Dr. Walters, it's nice to see you." She went around the room making introductions and Robin did in kind, introducing Nico as her friend.

"I've got some good news for you," Robin said, with a smile on her face.

"What?" Carla replied looking at her curiously.

"I found Maria Rodriguez! She's alive but she does have some amnesia. Doctors are hopeful that she will recover her memory."

Carla sat perfectly still in her bed and didn't say a word. Her face looked like a mask. A full minute went by before she spoke.

"You found Maria and she is alive?"

"Yes," said Robin.

Carla broke down into tears as her husband quickly moved to console her, along with their children.

"I'm so sorry, I didn't mean to upset you," Robin said. "I will come back another day when you're feeling better." She motioned to Nico that they should leave.

"No, no, please don't leave," said Carla. "I'm not crying because I'm upset. I am crying because I had accepted that my friend was gone and now you tell me she is alive. I am overwhelmed with joy."

Tears streamed down her face as Robin quickly updated Carla on Maria's status and location. Afterward, Robin and Nico prepared to leave but before she did, Carla wanted to leave Robin with one last thought.

"You know Josiah changed us all."

Robin turned and looked at Carla.

"He changed us all—me, my husband, Maria, Keshawn, even you. Everyone that child touched came away a better person; that is, everyone except his mother. I don't understand how you can be around that much light and it not affect you. I hope you end up with Josiah. I know you love him and he loves you. Some things are just right."

A tear slid down Robin's cheek as she thought about the Patricia Martin she had just witnessed with Josiah. She loved Josiah and didn't want to let him go, but she knew in her heart of hearts that Patricia was a changed woman and she owed it to Josiah and to Patricia to assist in every way she could to try and make that relationship a healthy and happy one.

"I believe God is going to answer Josiah's prayer and I will be right there cheering him on, no matter what, because I do love him. Not my will, but God's will be done. Thank you for all the updates, phone calls, and encouragement you gave me through the most difficult time in my life. You were a stranger to me, but your decision to help, made my life bearable as well as Josiah's. I'm not sure why all this happened, but if God allowed it, there is a greater purpose behind it and He will reveal it in his own time, but I need you to know how your decision affected my life. Thank you."

She walked over to the bed and hugged Carla Dixon and held her tightly. Saying a round of quick goodbyes to everyone, she and Nico walked out the room.

EPILOGUE

(six months later)

Simone, Jo, Amera, Tiffany, and Robin were all sequestered in Robin's bedroom while Robin put the finishing touches on her makeup. They were somber, but not sad because today was a very important day. A lot has happened in the six months since the storm.

Simone had shanghaied Cliff while he was in the hospital. She had insisted on going home with Cliff to take care of him, instead of him hiring a nurse. Cliff said the only way they could stay in the same house, was if they were man and wife. Simone said that was just fine with her. Jason, who was now Amera's fiancé, performed the nuptials right there in the room. Cliff's connections took care of getting all the correct paperwork signed and into the correct hands, so now they were man and wife and they were extremely happy. They had just closed on a new house only two months previous and they had all learned that Cliff was not the security/father they all knew and trusted but he revealed that financially he was well fixed and if anything were to happen to him, all his girls would be taken care of. He now had a wife and four daughters and he loved them all dearly and they loved him in return. They still didn't know how Cliff was connected to the White House, but they figured some things would just remain a secret. It really didn't matter.

All the girls were engaged and they were trying to decide if they wanted separate weddings or one big one. After much discussion, it was starting to look like one big off the chart wedding was going to be the consensus.

Simone was putting the finishing touches on Tiffany's hair and Amera was buckling Jo's shoe, as Robin looked around the room through the mirror. So much love in this room, she thought. She hadn't known she was lonely until they came. She hadn't known she was incomplete until HE came. She hadn't known she was in denial until Josiah came and now here they all were. She now had a mother, a father, sisters, a child, and a soul mate. She looked at the picture of her, Josiah, and Nico on her dresser. It had been taken at Cedar Point. Their faces were flushed with sun and laughter and it was obvious to everyone they were having the time of their lives. It was one of her favorite pictures.

Once the children returned to the group home safe and sound after the storm, Patricia Martin had kept her word and dropped the lawsuit. The sleazy law firm she'd agreed to let represent her in the case had advanced her almost $10,000 against the settlement they were anticipating from the Burke Center and Dr. Walters. When Patricia dropped the lawsuit, they attempted to sue her to get their advance back, but Robin had her attorney work out an agreement with Patricia's attorney and she paid them $3,000 dollars to close the case and forget they ever knew Patricia Martin, so that chapter was behind them.

Once the lawsuit was over, Robin was able to visit Josiah at the group home, so she and Patricia got to know each other. Josiah loved that the two women he loved most in the world were now friends.

She saw that Patricia was indeed a different woman and the relationship between her and Josiah continued to grow. Robin could see that Josiah was happier than she had ever seen him and the shadows she could always see behind his eyes were gone.

She'd met Patricia's friend Allison, and loved her immediately. She was opinionated and honest, and it was plain to see she loved Patricia like a sister. She told the story of how they had gotten saved together. Maria Rodriguez and Carla Dixon had both recovered from their injuries and were back at work. Greg Fisher, the basketball coach, resigned deciding to pursue a different career after the trauma of the storm. Robin became good friends with Maria and Carla, so now they too had their own connection and they all shared a love for God that had been tested, strengthened and everything in between because of the Josiah Effect. They had all come away with a deeper faith, a closer walk and a clearer understanding of what God's love really meant.

But today was a celebration of life and they were all there in Robin's backyard which had been beautifully decorated to celebrate the collective and individual journeys they had all been on. Patricia was awarded full custody of Josiah and today he was leaving the group home and would be going home with his mother. He was happy but sad as well because he had come to love so many people there, especially Keshawn. He hoped that maybe Dr. Walters would take Keshawn because the two of them now also had their own relationship and were very close, but no one had said anything so he was both happy and sad on this day.

Robin, Amera, Jo, Tiffany, and Simone all came through the French doors leading to the patio at the back of Robin's house. The backyard was full of people, including a band and a deejay. Everyone paused momentarily as the ladies came out onto the patio. They made a lovely picture, each in a beautiful summer dress that complimented their coloring. They all had a different look, but each one was so lovely. The guys all stood together and scanned the crowd trying to locate their better halves finding them as usual all together as they moved in concert toward them.

Before Robin could reach her destination, Keshawn and Josiah bum rushed her each grabbing an arm.

"Guess what?" said Josiah excitedly. "Shawn's getting adopted and we're still going to get to see each other."

She had half-heartedly considered adopting Keshawn because she had found him to be an excellent child and she had come to love him too, but the Spirit hadn't led her to do it. She discussed it with the girls and Simone and they had told her that God must have other plans for Keshawn and now she saw they had been right on the money.

She looked at Keshawn who held her right hand and at Josiah who held her left hand. They were both smiling away. They began to pull her, maneuvering through the tables and people until they came to a table. The woman at the table looked up and Robin was surprised to see that it was Nurse Earley. She was the one who had called Robin for confirmation of a medication dosage. Robin had gone to the hospital and met her that evening and thanked her for her diligence. They smiled at each other and Robin sat down. Not knowing their history, Keshawn introduced Robin to Gloria Earley. As they sat together talking, what Robin learned was very interesting.

She learned that Gloria Earley had tried to adopt Keshawn immediately after Josiah's hospital stay, but Keshawn had refused telling her that he couldn't leave until he knew Josiah was going to be alright. Nurse Earley told Robin that Keshawn thought that she, Robin, was going to get custody of Josiah, not knowing that Josiah's mother had been at the hospital every night he was there. Nurse Earley told Robin how she would often see her coming out of the chapel or out of his room in the wee hours of the morning so she had known the chapter with his mother was not finished.

"I knew God was working something out with both of these boys so I told Keshawn that was fine, and that he and I would use the time to get to know each other."

Now all the background investigations and paperwork were finally complete. Funny how it coincided with the date that custody of Josiah had been returned to his mother, Patricia Martin. Patricia and Gloria were often at the group home visiting their boys at the same time, so they had gotten to know each other pretty well. They each understood the connection the boys had formed and neither wanted to break it, so they had exchanged numbers and were on the way to becoming friends.

"I will be taking my son home today," she told Robin. God told me some years ago he was going to bless me with a son. When they told me I would never have children I thought I was going to have a child like Sara and Abraham, but as time went on I just kind of put that dream away but God never forgot it." She hugged Keshawn to her, feeling emotional for a moment.

"Mom! Not in front of everybody," Keshawn said, but he didn't move one inch.

Everybody laughed and hugs were given all around. Robin excused herself, telling them she would get back with them later. She moved toward her man and her family and they all began to move toward the staging area that had been set up for the band. Robin grabbed the microphone.

"Hey everybody, I want to welcome you to my home and I want to thank you for coming out. Everybody here is bonded together by love." She looked around the backyard full of people and saw people she knew and some she didn't, but she knew they were connected somehow to this thing that Carla and Maria had entitled "The Josiah Effect."

"Almost two years ago, God sent a child to me as a patient. I thought I was divinely selected to help this child through a difficult time in his life that he was experiencing, but I had no idea that he had been divinely selected by God to help me face a difficult time in my past so that I could begin a healing process which should have happened some twenty-seven years ago. Because of this child," Robin pauses for a moment voice heavy with emotion, "I stand before you today with no shadows from my past controlling me. I am free and now he is too. And we are not the only ones." She looked at Tiffany to her left and Allison in the front row and smiled. Today Josiah will go home with his mother because she too has been set free from the demons of her past. Today is a celebration of life!"

With that, everyone released the balloons they were holding watching them climb higher and higher while the band started playing and everyone shouted with joy. "*The Josiah Effect*" had accomplished what God had sent it to accomplish and because it had, they were all the better for it.